What the critics are saying...

Jude (Jude Outlaw)

"...characters are well developed...packs quite a sensual punch." ~ *Sinclair Reid, Romance Reviews Today*

4 *angels!* "...shows imagination and flair..." ~ *Rogue Storm Fallen Angel Reviews*

Luke (The Claiming)

5 *hearts!!* "...sex is sizzling hot with a blend of tenderness and inventive use of different situations and toys ..." ~ *Patrice The Romance Studio*

4 *stars!* "...will leave you hot and bothered and looking for delicious outlaw lovers of your own." ~ *Donna, eCataRomance*

4.5 *stars!* "...very hot, sensual...fast-paced, well-written, and an enjoyable read..." ~ *Dani Jacquel, Just Erotic Romance Reviews*

"...so hot and steamy...deft story of terror and love" ~ *Deshanna Heavelow, Coffee Time Romance*

"...it's absolutely hot...very intense and certainly captured my attention" ~ *Sinclair Reid, Romance Reviews Today*

JAN SPRINGER

JUDE OUTLAW LOVERS and LUKE

ELLORA'S CAVE
ROMANTICA PUBLISHING

An Ellora's Cave Romantica Publication

www.ellorascave.com

Outlaw Lovers: Jude and Luke

ISBN # 1419952188
ALL RIGHTS RESERVED.
Jude Outlaw Copyright © 2004 Jan Springer
The Claiming Copyright © 2004 Jan Springer
Edited by: Mary Moran
Cover art by: Syneca

Electronic book Publication:
Jude Outlaw, June 2004
The Claiming, November 2004
Trade paperback Publication: October, 2005

Excerpt from *A Hero's Kiss* Copyright © Jan Springer, 2003

Warning:

The following material contains graphic sexual content meant for mature readers. *Outlaw Lovers: Jude and Luke* has been rated *E-rotic* by a minimum of three independent reviewers.

Ellora's Cave Publishing offers three levels of Romantica™ reading entertainment: S (S-ensuous), E (E-rotic), and X (X-treme).

S-ensuous love scenes are explicit and leave nothing to the imagination.

E-rotic love scenes are explicit, leave nothing to the imagination, and are high in volume per the overall word count. In addition, some E-rated titles might contain fantasy material that some readers find objectionable, such as bondage, submission, same sex encounters, forced seductions, etc. E-rated titles are the most graphic titles we carry; it is common, for instance, for an author to use words such as "fucking", "cock", "pussy", etc., within their work of literature.

X-treme titles differ from E-rated titles only in plot premise and storyline execution. Unlike E-rated titles, stories designated with the letter X tend to contain controversial subject matter not for the faint of heart.

Also by Jan Springer:

Contents

Jude Outlaw

Chapter One

Gulf of Maine, United States,
Year 2020

"Come on out, Cate, or I'll break down this door!"

"Get off my boat, Outlaw!" Cate Callahan yelled back, her grip tightening around the knife.

Jude Outlaw chuckled, a free and easy laugh. It was a direct contrast to the fear running rampant through her body as she hid in the tiny engine room lavatory of the boat she'd stolen a couple of weeks ago when she'd run from the newly invoked Claiming Law.

"Your boat, Cate? My brothers catch you with it and you'll wish you were dead. They were really upset to find you gone, y'know. Come on, let's go home."

"And have the Claiming Law forced on me? No freaking way!"

Due to the death of most of the world's female population, a new law had been passed by the male majority in order to ease their sexual frustrations.

With the stroke of a pen, the newly re-formed United States government had taken away women's rights, turning them into nothing more than a piece of property that could be claimed by filing videos of a sexual consummation to the U.S. Claims Office. What made matters worse, she would be shared by more than one man. In the end, the woman would go to the largest group of men who produced the most creative sexual acts.

Jude Outlaw wouldn't have a chance in claiming her alone.

That's when he'd shocked her by sending a telegram explaining he was coming home from the Wars with four of his surviving brothers, Luke, Cole, Cade, and Mac. All had agreed to help him claim her.

The man she loved with all her heart expected her to be a wife to five men!

That had only been one of the reasons she'd run.

It was the thirty-day waiting period that terrified her more than being a wife to five men. The waiting period allowed any other group of men who wished to file a claim on her to sexually take her against her will.

"I know you're scared of the Barlow brothers wanting to claim you, too," Jude echoed her thoughts from the other side of the door.

Scared? That's an understatement.

"They're rich. They'll buy the judges," Cate hissed.

"Everything will work out fine."

"The hell it will, Jude. They bought their way out of the Wars. They can buy a judge to get me."

Even if the Barlows didn't get her, she knew in her heart Jude wouldn't look at her the same way if she slept with his brothers. The respect between them would be gone. Their special love would end. It was best if they never married under this new law.

"Either you come out right now or I'll lock you in until we get home. At least by then you'll be more...sociable."

A razor sharp fear zipped along her nerves. She had no food down here. And she was overdue for her medicine. Medicine she needed badly in order to stay alive.

It was another reason she'd stolen the Outlaws' boat. Selling it would give her enough money to buy medicine for a long time with enough left over to help her stay in hiding.

She tensed as his footsteps headed away from where she'd taken refuge.

If he locked her in, she'd be at his mercy in no time flat. She had to make her move now or she would never escape.

Quietly she unlocked the door and pushed it open just enough to get a glimpse of the man she hadn't seen in nearly five years.

Cate's mouth dropped open in sensual shock. Against her will, her body tightened with sexual awareness.

Heavens! The man had filled out quite nicely.

Standing at the base of the stairs, his broad naked back was turned to her. He stared up the staircase; apparently, deep in thought as to whether he should follow through on his threat of locking her in. Sweet unadulterated lust rammed into her cunt as she watched his thick sinewy biceps flex and bulge while he knotted his fists with apparent frustration.

Suddenly she wondered if perhaps she'd made a serious mistake in not being there to welcome him home.

Even from behind, the man looked lethal.

Drop dead gorgeous.

His sandy brown hair was just this side of unkempt and curled nicely against the nape of his neck. He possessed a pair of wide muscular shoulders. His torso was long, his waist slim.

Low hip-hugging jean cutoffs embraced a sensually curved ass. His large feet were bare, his legs long with powerful looking thighs.

Past experience proved he matched her own gentle and sweet sexual appetites but now he was a man and not a teenager. A man, who wanted to share her with his four sex-deprived brothers.

A fresh wave of fear scrambled through her system.

She would never submit to any man! She had to show Jude she meant business. All she needed to do was scare him enough so he'd allow her to go up the stairs.

Mind made up and knife held high, she shot like a bullet from her hiding place. In four quick strides she was halfway to him.

Unfortunately, he heard her coming and turned.

She moved faster.

Clasping the knife in front of her she gasped in shock as his arm came up in a defensive move slamming into the hideous blade. The edge sliced into the fleshy part of his arm just below his elbow. Crimson blood splashed out of the gash. His cry of pain shot fear and guilt through her every nerve and fiber.

Within the blink of an eye a strong hand clamped around her wrist. He squeezed so hard her fingers instantly went numb.

She dropped the knife and it clattered to the wood planked floor.

Momentary shock zipped through his face when he looked at her. As if he liked what he saw, his sensually curved lips curled upward. In response, her clit swelled with an overwhelming eagerness for his mouth to feast on her hot pussy.

"Long time no see, Cate."

He pushed her up against the wall, his fierce shaft pressing intimately between her legs, his bare chest squishing her breasts.

Anger, pain and lust flashed in his eyes. He bared his white teeth.

"You're going to be sorry you cut me, Cate. Very sorry."

Before she could mount a protest, he cupped her chin firmly in his large hand and lowered his head.

Scorching lips came down upon hers with such fierceness it took her breath away. Her body awakened as one nerve after another short-circuited. Lusty heat uncurled and shot lightning bolts deep within her belly and she couldn't stop herself from kissing him back.

His sensuous lips tasted of ocean salt and when she opened her mouth to him, she savored the taste of champagne on his rough tongue. Obviously, he'd been celebrating her capture before he'd boarded the boat!

A hand lifted the hem of her dress. Cool air brushed her clit. Hot fingers dipped between her legs and eagerly skimmed over the tight curls protecting her mons. When a firm, scorching finger slid against her large clitoris she jolted against him as a dizzying rush of blood shot straight into her vagina.

Her legs weakened and she grabbed his shoulders as if he were a lifesaver on a sinking ship.

She whimpered beneath his lusty onslaught.

At the sound, he broke the kiss and cocked an amused eyebrow at her.

"No underwear? You must have been expecting me."

Her face flamed. "Don't flatter yourself."

He grinned with a profound wickedness that made her heart thump with wild abandon.

In one fluid motion, he slid his finger between the folds of her passion-swelled labia lips. Heat seared against her vaginal walls as he dipped inside.

She gasped from the pleasure.

His eyes smoldered with fiery arousal.

"Never had a woman wet for me so fast. I won't have any trouble sliding my cock into you and fucking you senseless for the rest of today."

Son of a bitch! Is that all she was to him? Just a woman he could fuck?

Anger tore through her trapped frame. Instinctively her foot came up and she stamped hard on his bare toes.

He swore and let her loose.

She took off, scrambling up the stairs.

The instant she cleared the hatch, she slammed it down with a bang.

"Got you, Jude Outlaw!" she laughed as she secured the latch.

Adrenaline roared through her system and she found herself smiling at her good fortune.

She'd done it! She was free! And she had Jude Outlaw as *her* hostage.

"I guess my brother isn't as charming as I thought." The amused masculine voice drifted over her excitement like a cold wave.

Cate froze.

A tall brown-haired man who looked a lot like Jude stood right in front of her. A gun trained at her midsection.

Luke Outlaw.

"Don't look so shocked, Cate. My brother anticipated you'd put up a good fight. Brought me along as backup."

Amusement tipped his sensuous lips.

She didn't have time to be mad. Without warning the familiar wave of lightheadedness swept over her.

Damned cursed terrorist sickness! It always grabbed her when she least expected it.

Weakness zipped through her spine. Her legs buckled.

She fell hard to her knees.

"That's the perfect position for a woman about to be claimed," Luke chuckled.

Despite his humor, she read concern in his dark blue eyes. It gave her little comfort.

"I suppose you'll be needing some of that medicine?"

Cate nodded numbly as the weakness spilled into the rest of her body.

Furious pounding and shouts erupted from the locked engine room.

"I think we'll leave Jude down there until your medicine kicks in. I know you're going to need a rest before he takes you home."

Oh God.

She wished she could get up. Wished she could dive overboard. Escape the fear searing through her body at what awaited her back home.

But she couldn't move a muscle.

Her eyes grew heavy. Drifted closed. Her mind started shutting down.

She heard Luke swear softly and his hurried footsteps snapped against the deck as he went for her medicine.

Once again she cursed the aftereffects of the sickness.

Dubbed the X-virus, it had originally been developed to suppress destructive behavior in the hopes of easing certain mental behaviors. Unfortunately, a brilliant but rather loony scientist by the name of Blakely managed to get his hands on the experimental drug and altered its makeup. The resulting airborne virus was now specifically designed to attack estrogen-rich female bodies. Once contained within the female body, the virus attacked the brain, repressing independence while elevating the need for submission. Blakely sold the untried virus to a then little known, but richly endowed, terrorist group called the DogmarX, thereby providing them the means to put into motion their righteous plans for female submission to the male. DogmarX targeted select women's equal rights groups attending a convention in Afghanistan. The terrorists had sent a written warning to authorities informing them to cancel the convention or suffer the consequences. Unfortunately, the authorities had concluded the warning as just another hoax. The convention proceeded as scheduled. Within days, the women attending the convention began to exhibit signs of excessive sexual submission to men. The airborne virus spread like wildfire throughout the world mutating independently and destructively until more than eighty percent of the world's women had died. Instead of merely suppressing certain areas of the brain, the mutated virus painfully destroyed then consumed the brain before attacking other vital organs within the female body. Effectively acting like a cancer on speed. The survivors, she being one of them, were reduced to taking expensive medicines to stay alive. And by the way she was feeling right now she wouldn't be living for long.

Blackness closed in around her like a welcome blanket and she slipped into heavenly unconsciousness.

Chapter Two

Jude Outlaw winced at the pain shooting through his injured arm as he reached out and brushed a stray strand of hair off the unconscious Cate's flushed forehead.

When Luke had finally let him out of and Jude had seen her sprawled on the deck of the boat, his heart had frozen solid. He'd thought she was dead. Relief had swept through him when his brother told him it was the sickness and he'd already given her the injection.

He smiled down at her sleeping figure.

God, he'd missed her.

Had yearned to hold her in his arms. Had ached to touch her silky breasts. Most of all he missed plunging his rigid cock deep into her sweet cavern and listening to her sexy moans like when they'd been teenagers and before he'd gone to the Wars.

She looked so feminine, so soft and sultry as she lay on the bed where they'd carried her.

Her shoulder-length hair gave the appearance of a blonde halo splashed over the pillow. Her high pink cheekbones looked stunning. Sensually curved lips were red and slightly parted. Long eyelashes lay over her closed eyes.

Eyes that when open sparkled emerald green, like the ocean waves at sunrise.

He should have married her before he'd run off to fight the Wars. But everything had happened so fast. The terrorists had unleashed the final blow by setting loose a sexual virus.

Cate had been one of the millions who'd been hit by it. She'd almost died. Others hadn't been so lucky, like his and Cate's mothers. They'd died excruciating deaths.

That's when he and his brothers had joined the fight against terrorists. They'd battled overseas for five long years.

During that time, world economies collapsed in a dominoes effect. Governments could no longer sustain their armies' occupation of other countries. Soldiers were quickly being recalled. When Jude and his brothers received word they'd be pulling out, they'd been glad.

The fights had been tough and long.

They were tired. Anxious about the rumors they'd heard.

Rumors of the surviving women going into hiding to avoid the Claiming Law. Women barely existing off the land and stealing whatever they could get their hands on so they could buy the medicine that would keep them alive. Living like savages until captured by groups of men who would sexually claim them right then and there.

He'd feared for Cate's safety and when he and his brothers had arrived home they'd discovered Cate had run off, too.

She'd gone into hiding in order to avoid the new Claiming Law.

Jude sighed wearily.

She shouldn't have left. She should have waited for him. She should have given him a chance to tell her how much he loved her.

"You both okay?" Luke asked as he entered the cabin.

"Fine." Jude replied tightly.

"I'm glad we finally caught her. It'll make finding Tyler that much easier."

Jude gritted his teeth and closed his eyes as he thought of their missing younger brother. Up until a couple of weeks ago they'd thought he was dead, a casualty of the Terrorist Wars.

That is until Clay Barlow had told them different. The youngest brother of their closest neighbors, he'd snuck off to join the Wars a few years back. A couple of weeks ago he'd shown up at the Outlaw farm declaring Tyler alive. At first they'd all been stunned with disbelief. But when Clay Barlow shared information only Tyler could know, they knew Clay spoke the truth.

However, their happiness had been short lived. Clay Barlow revealed Tyler was rotting away in a prison somewhere but he wouldn't give his exact whereabouts unless he and his three brothers got something first.

They wanted Cate.

And that's when Jude had realized why Cate had run. The evil Barlows had told her they wanted her, too.

"She's turned into quite a pretty woman from the tomboy we used to hang with," Luke said softly.

"She sure has."

"Now that we have her you're not going to change your mind are you? We'll still use her to get the information about Tyler?"

Jude nodded his head slowly, bile clogging up his throat at what they planned to do with Cate.

"You sure? Because the longer it takes to find Tyler, the more he's gonna suffer."

"Dammit, Luke! I gave you all my word. It doesn't mean I have to like it. So back off!"

Luke sighed wearily. "When are you going to tell her the news about the deal we struck with the Barlows regarding Tyler?"

"I don't know."

"The sooner you tell her the better she'll be prepared."

Jude remained silent. How could he tell the woman he loved he was going to hand her over to those filthy bastards?

"She's going to wake up soon. You tell her. Prepare her. She might take it easier if the news comes from you."

"That's a laugh. Those Barlows are the cruelest men I know. They'd use her until there's nothing left but an empty shell of the woman I love."

Luke's eyes narrowed with determination. "There's no alternative. We have to find him as soon as possible. And the only way is to give the Barlow brothers what they want."

"Would you give up the woman you love?" Jude snapped.

Luke's face paled.

Jude cursed softly, instantly realizing his mistake. Years ago the authorities had taken Callie, Luke's girlfriend and Cate's sister, away for experimental testing.

Testing because she'd shown no signs of being infected by the terrorists' illness. The authorities had told Luke to never expect her back alive. He'd searched for her but had never found her.

"I'm sorry, I shouldn't have said that."

"I've docked *The Outlaw Lover*," Luke said tightly. "I'll go get the Barlows and bring them back here. I shouldn't be too long. Stay on board, okay?"

Jude nodded. He'd been so deep in his anger he hadn't even noticed they'd stopped at the newly rebuilt New Portland docks.

A minute later Luke was strolling down the wharf, his shoulders slumped, his head bowed. Jude didn't have to be a genius to know his insensitive words had gotten Luke to start thinking about Callie again. It was too late to take back what he'd said. Luke would just have to deal with it, just like Jude had to deal with the familiar anger churning deep inside him when he thought of the Barlow's ultimatum.

They had made it quite clear. If they didn't get Cate, then the Outlaw brothers wouldn't get Tyler.

That meant their youngest brother might be as good as dead.

* * * * *

The soft rumble of a boat engine drifted through the thick layers of Cate Callahan's sleep, prodding her to open her eyes.

"Nice of you to wake up," Jude said softly.

He sat on the bed beside her, his warm body heat zipping through the thin material of her dress and nestling wonderfully against her skin.

She fought against the need to move closer to him. Fought the insane hammering of her heart as his sexy earthy scent swarmed her senses.

Her eyes darted from the intensity of his dark gaze to quickly roam the length of the room.

Son of a bitch!

He'd secured her in the cabin of *The Outlaw Lover*, the Outlaw brothers' sixty-foot cruiser.

Situated high in the cruiser, the cabin had always appeared small and ultra cozy to her the few times Jude had brought her here before he'd left for the Wars. Now it seemed like a prison. Glass surrounded the entire room allowing her to look out at the sky darkened with bruised purple clouds. Screeching white seagulls sailed overhead and she saw nothing in the horizon but rolling gray ocean waves tipped with whitecaps.

Alarm zipped up her spine as she realized the boat was moving out into the ocean leaving Maine behind.

It was at that same point she realized her wrists were bound by soft velvet lined cuffs to the sides of the bed. Her legs were spread-eagled, her ankles bound.

Shit!

She pulled at her bonds. There was some give but not enough for her to break free.

"This isn't the way to treat a woman you say you want to claim."

He didn't say anything but her heart hammered insanely in her ears as he reached over and caressed her jaw with a long hot, callused finger. He slid his digit off her jaw and drew a hearty line of fire down her neck and over the top swell of her left breast.

"Where are you taking me?"

In response, he smiled warmly and she couldn't stop the tingles of excitement shooting through her body.

"We're going to get reacquainted."

Reacquainted? Sweet heavens!

Guilt assaulted her when she noted the stark contrast of the white bandage wrapped against the darkly tanned flesh of his arm where she'd stabbed him. Her guilt turned to a sweet sexual awakening as his finger intimately brushed against the tip of her nipple that poked eagerly against her dress.

"What are you going to do to me?" She tried to keep her voice tough. Tried to show him his hot touch didn't affect her but the cool knowledge in his eyes made her whimper.

"You have to ask?"

"Don't bother. I don't love you anymore," she lied.

"You'd better make me believe you, Cate."

"I won't be claimed by your brothers or any other man."

She saw the slightest tightening of his jaw.

"How can you live with yourself, Jude? Spreading my legs like a whore for you and your brothers. Do you call that love? If you cared a little…"

"I do care," he snapped.

"Then let me go."

"I won't let you go. At least not until I give you a taste of what you'll be missing if you decide to leave me again."

Oh sweet heavens! The heated arousal in his eyes scorched her body igniting a fevered anticipation she knew only Jude could extinguish.

"I'm missing nothing," she spat.

"You shouldn't have run, Cate," he said.

"How'd you expect me to react? Having to be a wife to five men. And others…"

He winced at her words. "The old days are gone, compliments of the terrorists. We're going to have to get used to it."

"I won't get used it!"

Ignoring her outburst, he whispered, "I've missed looking at your breasts."

An anxious shiver racked through her as his hands skimmed upward to the collar of her dress. Shaky masculine fingers opened one delicate button at a time, his gaze transfixed to hers. She tried to look away but found she couldn't.

He stopped just above her bellybutton.

"I've missed touching you." His voice sounded hoarse. "For years I thought about you. Thought about how you'd welcome me home. And now I'm going to find out…"

Ripples of fire rumbled through her as he spread the material wide open, allowing her breasts to spill out to his hungry appreciative gaze. His work-roughened hands slid erotically over her generous mounds, cupping them, making them swell. She couldn't stop the beautiful sensations racing through her breasts as his rough thumbs massaged her nipples until they became the size of marbles and a stiff pink.

"Your nipples are an enchanting color. Just like the color of sparkling champagne," he whispered.

He lifted a hot hand away and reached for a bottle she hadn't noticed settled beside him. Pulling the cork with his teeth, it opened with a loud pop and he took a generous swig.

His Adam's apple bobbed as he swallowed.

Then he looked at her. His gaze burned a searing path straight into her soul. "Now it's time for me to get a taste of what I've been missing."

Suddenly he tipped the bottle over her aroused breasts and she cried out at the impact of the gushing cool liquid.

Her heart thundered as he bent his head.

His hot tongue licked like a rough flame at the pink liquid seeping off her breasts. She shivered beneath his lusty licks, her breath came in sharp gasps and she found herself arching against him. When he took one of her hardened nubs into his mouth, the pleasure and heat torched a line straight to her cunt.

The scent of wine in the air and the steady pressure of his mouth suckling her nipple made her gasp in pleasure. Her body hummed and yearned for more.

"You bastard," she cried out and arched against him as she literally felt the last of her resistance slip away.

As he suckled, his large hand slid like a hot brand upward along her inner thigh.

She bolted against her restraints when a finger nudged at her cunt opening. Reality tried to seep back into her senses. She couldn't allow him to do this. Couldn't allow him to force her to remember how good it felt to have Jude Outlaw making love to her.

"Jude, don't..."

He tore his mouth from her pink swelled nipple with a popping sound and blinked at her. The mesmerizing grayness of his eyes hypnotized her, calmed her. Well, maybe calm was the wrong word.

"Your sweetly drenched channel says otherwise, Cate."

Damn him, he was right. She was wet for him. Wanted desperately to squash her pussy against his hot hand.

She'd always been wet whenever he'd looked her way. Had always been weak in his arms. He'd always been so gentle and sweet with her.

But this time was different.

Five years had passed and there was a new desperation in his touch. A wonderful confidence she couldn't ignore. A confidence that made a spear of jealousy shoot through her as she wondered how many of those conscripted women he'd taken to his bed while he'd been away. She'd heard about them. Women who were ordered to sexually pleasure the troops. She'd even heard rumors that some of those women had literally been kidnapped from their homeland and made into sexual slaves for the higher-ranking officers.

A thumb frayed against her pleasure pearl making all thoughts of the Wars vanish. She clamped her jaws together in an effort not to cry out from the fascinating sensations ripping through her senses.

She felt hot. Feverish. Felt the cream of her arousal seep from her cunt. A finger slipped into her tightly drenched channel making her whimper with want. He inserted two more fingers. Sliding in and out of her in an erotic rhythm, her cunt muscles clenched around his fingers. She couldn't stop herself from wiggling her hips or pulling at the restraints wanting more of his pleasure. It had been so long since she'd had sex.

Oh, yes! Keep going.

She moved her hips against his hand. Felt a fourth finger slide inside her.

The fit was tight.

So damned hot. Like pieces of velvet-covered steel impaling her.

His furnace-like fingers sent slurping sounds through the air as he thrust.

In and out of her.

Oh, yes! That's it!

Her breasts rose and fell as she inhaled with the escalating pleasure.

Her eyes closed readying her body to fly. She was almost there. Could feel the tension mounting. Just a few more strokes and she'd be there...

Without warning his fingers slid out of her.

"You always look so beautiful when you're about to climax, Cate. But you've had enough for awhile."

"No," she whimpered with frustration. Her eyes snapped open to find him standing.

His face had softened and a purely sensual look glazed his eyes.

Her heart clenched in remembrance. He'd always looked at her that way before he fucked her.

Oh God! Her mind screamed in desperation.

Don't stop! Don't leave! I want you, Jude. Please, fuck me!

He smiled warmly and then he was gone. She tried to pull her thighs together to bring some relief. To douse the furious fire he'd stoked but the binds held her legs tightly in place.

"Damn you, Jude Outlaw!" she cried out.

Her answer came in an amused chuckle that left her to whimper in frustrated sexual distress.

Chapter Three

Cate must have drifted off because when she awoke, she discovered Jude leaning over her. His eyes were glazed with lust as he stared at her bared breasts.

Then he was lifting her dress up over her hips, tucking the material in around her waist, exposing her cunt to his full view.

Her body trembled as his intense gaze latched onto her face.

Why he didn't rip the awkward clothes from her body and just plunge into her aching cunt, she didn't know. But the heated look in his gray gaze gave her the feeling he wanted to do just that.

"I'm so glad you remembered I prefer you without underwear," he cooed.

Her pussy clenched violently as his eyes drifted downwards over her breasts to land between her widespread legs.

It was then that she noted the bowl in his hand.

"What the hell are you going to do?" she asked as the earlier sexual frustration quickly returned to her body.

He tipped the bowl slightly. Her heart hammered as she spied the whipped shaving cream, a steaming cloth and a straight razor set inside.

"I only eat a woman who is bare," Jude commented huskily.

The idea of his mouth suckling her cunt made her stomach clench wonderfully.

The instant the steaming cloth hit her pussy she was forced to suck in a sharp breath. Inserting it snugly against her outer folds and around her labia lips, the fiery heat shot straight through her pubic area arousing her to new heights.

"How's that feel?"

"Go to hell!"

He grinned knowingly and she clenched her fists in frustration.

"Why are you doing this to me?"

He didn't say anything as he reached for the shaving cream.

"Are you sure you aren't preparing me for your brothers?"

His lips tightened at her words. Obviously, the Claiming Law didn't sit well with him either. That was an encouraging sign.

She held her breath as he tenderly ran his fingers through her tight blonde pubic curls. Her pleasure pearl throbbed with anticipation, eager for his touch. Her clit swelled and she could feel it drop past her pussy lips, betraying her.

"No need to be embarrassed," he chuckled as his fingers scorched and pinched her labia lips.

Her belly muscles clenched in reaction. "You sure as hell would be in my position!"

"Somehow I think I would enjoy you shaving me down there."

"Not in this lifetime," Cate lied.

He began to hum softly, obviously overly interested in what he was going to do to her.

"I don't see why you're so happy. You're only doing it for a group of men who want an easy fuck."

His humming stopped.

Cate smiled sweetly at the dangerous way his eyes darkened.

"Ouch! Did I say something wrong?" she purred.

"You might want to be careful at what you say, Cate," he warned. "This next part requires delicate concentration on both our parts."

"Oh you're so right. The last thing *I* need is a pussy full of nicks and cuts when all those men start raping me. Might make you look like a bad barber."

An angry muscle twitched in his jaw and he yanked the now warm washcloth away. Breezy air slammed against her flesh making her grimace.

His hand was rough as he liberally lathered the cool shaving cream over her entire crotch area. The soothing sensation tickled and sent pleasing vibrations cascading over her flesh.

The razor was sharp, the raspy sound proof as the blade cut through each and every strand of pubic hair. When his fingers touched her labia lips, she couldn't stop herself from sucking in a tense breath.

"Nice and puffy," he chuckled.

He was precise as he pushed a nether lip this way and that way allowing the cool blade to intimately graze the skin of her outer folds. To her shock, the blade slowly lowered and scraped the fine hair around her tight anus.

Sweet heavens! What did he have in store for her?

Her sensitive skin tingled as he wiped at her shaved area with the warm wet cloth.

Her face flamed with both anger and arousal as he inspected his work of art.

"No need to be embarrassed Cate, you have a beautiful pussy. Nice and naked. I'm sure I'm going to enjoy every delicious bite."

Enjoy every delicious bite! Her vaginal muscles contracted wonderfully.

No way. He'd never been interested in doing *that* to her in the past!

The air grew tight with tension as she watched him casually stroll to the foot of the bed, an impressive bulge pressed against his tight jean shorts.

Damn him! Why didn't he just pull out his gorgeous cock and bring her the pleasure he wanted. The pleasure she now craved.

She couldn't stop the fevered excitement from sweeping through her body as the mattress moved and he kneeled between her widespread legs. Slipping his hot hands intimately under her buttocks, he tilted her hips upwards and shoved two soft pillows beneath her ass.

This maneuver made her legs pull against her restraints, not painfully but tight enough for her to remember she was totally at his mercy.

Grabbing the champagne bottle, which was a quarter full of pink liquid, he slid the bottle between her legs.

Goodness!

The coolness of the bottle felt wonderful against the hot skin of her inner thighs.

"Jude? What are you doing?"

"Shh, you'll enjoy this."

Her eyes widened as he tenderly caressed her sensitive clitoris with the open smooth bottle mouth.

Her pleasure pearl immediately reacted. Blood flowed into her quivering clit. Her body tensed with desire. Wetness seeped from her cunt. Her hips arched.

"Yes, that's it, Cate. Move your hips for me."

Oh God!

The lip of the bottle teased her vaginal opening making flames of want rage through her system.

Stick it inside! Please stick it inside.

His knowing eyes met hers, dark with desire.

Her body and mind weakened. She wanted to pull his cock from the restraints of his shorts. Wanted to see his red-hot arousal pulse — just as he was seeing hers.

The mouth of the bottle circled her hot bundle of nerves until it made her thrash on the bed.

"Jude," she managed to croak, wanting him to stop this exquisite torture.

No, don't stop. Just fill me with pleasure. Fill me with your cock!

"Just enjoy it, baby."

She twisted against her restraints as he inserted the long smooth neck of the bottle into her steaming slit. Velvety cunt muscles eagerly clenched hold of the foreign object and her wetness allowed it to slide easily inside.

He tilted the bottle slightly.

Cool wine seeped into her vagina, some of it gushed out and dripped over her anus pooling in the pillows beneath her buttocks.

He left the neck of the bottle delectably stuffed inside her quivering pussy and leaned over to kiss the insides of her knees.

Have mercy!

Hot lips tenderly kissed their way up along her inner thighs. She tried hard not to cry out as the stubble from his five o'clock shadow grazed erotically against her tender flesh. When his face delicately touched the end of the bottle, he stopped and gazed at her.

"During the Wars, I had lots of time to think up ways of pleasuring you," he whispered tenderly. "Sipping wine mixed with your cum was one of them."

The man was deliciously mad!

"You want to know what else I'm going to do to you?"

Her eyes widened at his words. Heated blood raged through her veins. She wanted to shake her head no. Wanted to pretend she didn't care one way or the other what dark desires his heart craved. But she couldn't deny it. She wanted him to do savage and sensual things to her body.

Wanted him to take her any way he wished.

"Do you want to know?" he prodded and delicately kissed the end of the bottle making it wiggle ever so wonderfully inside her clenched channel. His gray eyes gazed so intensely at her she found herself nodding.

"How about I show you instead?"

"Jude, please," she whispered meekly.

She didn't know how much more of this exquisite torture she could put up with.

He pulled the head of the bottle out a little. Her body tensed as his finger slid firmly against her swollen clitoris. Fire crawled through her clit and flamed outward into her belly.

He slid the long neck of the bottle deeper into her pussy. She could feel her vaginal muscles clamp frantically around the smooth glass walls. His fingers groped her labia lips pulling them apart until a sweet burn swept into her clit.

Then he let go, sliding his finger over her swollen clitoris dampening the fire and increasing the pleasure all the while whispering to her in a calming voice as she whimpered her sexual frustration.

Her legs trembled beneath his torturous touches. Her breath became heavy.

Her heart beat out of control.

When he finally looked up at her from between her legs, his pupils were large and dark with desire. His sensual lips parted in a sexy smile.

"This is the way I want to see you, Cate. Naked. At my mercy. Your face all flushed with arousal. Your pussy soaked with desire and readying itself to take me."

Oh God!

"Do you want me to take you, Cate? Do you want me to fuck you?"

"Yes," she found herself whispering.

"Say it, Cate. Say that you want me to fuck you. That you want it bad."

"I want you…to make love to…me," she hissed.

The bottle slid out of her with a sharp pop leaving her pussy weeping and longing to be filled by his pulsing penis.

But he didn't pull out his lusty cock from his shorts. Instead, his hands slid to the outside curves of her hips, his fingers dug into her sensitive flesh holding her still.

"First I will administer your punishment for leaving me," he whispered.

She cried out as his hands tilted her hips a little higher and his head lowered between her trembling legs.

His feather-soft hair brushed erotically against the insides of her widespread thighs increasing the sexual tension in her body. The instant his mouth fused over her ravished clit the climax hit and it hit hard.

Her cunt exploded.

Her mind and body shattered in such an overwhelming wave of pleasure. She could do nothing but allow her limbs to twist against her restraints and undulate her hips uselessly against his powerful hands.

His moist lips suckled her labia. His hot tongue flicked against her pulsing pleasure pearl with strong swirls and metrical motions.

She'd never known she could be like this. Never knew sex could be so wickedly wild. That she could be so crazy with desire.

Her breath seared her lungs. Her body grew to a feverish pitch as she thrashed beneath his onslaught.

Her breasts swelled tighter. Her nipples stabbed into the air wanting to be touched too. But he stayed between her legs.

His mouth sipped her cunt with loud slurpy sounds. His sexy groans encouraged her to arch harder into his face. And when his heated tongue plundered into her vagina, she keened as her muscles spasmed magically. She could literally feel the slick cream of arousal slide down her heated channel and onto his tongue. Slurping sounds mixed with his masculine moans as he devoured her cunt.

Devoured her as if he were a famished man.

His mouth sucked harder and she twisted against the agonizing pleasure, her body convulsing with a mind of its own.

Heated blood raged through her veins. Ecstasy pulsed through her nerve endings.

His heated tongue slammed like a breathtaking probe deep inside her vagina.

Hot and prodding. Gentle yet harsh.

Oh, she was going to die inside this incredible bliss.

Blackness hovered at the edges of her sight. She cried out as yet another climax hit making her shudder against her restraints.

She was flying, her body totally under his control.

Through heavy lids she barely saw him pull away. Barely saw his face, all flushed with arousal, his lips wet with her cum.

He grinned with the utmost satisfaction as he slipped off his shorts. His magnificent cock nestled in his hands.

Chapter Four

Her eyes widened with surprise.

His cock looked so long.

Unbelievably huge.

He was even bigger than she remembered! The purple mushroom shaped head pulsed with desire. The slit covered with precome.

Fierce looking veins bulged along his entire length. And his balls hung heavy and near to bursting, the contents ready to be emptied into her.

Oh sweet God! He looked magnificent!

"That's right, Cate. I'm a man now. Not a gangly teenager anymore. I've got a man's cock. A man's needs. Not clumsy little boy wants."

Her breath jammed up in her lungs at his hushed voice. Her cunt clenched and spasmed wonderfully as her gaze became magnetized to his sex.

He rose above her. His pupils were wide and black. Perspiration glistened his splendidly naked body.

He eased down on her.

His body lay upon hers, every muscle molding into her soft curves. His hipbones sidled against hers.

Cate trembled with lust as his thick head slid into her wet entrance stretching her vaginal muscles to an unbelievable width.

His chest sizzled against her breasts, flattening them as he lowered more so onto her.

His hot male breath fanned her face.

"Even while my brothers are fucking you, you will still be my woman." There was a desperate, erotic edge to his voice. "They can bring you the ultimate joy, Cate."

His mouth brushed lightly against hers and her world tilted wonderfully as she tasted her cum on his lips.

"Their cocks plunging inside you while I watch. Your moans and cries of arousal ripping through our bedroom while their mouths suckle your breasts."

His words rocked her to her very core. Unbelievably, this time though she wasn't afraid. The thought of him watching her getting fucked was turning her on!

He rocked his hips a little. His hot flesh slid deeper into her vagina making Cate gasp. The sexual tension inside her body kept growing.

He grinned as if knew what he was doing to her.

"Bastard," she whispered not wanting him to know that maybe, just maybe, she wouldn't mind experimenting with several men pleasuring her. Deep in her heart, though, she truly craved only Jude.

"I'll not have your brothers fucking me," her voice sounded aroused. Too aroused.

His eyes sparkled as if he knew what she'd just been thinking.

"It's the new law, Cate. Besides I know you'll enjoy it. No woman can resist an Outlaw cock."

She sure wasn't going to deny it but she sure as hell wanted to if only so Jude wouldn't get away with his arrogance.

She moaned as he drove his rod straight to the hilt, his cock lighting a burning fire inside her body. Her cunt muscles contracted beautifully and squeezed around his thick shaft. Big hard balls pressed solid against her flesh.

"We fit together." He slid out of her, quickly slamming into her again creating wonderful spirals of heat.

His mouth clamped over hers catching her cries of pleasure.

She kissed him back fiercely with all her pent-up hostility, her confined desires. Allowed herself to descend deeper toward the gratification he offered as he continued to piston into her.

"I'm glad you waited for me," he ground out and slammed into her body yet again.

"Who says I waited," she gasped as her cunt muscles clenched readying for an orgasm.

His eyes flashed at her answer.

"You're too damned tight, that's why, darling. Besides, you're a loyal woman. You wouldn't be protesting multiple lovers if you weren't."

Damn you!

"Yes! That's it! Harder!"

Pleasure racked her. Her inner muscles constricted madly around his thick intrusion.

"You're so beautiful. I don't want to share you," he groaned. His lips lightly brushed her quivering mouth.

He didn't want to share her!

Her cheerfulness disintegrated as he pumped her pussy faster driving her toward her release.

Perspiration drenched her. His hot muscular body pulsed over her.

God, she'd missed sex with Jude. She'd missed it so much.

But according to the Claiming Law he had to share her with his brothers. If his brothers were half as good as Jude was...

Her breath caught as the explosion tore through her body.

Sharp. Agonizing. Beautiful.

It zipped along her vaginal muscles. Clenched her lower belly. Shuddered through her whole body until she cried out from the magnificent impact.

His heated length pulsed inside her with warning. His corded muscles tensed and he shouted as he reached his own climax.

It was a fantastic guttural sound.

Primitive. Sexy.

He cried out again and she felt his hot sperm drive into her very depths.

Afterwards, he lay on top of her, his softened flesh still buried inside her. His hot breath framing her face as he fell asleep.

Cate smiled. He'd always done that. Fallen asleep after making love to her.

Rest up, darling. Rest. For when you wake up, I want you to fuck me over and over again.

Cate shuddered. Realization washed over her.

Despite the Claiming Law being thrust upon them she now knew in her heart that no matter who fucked her, her body would only belong to Jude Outlaw.

* * * * *

When she awoke, Cate discovered her bindings had been removed and a warm blanket covered her nude body.

There was no sign of Jude.

And she immediately knew why.

The boat was dipping and rising so badly it tugged a sour knot of nausea at her stomach. A quick look out the rain-streaked windows confirmed her suspicions.

A storm had hit.

Giant frothing white waves splashed over the bow and decks of the cruiser. Beyond, she saw nothing but gray mist and silvery sheets of rain.

Scrambling out of bed, she ignored the gentle ache between her legs and quickly donned a thin white cotton peasant-style dress she found on a nearby bolted chair before rushing outside.

Cool rain slashed over her and a strong salty wind blew against her as she headed up the metal stairs to the pilothouse situated directly on top of the sleeping quarters.

She found Jude struggling at the wheel. Rain slanted beneath the awning pummeling his body.

Immediately she noted the blood staining the bandage on his lower arm. Guilt assailed her for doing such a horrid thing to him. But this was no time to feel guilt. She had to do something to help him fight the storm and she had to do it fast!

An idea quickly formed and she headed toward the coiled rope in a corner of the pilot-house.

When he spotted her, he yelled angrily, "Go down below! Stay there!"

"No!" She screamed back, wiping the rain from her eyes and sifted through the oily smelling coil frantically looking for one end of the rope.

"I said get your ass below!" He shouted again.

She ignored him and found what she was looking for. Looping the end of the rope through a hook bolted into the floor she secured it.

Beside her Jude swore. "Dammit, woman! Listen to me! Get your ass into the engine room and stay there!"

"What? I can't hear you?" she lied.

Fumbling through the coiled rope, she found the other end. Tugging it along with her she quickly looped it around Jude's waist and tied it with another knot.

Damned if she was going to lose him now.

He cursed again but she knew he was helpless to stop her. If he removed his hands from the wheel there was no telling what would happen to the boat.

"For God's sake at least tie yourself down too," he cried frantically as the wheel jerked in his hands. "I don't have time to worry about you!"

She nodded and searched for another coil of rope. Finding one inside a cabinet, she quickly pulled it out.

A moment later she had herself secured and joined him at the wheel. He seemed relieved when her warm hands slid over his cold ones.

The wheel miraculously steadied.

To her surprise, he smiled at her.

Stubborn man. Didn't he know that a woman was just as strong as a man?

Another ocean wave heaved itself over the bow, spilling water in a V above the decks and into the pilothouse slamming into both of them with such a fury she tumbled against Jude.

"Spread your legs! It'll give you balance!" he shouted above the screeching wind.

Cate nodded her understanding and did as he instructed.

They fought the storm that way for hours. Their hands gripped tightly to the wheel. She stood behind him using his body for much needed warmth against the cold elements. Finally, when the storm eased a little, they'd taken turns at the wheel. While one manned the boat, the other rested in the nearby captain's chair.

Just as Cate was doing now.

Damn her! She looked so cute in that dress.

Jude's grasp on the wheel tightened and his cock pushed hard against the restraints of his jean shorts as he watched her sleep. If the ocean still wasn't so rough, he'd be untying that safety rope from her waist and nibbling on those bare feet she'd tucked beneath her cute ass when she'd climbed onto the captain's chair.

His heart picked up speed as he observed her generous curves outlined against the simple dress he'd laid out for her. He'd purchased the pretty peasant-style dress through Soldiers Mail-Order Catalog service a couple of years ago. He'd kept it with him while he'd driven the tanks through the hot dusty deserts. He'd taken it out every night, touching its softness, imagining it on Cate.

The thought of her wearing the simple dress at their own wedding had saved his sanity amidst the harsh fighting of war. It had eased his sorrows as the painful cries of his fallen comrades had seared through his brain and it had dampened the sounds of sniper fire exploding all around them through yet another terrorist attack.

Jude shivered at the gut-wrenching memories.

He forced aside his sadness and drew his thoughts back to his sensual Cate.

The dress fit her perfectly and it looked a whole hell of lot better on her than he could ever have imagined.

With a low daring neckline, the simple dress gave her an innocent sexy look.

The drenched cotton material embraced her lush breasts, barely concealing those big sweet-tasting nipples from his view.

While she slept, her wet golden hair was tangled over her face; her cheeks were flushed a pretty pink from the wind and her stunning mouth pouted at him.

His cock throbbed as he remembered the snugness of her pussy.

God! She'd been so achingly tight. Her slick velvety vaginal muscles had trembled like a virgin around his flesh. The deeper he'd dove into her the more intense the pleasure.

He'd held his own gratification at bay as he'd concentrated on making her come over and over again, totally transfixed at the exquisite delight etched in her face. When she'd cried out her enjoyment, he'd finally come undone and sought his own pleasure.

Jude closed his eyes and inhaled the salty air. God, he'd found such superb satisfaction in her body and he'd find even more when this storm was fully gone.

The boat pitched against a wave and he held tight to the wheel wincing at the soreness in his arms. They'd worked well together and they'd put up a good fight against the storm.

He frowned, his heart heavy with sadness as he thought of the Barlow brothers waiting for him to show up with Cate. She was the bargaining chip to get his brother Tyler back.

Taking her away in the boat had been a spur of the moment selfish last-ditch effort to bring both of them some pleasure before he turned her over to those wicked men.

Ah shit! Who was he kidding? He'd whisked her away because he'd been terrified. He wanted her safe. Deep in his heart he knew there was no way in hell he could turn her over to the Barlow brothers even if it meant saving Tyler's life.

Narrowing his gaze, he noticed a ray of sunshine beaming far ahead on the ocean's wavy horizon. Soon the sun would shine again and he would have to face reality.

The reality was, when he returned to shore, he would set Cate free.

His heart felt heavy in his chest when an hour later the sea shone as calm as a mirror and Jude's arms ached so badly he could barely lift his sleeping Cate off the captain's chair. Bright sunshine streamed through the salt encrusted windows and bathed him in a warm glow as he carried her into the sleeping quarters.

He was exhausted yet his cock stirred violently as he quietly stripped away her wet dress and admired her shaven pussy, her plump pink nipples and those luscious breasts that felt like silken globes when he held them in his hands.

As if sensing his thoughts she smiled and mumbled something but didn't wake.

Unzipping his wet jean shorts, his cock sprang free of its prison. His erection pulsed thick and hot and despite his exhaustion he was ripe and ready for a good fucking. He flirted with the idea of kissing her awake or playing with her clit until she was so wet he could slide inside her and bring himself relief.

He did neither.

He didn't deserve her. She was too good for him.

He'd lost any future when he'd kidnapped her, tied her down and fucked her.

Shoving his shorts off, he climbed into bed and spooned himself around her backside, his pulsing cock pressed between her ass checks and poked intimately against her back door.

Sighing he draped the warm blankets over both of them and cuddled Cate's sleeping body into his arms.

She felt so right nestled against his body. How would he be able to live after she left him?

His chest tightened with anxiety and it suddenly felt hard to breathe.

"Darling, I have to set you free," he whispered as he buried his face into her tangled damp hair and inhaled her sweet scent.

Catching a sob in his throat at the horrible thought that this could very well be the last time he would hold her in his arms he forced himself to relax.

There was nothing he could do right now. He needed to rest. Needed to think things over again when he could think straight. Maybe there was another way out of this mess. Exhaustion soon overpowered him and he drifted into a restless sleep.

Chapter Five

Jude awoke to the dull throbbing of odd aches and pains in his arms and legs and also to an unusual tickling sensation prodding the feverish head of his cock.

He gritted his teeth to the killing pleasure and opened his eyes to find himself lying totally naked on the bed with Cate seated cross-legged between his own widespread legs.

She wore nothing but the cutest little smile.

The she-devil!

Obviously, she'd been having her way with his cock while he'd slept. His arms and legs were tied to the bedposts and his erection was in full swing. Thick and hot, his shaft stuck up like a solid pole from between his legs.

His entire body tensed as she fanned a plume across the rounded head of his pulsing penis.

"Glad you could join me for the festivities," she purred.

Jude swore softly. The tables had turned and now he was at her mercy.

"What are you up to, Cate?"

Stupid question. He knew what she was up to.

Revenge.

"I could tell you but I'll show you instead."

Her eyes smiled as the feather tenderly crisscrossed the powerful weave of veins in his throbbing cock.

Jude's shaft twitched quite pleasantly and he smothered the need to groan.

When she reached the thick base, she slid the plume lower brushing it to and fro across his bulging sack. Lust shot through his heavy balls, spreading upward and spiking his erection with such sweet pain he couldn't stop the groan from escaping his lips.

"You appear to be in distress," she whispered.

"Perhaps you should come to my rescue, Cate."

"Perhaps you should come…"

Shit!

She dropped the feather. Her lips tilted upward into a delicious smile. His body burned as he looked at her mouth. It made him think wild thoughts. Made him want her lips wrapped tightly around his cock, her hot little tongue licking his balls.

He wanted to be loose, to ask her do these things to him.

"Cate, I want…"

Her hand felt soft and warm as she clamped it over his mouth silencing any requests. He noticed the soft dusting of freckles across her nose, noticed the seductive way her green eyes sparkled as she gazed down at him. His chest constricted at her natural beauty.

"Shh, I've had five years to think of things I want to do to you too, Jude."

Her soft words made his body hum.

Holding her hand tightly over his mouth, she reached out with the other hand and cupped his testicles. Despite his best efforts to keep himself under control his body tightened with tormenting need.

It wasn't supposed to happen this way. He was supposed to be the one in control. The one who would make her beg him to fuck her and not the other way around.

Gentle fingers kneaded his balls until a moan slid up his throat.

He cursed softly when she let go of his scrotum and lowered her head. Taking a rock-hard ball into her hot little mouth her velvety tongue poked diligently and her sharp teeth nibbled at his flesh.

His cock sparkled with fire. Heated blood shot through his veins until he felt as if his entire body might explode.

Suddenly she let go of one ball and started in on the other. Within seconds, she had both his testicles on fire, his cock primed and his entire body shuddering with anticipation.

The instant she lifted her hand he hissed hoarsely, "C'mon Cate, quit torturing me."

She smiled sweetly and he fought against the desires swamping his body.

"You're trembling like a man who hasn't been properly fucked in years but I'm sure you've had your share of *those* women."

"I stayed true to you, in my mind," he admitted.

She grinned, obviously pleased with his answer. In the beginning, he'd tried to stay faithful to her but eventually sex had become a required part of R&R for a soldier. Some women had volunteered for the duty of satisfying the troops. Others had been conscripted, drafted by the homeland or even kidnapped by recruiting officers and trained as sex slaves. He'd always made it a point to seek out the women who'd come voluntarily. He'd learned so much from them.

"They taught me things, Cate. How to please you in so many different ways. Besides, I didn't hear any complaints from you earlier," he growled.

She laughed and winked. "And you won't either."

Her bare breasts jiggled wonderfully as her blonde head dipped again. She licked the underneath part of his shaft all the while purring sweet erotic sounds.

Perspiration tingled over his flesh.

Her scorching moist tongue swept over one side of his bulging head and down the other side and then she whispered, "I wanted you the minute I saw you again."

She'd wanted him? A zip of relief shot through him and niggled away the guilt he'd been feeling at tying her down.

"Don't you remember how wet I was for you when you first slid your finger into me down in the engine room? I haven't worn any underwear since you left. Every time I thought of you all I had to do was reach down and pretend it was your finger…"

She opened her legs wide allowing him to see her wet cunt. Allowed him to watch her slide her hand over her bare pussy, between her swollen labia lips. Her purple aroused clitoris all wet and gleaming and dropping past her lips.

His cock pulsed with excitement and he groaned as her finger disappeared inside her tight slit.

With a sucking sound her finger slid out of her vagina. It looked moist and gleaming in the sunshine.

"I still love you with all my heart. I was just scared of this Claiming Law."

A dark uneasiness zipped through him. Maybe he should tell Cate everything. Tell her about the deal his brothers had made with the Barlow brothers.

No, he wouldn't tell her.

It would be easier for her if she never knew how close they'd been to betraying her.

"Change always scares people," she continued. "At least it's always scared me. But past experience has shown me that things don't usually turn out as bad as I fear. A lot of times change brings better things into someone's life."

Her ocean green eyes sparkled. Her hot velvety hands slipped around the root of his shaft and she lowered her head again kissing the tip of his bulging penis with her warm pink lips. Jude closed his eyes as a white-hot fire raged down his shaft and rumbled through his balls. He could literally feel his sperm building. Could feel his love for her swelling inside his chest.

"I want to come back home with you, Jude. I want to be claimed by the Outlaws." Her hot breath caressed his swollen flesh. He could barely hear her soft whisper as the heated blood roared through his ears.

He should tell Cate the truth. Tell her she couldn't come home. He wouldn't allow it. Wouldn't allow her to be turned over to the Barlow brothers.

He sucked in a harsh breath as her satiny soft lips fastened over the head of his cock making all coherent thoughts vanish.

Ah hell, he could tell her later.

Arching his hips, he pressed his swollen aching flesh deeper into the velvety depths of her hot mouth.

He groaned as her teeth scraped his sensitive skin. Her tongue lashed his shaft and he could feel the tip of his aching cock touch the back of her throat. The insides of her satiny cheeks pressed intimately against his engorged flesh as she eagerly suckled him.

His body tensed wonderfully and he slid quickly to the sharp edge of a climax.

She withdrew her mouth and then she pushed in over him again.

"Oh, Cate! You're so damned good!"

Once again her succulent mouth tightened around him. Her hot tongue branded his cock.

She sucked harder.

He growled as the arousal built to a feverish pitch, threatening to explode at any second.

He groaned and pulled on his restraints wanting to be free. Wanting to grab her by her shoulders. Aching to push her down onto the bed so he could mount her. So he could take her over and over again until they both screamed with arousal.

Her hands slid off his shaft and he inhaled sharply as her fingers curled over his swollen balls.

His abdomen tightened.

Her mouth released his cock again.

"Come for me, Jude." Her hot breath whispered against his penis before she slid her lips over his shaft again.

He groaned.

Her warm fingers squeezed his aching balls in a gentle motion. The pressure inside his scrotum doubled instantly and built to an intoxicating ache until he thought he'd surely explode.

The sweet warmth of her mouth enveloped him again.

"Come for me, Jude," she whispered as she released him.

His entire body trembled and tensed as she drew him in and sucked harder.

"Oh God!" He shouted his warning and lost control.

The orgasm shot through him like a scorching bolt of lightning. Forking through his veins, blazing down his shaft into his balls and crashing through his body in mind-numbing explosions.

His limbs trembled against his bonds. His lungs labored for air. His cock shook valiantly and he released his hot load into her beautiful waiting mouth.

She sucked on him hard. Real hard. Draining him of his sperm until he was bone dry.

When she finished, she rested her head on his thighs, her fingers still curled around his pulsing balls.

He wanted to lift his hand and touch the blonde tangles of her hair. Wanted to reassure her that he would return the favor but he needed to recuperate from the fantastic orgasm.

Instead, he smiled and closed his eyes.

Damn but she was good!

* * * * *

"I hope you've learned your lesson, Jude Outlaw," Cate mumbled as she untied the bonds from the sleeping man's ankles and wrists.

A soft snore answered her.

Damn him!

She'd gotten herself all hot and bothered sucking his cock, bringing him to climax and now he'd fallen asleep on her.

Her drenched cunt quivered and wept against the sheets.

She sighed in frustration and sat cross-legged between his widespread legs frowning at his semi-erect cock. Veins bulged and pulsed up his entire length and his balls were hardening again.

Hmm! The man appeared to be aroused in his sleep. Perhaps she could use his semi-erect cock to her advantage? A partial erection was better than no erection.

No, she wouldn't take him while he slept. She wanted him wide-awake. She required the full power of his strength as he pistoned into her.

In the meantime, she'd use her vibrator.

Cate grinned. She never went anywhere without it. It had become her best friend over the past few years while Jude had been away.

Until he decided to awaken, she'd amuse herself. Just like old times.

Reaching overhead, she popped open a compartment and drew out the trusty old friend she'd stashed up there when she'd stolen *The Outlaw Lover*.

The plastic vibrator felt smooth in her hands and a tingle of excitement zipped up her spine at the thought of masturbating right here in front of Jude while he slept.

She was so hot and bothered, so on the edge that she knew it only would take a few quick thrusts deep into her aching channel with the built-in clit stimulator rubbing against her clitoris and she'd be riding the rod into a climax in no time flat.

Her finger slid onto the switch and her body hummed in anticipation. She was just about to flick it on when a strong hand clamped over her wrist.

"Not so fast, Cate," Jude's strangled whisper curled around her sending shivers of excitement zipping along her nerves.

He sat up on the bed, his hair all ruffled and damp with perspiration, his gray eyes flashing brightly with lust, his lips puffy from their earlier kisses.

"You're awake!"

"I've got something better than masturbation planned for you." He grinned and took the vibrator away from her.

"Turn around. On your knees. Ass in the air. Face into the mattress."

Cate swallowed. Excitement knotted her belly as she spied his cock fully erect and primed for another delicious fucking.

"What are you up to Jude Outlaw?"

"If you want to find out, you'll do as I say. And don't forget to spread your legs wide for me."

Feverish heat flared inside her. "You can be a demanding fellow can't you?"

His dark eyes locked with hers. "Years without my woman can do that to a man."

"Years without her man can do that to a woman too," she breathed.

Turning around she got onto her hands and knees and wiggled her bare ass in the air for him.

"Your face all the way down, Cate."

She felt her body flushing hotter at his soft command. Placing her arms down against the mattress, she nestled her face sideways against the cool sheets and spread her knees wider.

"Fuck me, Jude. Fuck me hard and fuck me now," she demanded.

Cream dripped from her channel and her heart crashed against her chest as the bed moved and he got into position behind her.

She heard the vibrator hum to life.

Here we go!

Her eyes widened as the tip of the vibrator sunk into her vagina in one quick fluid motion.

"Not wasting any time are you?" she gasped as he slid the plastic rod out of her and rammed it into her again. Every muscle in her body tensed as the clitoral stimulator on the machine massaged her clit and the vibrator shivered against her pussy walls. Her vaginal muscles already stimulated from her earlier session of orally pleasuring him clenched tightly around the plastic object. The scent of her arousal pierced the air.

"I'm sure we're both too impatient this time around," he chuckled as he withdrew again.

It was true. This would be the first time they were both free of their bonds and she was just as eager as he was to get quick satisfaction this time around.

She scrapped her sore nipples against the soft bed sheets, imagining it was Jude's roughened tongue lapping at her.

He withdrew the vibrator again. This time though he slid it intimately between her ass cheeks. Her legs trembled with the realization he wanted to take her anally with the vibrator.

Her pulses skittered as he dipped the moistened tip inside her ass. He eased the plastic object into her slowly, carefully, every soft stroke going deeper into her snug ass. She forced her muscles to relax. Forced herself to keep calm. To float with the odd sensation of being filled like she'd never been filled before. By the time he stopped the insertion, she was shivering and poised on the edge of something untamed and new.

"I've wanted to do this to you for as long as I can remember, Cate. I've wanted to be the first to double-penetrate you." he whispered as he eased the hot tip of his cock between her drenched labia lips and entered her too-tight sheath.

A mixture of both fear and excitement slammed into her and her breath caught in her throat.

Oh God! Double penetration!

He was preparing her for his brothers! He was getting her used to the idea of several men fucking her at once.

Double penetration. It was a requisite of the Claiming Law.

Double penetration by two men and a third coming in her mouth.

Madness!

Sensational madness!

She could get used to this awesomely stuffed feeling of being double penetrated.

"You're so tight," he groaned as he slid deeper. "So beautifully tight. I never imagined you could feel like this."

He thrust his hips slowly in a gentle but powerful rhythm forcing her channel to accustom quickly to the double penetration.

Fire zipped up her cunt and soon her muscles gave way surrendering to his thick cock as he plunged the rest of the way into her. Her fear about why he was doing this quickly vanished into arousal as his finger massaged her quivering clit. Incredible pleasure drenched her. Automatically she bucked her hips backwards into him allowing his cock to slide even deeper into her womb. Her inner body clutched frantically at his searing flesh.

When his cock lay buried deep inside her, he whispered into her ear.

"We belong to each other."

He spoke the truth. She did belong to him.

He'd taken her heart a long time ago. She understood that now. Knew she could go back home with him. Recognized that their bond was stronger than a manmade law.

She would allow his brothers to fuck her. She would accept their straining cocks inside her. But that's all it would be for her. Just sex.

Pleasure with sensual men she'd always cared about but had never loved. At least not loved in the sense of wanting to sleep with them.

Except with Jude it would be more than sex. It would be true love. She would do anything to be with him and if she had to be the wife to his brothers too, so be it.

As she accepted her new way of thinking, she literally felt the last of her resistance dissolve and her love for Jude grow.

"I love you, Jude," she whispered.

"I've always loved you, Cate," he replied. "Believe me when I say I don't want to share you with anyone else."

"I believe you."

He withdrew his cock and impaled her again to the hilt, his balls squashing against her.

Passion cradled her body as he plunged in and out of her in a steady rhythm and at the same time leaving the vibrator firmly impaled in her ass.

He plunged into her tightness with long heated strokes that left her gasping. She could literally feel herself becoming lost in his masterful thrusts. Could feel how her vaginal walls clenched around him.

Soon her body dripped with perspiration and her anguished moans of pleasure intermingled with his groans.

She pushed harder against him straining toward her climax. Her muscles tightened. Her body shuddered. His rhythm increased and she struggled to breathe.

Closing her eyes, she slipped over the edge.

White-hot pleasure raged through her double-penetrated body.

From somewhere far away she heard herself scream out Jude's name. Heard herself begging him to never leave her.

She heard his hoarse affirmation, as his cock spewed his heated release deep into her womb.

Chapter Six

Wrapped warmly in his arms, Cate couldn't stop the smile from sliding over her lips and her heart filled with happiness.

Jude Outlaw was a fabulous lover, better than she remembered.

"You're almost due for another shot of medicine," Jude's soft whisper caressed her cheek.

"I know."

"I heard they're coming out with something new. Instead of daily injections you'll be able to take the medicine in pill form once a day."

"I just wish they'd come up with a cure for it," Cate sighed and snuggled deeper into his embrace.

"The researchers are working on it. They say it's only a matter of time. They just have to find out how to stop the trigger that switches on the sickness in the DNA. Once they find it they can turn off the switch then no more sickness and…"

"No more medicine. Y'know sometimes when the sickness hits I wish…"

"What?"

"Oh, never mind."

"Tell me," Jude nuzzled his raspy five o'clock shadowed face against the nape of her neck.

"Sometime I wish I would just die."

Every muscle in his body tensed against her.

"Don't ever say that again. Don't even think it, do you hear me?"

"Why? Would you have missed me?"

There was a long hesitation before he replied in a soft tone. "If you had died, I would have been walking around like a zombie. Just like Luke's been doing these past few years. He was so careless in the Terrorist Wars he almost got his head blown off a few times. Cripes, he was in the hospital more times than I can count."

"He still misses Callie."

"A love like they had never dies."

Cate worried her lip. Now that talk had turned to her sister, Callie, she figured it was time to tell him something she hadn't had a chance to tell him.

"I promised I'd never say anything about this but I think I better say something about Callie."

"Is she dead? Did they send you word?"

"No, she's not dead. She escaped from an experimental facility."

"What? You're kidding? You've seen her?"

"No, but my other sister, Laurie, spoke to her."

Jude unwrapped his arms from around her and bolted upright in the bed. His eyes blazed dark with excitement.

"Where is she?"

"I have no idea."

"Shit, Cate! When did all this happen?"

"She dropped by Laurie's place a few months ago. She needed some money. Laurie gave it to her and Callie left without telling her where she was going. She said she didn't want to put anyone's life into danger." Cate forced back the stab of intense worry she'd felt for her sister.

"Did she at least say how she can be contacted?"

"She said she'd be in touch with Laurie. I don't know where she went, Jude. She said the authorities were after her."

"Shit!" Jude stood up and began getting dressed.

"What are you going to do?"

"Heading back to shore. Luke has to be told."

A shiver of nervousness skittered up her spine. They were going back. Back to reality.

When he was dressed, he sat down on the bed beside her and caressed her hair.

"You're due for an injection. I'll give it to you and then I want you to rest. I'll wake you up when we get back."

Cate nodded.

He quickly left the cabin to retrieve her medicine from the kitchen.

She bit her bottom lip and stared out the windows at the cheerful sunshine streaming down onto the ocean.

She hoped Laurie would forgive her for telling Jude about their sister, Callie. Cate shivered and hugged herself. She'd heard horror stories about those experimental facilities and she didn't want Callie to get caught and sent back there.

"Everything is going to be okay, Cate. Trust me, Luke will find her and protect her," Jude said as he re-entered the room with her medicine.

There was an odd look in his eyes that unsettled her but he smiled and the look quickly vanished into something beautiful she could only call love.

He unwrapped the plastic from a new needle and jabbed the point into the vial of pink medicine sucking up the required amount that she needed to take every day in order to stay alive. She flinched as he injected the medicine into her shoulder.

"Rest now my lady. Rest."

She nodded and he tucked the blankets in around her naked body and left.

* * * * *

She didn't know how long she slept but when she awoke the sky was pitch black and she heard two men's voices drift through the nearby open window from the cockpit directly above where she slept.

Looking through the windows she noted the familiar silhouette of the New Portland skyline and the buttery lights glowing in some of the building's windows.

Obviously, they were docked at the wharf and Jude had picked up his brother, Luke. It meant they'd be heading to the Outlaw farm and she would begin her new life as their wife.

She sighed heavily. Doubts swirled.

Could she handle it? Could she handle having several men making love to her? Cate squared her shoulders in defiance. Of course she could. It was a new way of life for all of them. Besides, she wasn't in this alone. Jude would be standing by her side.

Confidence soared inside her. With Jude behind her, she could do anything.

If he felt certain that he could protect her from the Barlows and that their relationship could survive this new Claiming Law she would put her trust in him.

Head held high with pride, Cate pushed open the cabin door and halted when she heard Luke's voice sail through the night air.

"It was the agreement we made with the Barlows, Jude. Cate was to be theirs."

Cate's blood ran cold.

What agreement with the Barlows? What did he mean Cate was to be theirs? Were the Outlaws giving her to the Barlows?

Sweet God! No!

She stood stiffly in the doorway barely feeling the cool breeze blow against her shivering body.

Anxious minutes drifted by as she awaited Jude's response.

Say something, Jude. Tell Luke what you told me! Tell him the Outlaws would protect me!

She didn't hear him answer.

Son of a bitch!

Her legs wobbled and threatened to collapse. Hot tears of rage bubbled into her eyes.

She shut the door behind her and flung herself onto the bed burying her head into the pillow to stifle her sobs.

How could he? How could Jude betray her like this?

When was he going to tell her? Or was he simply going to let her think she was heading back home to the Outlaw brothers and when they got there they would hand her over to the Barlows?

She'd honestly believed he'd loved her. Instead, he'd used her for his own sexual gratification.

A few good fucks to remember him by?

The bastard had betrayed her. She would kill him. That's what she'd do. She'd cut off his...

She cringed as a hand curled gently over her shoulder.

"I'm sorry we woke you, Cate. I saw the light switch on. I guess you heard us talking." Jude said softly. "I should have told you."

Whirling up in the bed Cate couldn't stop the red-hot anger from screaming through her as she slapped him against his cheek.

The sharp sound of her sudden violence, the surprised look on his face and the sting to her palm did little to dampen her hurt.

"Yes, you should have told me you were betraying me, you bastard!" She wiped away the tears streaming down her face. "God! How could I have been so stupid in trusting you? The only reason you were fucking me was to prepare me for those cruel men. God! I was so naïve. So pathetic. Clinging to your lies like an idiot. I thought you loved me. What a laugh."

"I do love you, Cate. I love you with my whole being."

Cate shook her head with puzzlement.

"Why then? Why are you so casually throwing away what we feel for each other?"

"He's not, Cate."

Anger burned anew when she spotted Luke Outlaw standing in the cabin doorway.

His sharp eyes gazed back at her. He looked uncomfortable. Maybe even ashamed?

Good!

"You're no better than he is," she spat.

"He didn't meet the deadline, Cate. Jude took the damn boat and took you and left me high and dry back here to deal with the Barlows. They came and they went. They called off the deal."

Jude reached out to caress her cheek but he flinched as she pushed him away. "I wanted to tell you, Cate. Wanted to tell you about the deal with the Barlows. About Tyler. About our plan."

"We would have gotten you out after they had given us the information." Luke explained.

Cate's head spun with confusion. "What deal? What information? What news about Tyler? I thought he was dead?"

"The Barlows have information about Tyler. He's alive but they wouldn't say where he was unless they got you by the end of this week. When they showed up tonight they said the deal is off. They're rich men and apparently their money attracted a woman who willingly wanted to be claimed by them. Apparently they've already claimed her."

Jude sighed with relief. "So they've no reason to not tell us about Tyler. Where is he?"

"They won't say yet."

"Shit!" Jude cursed.

Luke smiled at her. "At least Cate is safe."

Jude squeezed her closer to his side. "Besides, if Tyler had found out we'd thrown his woman's sister to those bastards just to try and free him, he would have killed us all. I may just have saved all our lives."

Luke grinned. "You sure are right about that."

Suddenly he reached for Cate's hand and shook it. "I want to thank you for telling Jude about Callie."

"You're going to look for her, aren't you?"

"Yes. But before I go I have to say welcome to the Outlaw family. My brothers are tough on the outside but big romantic teddy bears on the inside."

"Cate's not going to be claimed by any of our brothers," Jude said softly.

She couldn't help but tremble with excitement at his words.

Luke blinked in shock. "But the Claiming Law…"

"Screw the Law. I'm not taking her home," Jude said.

"But where will you go? The entire world is adopting the Claiming Law. All the states have agreed to it. It's north and south of the borders. The authorities will question you wherever you go. You'll need papers to show she's been claimed. If they suspect she isn't claimed then they'll take her away and give her to anyone…"

"It's a chance I'm willing to take," Cate said quickly.

"And I am too." Jude agreed. "Besides, we've made connections during the Wars. Claiming papers can be forged."

Luke chuckled and slapped his brother on the back.

"Okay, stay put in New Portland for a couple of days. When I get back home, I'll wire you money. In the meantime…"

Luke reached into his back pocket and dug out a wad of bills. He held it out to Luke. "Here take this. You're going to need it."

Jude's arm snuggled warmly around her waist. "No. You keep it. Use it to help find Tyler and Callie. I've got enough money to keep us going for a while. We'll live on the boat. Maybe find us an island somewhere and stay low. But first we'll bring you back home."

"No, you stay with your lady. You two have been apart long enough. Don't worry about me, I'll be fine. Just make sure you send word home every once in a while that you two are okay."

"Will do," Jude agreed.

His arm around Cate's waist tightened and suddenly she couldn't wait for Luke to leave. Couldn't wait until Jude was nestled snugly between her legs again.

The man truly did love her. He'd sacrificed his own brother in order to keep her safe. Yet it pained her that Tyler would suffer because of the Barlow's greed.

She watched as Luke closed the cabin door. With a final wave through the windows, he disappeared into the night.

"Why the frown? I thought you'd be happy?" Jude whispered in her ear.

"I'm thinking of Tyler. All this time and we thought he was dead. My sister Laurie loved him. It broke her heart when she was told he was dead. We have to get word to her."

"Luke said he'd tell her. We'll find another way to get him back. I just pity the woman the Barlows claimed. But I'm glad it wasn't you. Just wish I had told you everything that was going on about Tyler. I'm a sorry son-of-a-bitch, Cate. Will you ever forgive me?"

"Oh I don't know," she breathed. "Why don't you ask me again when you've put me into a better mood?"

Cate curled her fingers against the zipper of his jeans shorts. Lowering it, she grinned at the sharp grating sound. His mouth-watering cock sprang free. It was long and thick and deliciously swollen.

Her blood heated at the gorgeous sight.

"Not wearing any underwear, Jude? You must have been expecting me," she teased.

He inhaled sharply as her hands curled around the base of his cock.

"Never had a man ready for me so fast, Jude. I won't have any trouble sliding you into my wet cunt and fucking you senseless for the rest of the night."

He grinned at the similar words he'd used on her only yesterday morning when he'd first caught her trying to escape him in the engine room.

"Fuck me, Jude Outlaw," she commanded as she pulled his cock closer to her.

"I never say no to a lady's demands."

His head lowered and his sizzling mouth clamped over her lips in a searing fusion of love.

The Claiming

For Mary Moran—a wonderful editor and a great friend. Thanks for all your support.

Prologue
Barlow Ranch — Maine, USA —
August 14, 2020

The scent of sex hung heavy in the air as Luke Outlaw pushed the bedroom door open and stared in shock at the scene in front of him.

They were all naked.

Three Barlow brothers.

And one very familiar woman.

Her long blonde curls were spread out on the black satin pillow like a golden waterfall, her eyes closed tightly in apparent erotic bliss.

He couldn't believe it was *her*.

The woman who'd sworn to love his brother Tyler for all eternity was having sex with his brother's worst enemies.

Never mind that she thought Tyler was dead.

It was no excuse to sell her body to these devils.

Yet here she was lying on a double king-sized bed, her naked body splayed out on black satin sheets, her wrists and ankles tied securely with long velvet straps that led to wooden bedposts shaped like a woman's breasts.

Moans of pleasure and slurping sounds drifted through the air as Clay, the youngest of the Barlow brothers, had his blond head buried between her legs, his long tongue eagerly lapping up her pleasure juices. Another Barlow tended to a swollen breast, massaging one full globe while actively sucking on a plump red nipple as if it were a lollipop.

A third Barlow, his plump lips twisted with pleasure, kneeled on the bed near her flushed face, his short cock plunging in and out of her eager mouth.

He knew the Barlow brothers had claimed a willing woman.

But this one?

By God, how could this be possible?

How could she betray his brother?

How could she volunteer to service the four Barlow brothers? And seemingly enjoy doing it?

Luke's stomach twisted with sudden anxiety.

Wait a minute. There were only three men here.

Where was the other one?

The tiny hairs on the back of his neck prickled a warning a split second before he heard the sharp sound of a gun cock.

Oh, shit!

Before he could so much as move, a gunshot seared through the air. Something hard and painful slammed through his shoulder spinning him around and tossing him into the bedroom.

He hit the plush white carpet hard, pain biting into him like a hot poker, bringing with it a thick black wave of nausea.

From somewhere far off he heard her scream. Heard the Barlows' shouts of surprise and anger.

He didn't know how long he lay there fighting the black waves threatening to engulf him before her concerned face hovered into view.

Gosh she looked quite pretty when she got upset, a cute little worried wrinkle nestled between her perfectly arched eyebrows. He could understand why his brother Tyler had fallen in love with her.

"Luke? Oh, my God! You shot Luke Outlaw!"

"What the hell is an Outlaw doing here?" one of the Barlows snapped angrily from behind her.

"Kill the bastard!" another snarled.

Shit!

He needed to tell her the truth. Needed to tell her she didn't have to be a sex slave to the Barlows. He needed to tell her that Tyler wasn't dead.

He had to tell her the truth before he died.

"Get me something to press over his wound!" she yelled at the brothers.

The words formed in his brain but when he opened his mouth excruciating pain sliced into him as she pressed something against both sides of his shoulder.

Oh man, this felt bad. Real bad.

The black waves swooped in for the kill, suffocating him, preventing him from telling her the truth.

He fought them. Truly he did.

But they were too powerful, slamming into him from all directions.

He had no choice but to give up the fight.

Promptly, he passed out.

Chapter One

Outlaw Farm — North Section, Maine, USA
August 15, 2020

Callie Callahan had just finished rinsing her dinner dishes when an odd sound split the silence of the rustic one-room cabin she was hiding in.

Over the last several weeks since she'd escaped the government research labs she'd trained herself not to panic at every little noise but that didn't stop the icy shiver of fear from slicing up her spine this time.

Taking no chances, she doused her candle plunging the room into semidarkness. Pulling the gun out of the waistband of her jeans where she always kept it, she slid her lean frame against the wall and peeked out the only window that wasn't boarded up.

Scanning the dusky shadows, her heart thundered against her chest.

Nothing moved out there in the dense Maine woods.

Yet, every cell in her body screamed danger lurked nearby.

Her finger tightened on the trigger.

Recent events with the newly introduced Claiming Law had her nerves on edge. Simply because the law said that a group of men could capture themselves a woman, videotape a sexual consummation and then lay a claim on her as their personal property, didn't mean she was eager to be found, fucked and claimed by anyone who discovered her hiding place.

Not only did she have to be on the lookout for horny men, she was also on the government laboratories "most wanted" list for being one of the few remaining women who was naturally resistant to the X-virus.

Discover for yourself why readers can't get enough of the multiple award-winning publisher Ellora's Cave. Whether you prefer e-books or paperbacks, be sure to visit EC on the web at www.ellorascave.com for an erotic reading experience that will leave you breathless.

www.ellorascave.com

THE
ELLORA'S CAVE
LIBRARY

Stay up to date with Ellora's Cave Titles
in Print with our Quarterly Catalog.

TO RECIEVE A CATALOG,
SEND AN EMAIL WITH YOUR NAME
AND MAILING ADDRESS TO:

CATALOG@ELLORASCAVE.COM

OR SEND A LETTER OR POSTCARD
WITH YOUR MAILING ADDRESS TO:
CATALOG REQUEST
C/O ELLORA'S CAVE PUBLISHING, INC.
1337 COMMERCE DRIVE #13
STOW, OH 44224

NEED A MORE EXCITING
WAY TO PLAN YOUR DAY?

ELLORA'S
CAVEMEN
2006 CALENDAR

COMING THIS FALL

www.cerridwenpress.com for customer recommendations we make available to new consumers.)

3. *Mobility.* Because your new library now consists of only a microchip, your entire cache of books can be taken with you wherever you go.

4. *Personal preferences are accounted for.* Are the words you are currently reading too small? Too large? Too...**ANNOYING**? Paperback books cannot be modified according to personal preferences, but e-books can.

5. *Instant gratification.* Is it the middle of the night and all the bookstores are closed? Are you tired of waiting days—sometimes weeks—for online and offline bookstores to ship the novels you bought? Ellora's Cave Publishing sells instantaneous downloads 24 hours a day, 7 days a week, 365 days a year. Our e-book delivery system is 100% automated, meaning your order is filled as soon as you pay for it.

Those are a few of the top reasons why electronic novels are displacing paperbacks for many an avid reader. As always, Ellora's Cave and Cerridwen Press welcomes your questions and comments. We invite you to email us at service@ellorascave.com, service@cerridwenpress.com or write to us directly at: 1056 Home Ave. Akron OH 44310-3502.

Why an electronic book?

We live in the Information Age—an exciting time in the history of human civilization in which technology rules supreme and continues to progress in leaps and bounds every minute of every hour of every day. For a multitude of reasons, more and more avid literary fans are opting to purchase e-books instead of paperbacks. The question to those not yet initiated to the world of electronic reading is simply: *why?*

1. *Price.* An electronic title at Ellora's Cave Publishing and Cerridwen Press runs anywhere from 40-75% less than the cover price of the <u>exact same title</u> in paperback format. Why? Cold mathematics. It is less expensive to publish an e-book than it is to publish a paperback, so the savings are passed along to the consumer.

2. *Space.* Running out of room to house your paperback books? That is one worry you will never have with electronic novels. For a low one-time cost, you can purchase a handheld computer designed specifically for e-reading purposes. Many e-readers are larger than the average handheld, giving you plenty of screen room. Better yet, hundreds of titles can be stored within your new library—a single microchip. (Please note that Ellora's Cave and Cerridwen Press does not endorse any specific brands. You can check our website at www.ellorascave.com or

About the author:

Jan Springer is the pseudonym for an award winning best selling author who writes erotic romance and romantic suspense at a secluded cabin nestled in the Haliburton Highlands, Ontario, Canada.

She has enjoyed careers in hairstyling and accounting, but her first love is always writing. Hobbies include kayaking, gardening, hiking, traveling, reading and writing.

Jan welcomes mail from readers. You can write to her c/o Ellora's Cave Publishing at 1056 Home Avenue, Akron OH 44310-3502.

She blinked in shock.

What in the world was she thinking?

She couldn't allow herself to be fucked by a male.

She had to speak with The Breeders about this. Needed to remind them that queens did not mate with males.

It was unheard of. Scandalous. Illegal.

Absolutely delicious.

Her enemies were about to give her something she'd dreamed about for as long as she could remember.

Why deny herself a taste of her deepest fantasies? Her darkest desires?

Frustration screamed through Queen Jacey's naked body, making her yank hard at the velvet bonds securing her up-stretched arms and spread-eagled legs.

Nothing budged.

She might as well relax. No use in wasting her energy. She'd need all of it when the time came to endure whatever form of sexual torture her enemies, The Breeders, had planned for her.

A whisper of uneasiness tingled up her spine at the sound of footsteps.

Two sets of footsteps.

Okay, two against one. She could handle it. She was a Queen after all, trained to resist torture.

Swallowing the lump of fear clogging her throat, she braced herself against her restraints and kept her eyes glued to the door of the tiny stall they'd brought her to.

Suddenly the door swung open and a male was quickly shoved inside.

Not just any male, but a tall, golden-brown-haired male.

And he was totally naked!

Stormy blue eyes ringed with thick black lashes snapped with desire the instant he saw her. His delicious-looking lips curved upward into an appreciative smile making Jacey's breath back up in her lungs. He had an exquisite masculine face with a straight nose, strong jut to his jawline, and a square chin.

He possessed a sensual neck, broad shoulders and a muscular chest with a generous spattering of curly golden-brown hair that arrowed down over his taut belly and...

Every nerve ending in her body sparked to life as her gaze drew straight to the rock-hard looking balls and the massive eight-inch cock stabbing out at her from between his powerful legs.

Goddess of Freedom!

The male looked so tasty she couldn't wait to wrap her mouth around his thick pulsing rod or kiss his tan nipples.

Only one man knew she was here and he'd sworn he'd never come unless it was their prearranged appointed meeting especially after she'd warned him she was on a shoot-to-kill and ask questions later schedule. It was the only way she could keep herself from being caught by the government scientists or claimed.

If someone was lurking around out there, he or they were walking dead men because she wasn't losing her freedom without one heck of a fight.

The silence rattled her and she moved the gun closer to the window turning her head to scan the interior of the cabin. From this vantage point, she had a visual of each boarded-up window plus the front and back doors.

If anyone came through anywhere, she'd plug him full of bullets.

An ear-shattering crash from right beside her made her jump in surprise as the window disintegrated. Numbed by the sudden attack she watched helplessly as an arm reached inside and snatched the gun right out of her fingers.

Oh, my God!

They're here!

All the calm she'd so carefully gathered over the past few weeks untangled in one fell swoop turning her into a bundle of helpless nerves.

What should she do?

She stared at the front door.

No! She couldn't go that way. They would expect her to go out one of the doors.

For a split second, she considered breaking the glass on a back window and pushing away the boards then diving through, but that would take too long.

A second later the back door burst inward with a deafening crash. In the darkness she made out the forms of two men standing side-by-side effectively blocking her escape route.

Blocking her bid for freedom.

Sheer terror made her sob in frustration.

They'd found her! They'd force themselves on her now. Claim her as their sexual property.

Virgins were always placed with the group of men who first took them.

A rage of defiance sifted through her.

She hadn't saved herself all these years for one special man just so a pack of strangers would lay claim to her. She'd die before she let that happen.

Her gaze flew to the butcher knife on the counter. She could sink it into her heart with one swift plunge...

"Callie. Don't be scared," one of the men who stood in the doorway said. Immediately she recognized his voice.

Sweet Pete, it was the preacher. The only man she'd allowed herself to have contact with since she'd escaped, her one link to the outside world.

The one who'd promised never to come here unless it was their scheduled meeting time.

"Oh, for heaven's sake!" she yelled at his shadowy figure. "What the hell are you doing here? You scared the crap out of me!"

Sweet mercy! She was actually safe!

And she was boiling mad, too.

"You're not supposed to come 'til next week. What's the matter with you? Why'd you break the window?"

"I didn't." The preacher pointed to the newcomer. "He did."

He?

She cast her gaze to the tall figure who stood beside the preacher.

He looked so heart-stoppingly familiar she almost forgot to breathe.

It was *him*.

She knew it in the elegant way he held himself. Knew it, even though his features were shadowed, that his hair would be a wavy brown with golden highlights, his eyes would be a dark chocolate and he'd have the cutest laughter crinkles at the sides of his sensually shaped mouth.

Despite that fact, her mind refused to admit he'd found her.

Could God be so cruel? Could he have brought Luke Outlaw, the man she loved with her entire being, back into her life?

"Callie? Is that really you?" The sound of his tortured whisper made her cry out in shock.

It was him!

"He's been shot," the preacher said quickly. "He tricked me into bringing him here. And he's drunk. He polished off a bottle of whiskey in the car. Purely medicinal purposes, of course."

Luke hiccupped and scowled at the preacher. "You're a goddamn son of a bitch for not telling me she's been living right here on Outlaw land and right under my nose."

He gave the preacher a rough shove into the cabin.

Then he stepped inside, closing and bolting the door behind him.

That's when she noticed the guns he carried in each hand.

One was aimed at the preacher.

One pointed at her.

Oh, my gosh!

"You are supposed to be dead," his voice echoed in the semidarkness as he waved one of the guns at her. "Or, at the very least, some crazed guinea pig hooked up to some government's experimental lab so they can figure out why you never got the X-virus." Hiccup. "Yet, here you are…hiding in what would have been our…home," he frowned. "And as healthy, and prettier than I remember you…" Hiccup. "As if you

never even left. As if you'd never been taken away all those years ago. As if you're a dream."

Callie's lungs tightened and concern rushed her senses. The preacher had said Luke had been shot. How serious was the injury? It couldn't be that bad if he was still standing, could it?

He swayed dangerously, his eyes narrowing with anger.

"Are you a dream, Callie?"

"Luke, please sit down before you fall." She stepped toward him and froze as Luke shot a bullet into the ceiling.

"Not so fast, honey." He blinked rapidly as if trying to clear his vision. Perspiration peppered his forehead and pain etched the shadows of his face. In the darkness, she noticed a dark patch staining his white T-shirt in the area of his left shoulder.

Blood.

Anxiety for his health swarmed her.

"How bad is he hurt?"

"Bad enough," the preacher said. "He mumbled something about the Barlows shooting him. Don't know why, but the bullet went clean through his shoulder. The only medicine I had was painkillers. He wouldn't take them. So I gave him a whiskey bottle that one of my parishioners gave me a long time ago."

"Even if you're a dream," Luke sang out waving the gun at her as if it were an admonishing finger, "you're not getting away from me this time. Light some candles, woman. I want to get a good look at my fiancée."

Callie stiffened.

It had always irritated her on the odd occasion when he'd tried to order her around. He was doing it now. And she was getting a touch pissed off.

"Do as he says, Callie. Alcohol doesn't seem to mix well with his mood. He might shoot off another round and there's no telling where the next one might hit or if there's someone out in the woods who might hear the commotion."

Callie nodded.

The preacher was right. The last thing she needed was for anyone to hear gunshots out this way.

Her hands trembled as she searched for the matchbox on the counter. It took her several attempts before she had a candle glowing. Setting it in the middle of the kitchen table, she turned around and found him now sitting on her bed and the buttery candle glow had chased away the shadows to his face.

She almost wished he'd stayed in the darkness of the room.

Maybe then her heart wouldn't have tightened so hard at the sight of the rough stubble on his face, the strong column to his tanned throat, the wide shoulders and the strong chest muscles straining against his T-shirt.

Sexual awareness glittered in his dark brown eyes as he stared at her in an intoxicating way that made heat spread through her pussy. She could literally feel the warm cream seeping past her plump folds to wet her panties.

Sexual tension thickened the air around them.

Callie swallowed tightly.

"How…how bad are you wounded?" She admonished herself for the overwhelming concern she felt for a man she thought she'd forced out of her heart, and once again stepped toward him.

"That's far enough, Callie. Stop right there. Let me take a look at you." The steely cold in his voice made her halt.

She tried hard not to shiver at the erotic way his heated gaze roved along the fullness of her breasts as they pushed up against the tattered shirt she wore.

"Very nice," he whispered. "Very nice indeed."

She followed to where he was looking and noticed how her nipples were poking proudly against the thin material.

Inhaling softly, she watched his eyes travel over her curvy breasts, down her belly to the area between her legs.

Her pussy quivered with excitement against her tight jeans.

Thank God, the preacher was behind her and he couldn't see how she was responding to the scorching way Luke was looking at her.

"I've come to claim you, Callie," he said softly.

Claim her?

"That's not possible, Mr. Outlaw." The preacher echoed her thoughts. "I already told you that you can't marry her—"

"Shut up!" Luke's eyes blazed fiercely but he kept his gaze fixed upon her. "I came here to marry her and I'm going to do it the old-fashioned way. Legal or not."

Callie's heart thumped a mile a minute as she digested what Luke had just said.

Marry her?

Was he seriously demented?

Delirious? Yes, he must be delirious.

"Preacher man!" Luke snapped and waved the pistol in warning. "You marry Callie and me. Now!"

"Luke... I don't think that's a good idea," she said.

"Callie, just stay there in the candlelight. God, you look so beautiful."

Her? Beautiful?

She hadn't run a comb through her short auburn tangles all day. Her shirt was covered in flour from making bread and she didn't even have any makeup on.

She resisted the urge to primp her hair into a more orderly fashion.

Oh, heavens! Why did she even care what she looked like? She had no future with this man. All their dreams were gone. All because of the one mistake she'd made.

Despite that fact, she couldn't stop herself from blushing at his comment.

He thought she was beautiful.

The gun in his right hand suddenly lifted and Luke pointed it at the preacher's head.

In response, the preacher squealed in fright. "Good heavens! Please, Mr. Outlaw, don't shoot me."

"Luke, you're delirious," Callie tried to keep her voice soft and steady. Inside, she trembled. If he was delirious, Luke just might be sick enough to shoot the man. "Put the guns down, please."

He shot another round into her roof, the echo piercing through the air like a missile.

Damn him!

"The gun doesn't go anywhere, sweetheart. Not until we're married. I've been dreaming of this day for more than five years...since you disappeared."

"I...I...I can't m-marry you two, Mr. Outlaw," the preacher stammered with anxiety. "It...it's against the law for a single man to marry a woman. The old ways are gone. She must be properly claimed...by at least four men...perhaps your brothers would be interested in joining you in the festivities?"

"She's mine," Luke snarled. His white teeth gleamed sinisterly in the candlelight. "Marry us, or so help me God, I'll kill you right where you stand."

"Yes, sir." The preacher promptly produced a bible from the folds of his black suit.

Callie's head whirled.

"This is ridiculous," she muttered as Luke's gaze continued to graze over her breasts sending a wonderful awareness coursing through her heated veins.

Her nipples hardened even more against her thin shirt, little rosebuds that were dying to burst free. Aching to pop into Luke's moist mouth.

"Luke, put the gun down. I've had enough of this." She tried to sound stern, but there was a sensual edge to her voice that she found irritating.

"Uh-oh, the groom-to-be is in trouble." Hiccup. "Not a good thing for the wedding night."

He chuckled and winked at her.

Oh, dear.

The preacher's quickly spoken words broke into the foray.

"Callie Callahan, do you take Luke Outlaw to be your lawfully wedded husband? In sickness and in health? For richer? For poorer? Will you honor and cherish him for as long as you both shall live?"

"She does. Now continue," Luke mumbled.

She had the sudden urge to grab a nearby frying pan and smack it over his head. How dare he assume she still wanted to marry him!

"This has gone far enough—" she protested.

He lifted the gun cutting her into silence. She stiffened as he kissed the open barrel to his lips.

"Shh, the preacher is marrying us."

"It isn't legal," Callie stated defiantly.

"Yes, it is," the preacher hissed back. "The government is still in the process of revoking our licenses. Mine is still valid."

Oh, God!

"Do you Luke Outlaw take Callie to be your lawfully wedded wife? In sickness? In health? For richer? For poorer? To honor and cherish for as long as you both live?"

"Damn straight I do."

Callie's stomach plummeted.

"The rings? I need the rings to make this official," the preacher replied quickly.

Oh, thank you, God!

No rings. No marriage.

"I have them right here," came Luke's quick reply.

To her horror, he slid the gun barrel inside the collar of his T-shirt and pulled out a chain necklace. Dog tags tinkled and behind them, she saw two glittering gold rings.

Their wedding rings!

He still had them. Even after all this time.

The preacher hurried over to him and helped remove the chain necklace and subsequently the rings.

A quick blessing over them and both Luke and the preacher were waving at her to come closer.

Callie swallowed hard.

This cannot be happening!

The thought of escaping rushed through her mind. She doubted Luke would shoot her. Doubted if the preacher could catch her.

It was as if Luke knew exactly what she was thinking for he pointed the gun at the preacher again who whimpered his distress. "Please, Callie. I don't want to die. I have to christen a baby tomorrow. Please, don't let Mr. Outlaw shoot me. And I still have to visit with the Barlows and their new wife the day after. They always offer such tasty food."

She noticed Luke stiffen at the mention of the Barlow brothers and wondered what pitiful soul those evil boys had captured for their wife.

"Get over here, Callie," Luke commanded. Red-hot anger flashed bright in his eyes.

In the time she'd known him before everything had fallen apart she'd rarely seen him angry. His calmness had been one of the many things that had attracted her to him.

But the anger contorting his face frightened her.

Something was seriously wrong and that unwanted compassion overwhelmed her again.

She did as he said. On rather wobbly legs, she walked over to the bed.

"Sit beside me."

She sat down, the mattress sagging beneath her. Even though the guns he held in his hands made her uneasy, she enjoyed the waves of sexual heat cascading through her at being near him again.

"Please," the preacher said quickly. "Hold out your hand, Mr. Outlaw. Callie, please place the ring on his finger."

Callie's eyes were drawn to the magnificent muscles that strained against Luke's shirtsleeves as he deposited one of the guns on the other side of him and lifted his free hand, wiggling his fingers in anticipation.

She took the larger ring from the preacher, trying hard to ignore the pleading look in his eyes for her to go along with this farce of a marriage.

This was crazy!

And yet Luke's nearness intoxicated her and she couldn't resist sliding the gold ring onto his finger.

"And now you, Mr. Outlaw."

Luke's face broke into a big smile allowing those cute little laughter lines around his mouth to blossom.

Something erotic and exciting sizzled to life deep inside her womb and she found herself holding out her left hand.

Without hesitation, he slid the ring onto her finger.

Oh, dear. A perfect fit.

The instant the ring slipped onto her finger, she could literally see the tension leave Luke's body.

"With this ring, I thee wed," Luke slurred as he thankfully placed the remaining gun onto the bed.

The flash of lust in his eyes made Callie shiver with a pleasure she'd thought long dead.

The preacher broke in, "I now pronounce you man and wife. You may kiss the bride."

Silence split the air.

Callie held her breath awaiting Luke's next move. An odd tingle swept through her at the thought of actually being married to him. It had happened so fast, her head was literally spinning.

Her breath caught in her lungs as he moved closer.

His full lips parted.

She found herself whimpering with pleasure the instant his hot seductive mouth claimed hers.

His lips were moist and rough against hers with an erotic desperation. His hands came up to cup both sides of her head, his long fingers spearing through her short hair. He kissed her so deeply, so soundly, so hard, she felt as if he were branding her his forever.

To her surprise she melted against him, the tension she'd been carrying around inside her for so many years disintegrating. She felt as if she'd finally come home, as if she finally belonged somewhere.

Belonged to him.

In total contrast, sexual heat spread through her pussy.

Her cunt creamed with arousal, the slickness drenching her panties. She wanted his head between her legs. Wanted his tongue to lance at her throbbing clit.

Her heart thundered madly in her ears, her hard nipples raked against his chest, her breasts felt so unbelievably swollen and heavy.

Five long years she'd dreamed of this moment, but nothing had prepared her for the sensual assault that zinged through her as she opened up to him allowing his strong tongue to slip inside her mouth.

He groaned and tore his mouth away.

She cried out in protest.

Breathing harshly, his head dipped sideways onto her shoulder.

"Don't leave me again, Callie," he whispered into her ear.

"I won't," she found herself answering.

"Promise?" his voice was so soft she barely heard it.

"Yes," she said, surprised that she hadn't hesitated in her answer.

"Is he dead?" The preacher's question snapped her out of the magical spell Luke had woven around her and she looked up to see his eyes wide with shock as he held his bible clasped tightly in his hands.

"You need to go to the Outlaw farm to find his brother Colter. He's a doctor. He'll know what to do."

The preacher nodded and quickly headed toward the door.

"Reverend!"

He stopped, his face deathly pale as he turned around.

"Don't tell anyone else. Only Colter. I'm putting my life into your hands to do as I ask."

"You can count on me, Callie. You know that. Don't worry. I'll get him and bring him here."

And then he was gone, the rustle of black clothes disappearing as he slipped out the back door, plunging the cabin into a deafening silence that made her terribly uneasy.

"Luke? Can you hear me?"

A groan was her answer.

"I'm going to have to take your shirt off to see the wounds. I'll try not to hurt you."

Another groan, his eyes flickered slightly.

"Is it really you?" Disbelief etched his voice.

She hesitated. Maybe she should just leave him here and go on the run again?

His brothers only lived about five miles away. They'd be here within the hour. Luke would think she'd just been a figment of his imagination. The preacher would back her up when he realized she'd left.

"Callie?" he mumbled and nuzzled his moist lips against her neck.

God! He felt so hot and masculine snuggled against her.

So handsome, and so unbelievably sexy.

She'd forgotten how dark and finely shaped his eyebrows were. Forgotten how thick his dark eyelashes were. But she hadn't forgotten the way his long callused farm-worked fingers used to part her labia and massage her clit until she was moaning and begging him for sexual relief.

Callie shook the thoughts away.

Luke was seriously injured. She couldn't leave him here alone. Not even for a moment.

"Yes, it's me."

A sensuous smile tugged at the corners of his mouth bringing with it those wonderful laugh lines she remembered so well.

Her heart swelled with warmth and she broke into action.

It was hard keeping him steady as she tugged his shirt off. Every movement made him groan and curse at her but eventually she had his upper torso naked.

She cringed at the sight of blood bubbling out of a hole in his shoulder and found herself praying that Colter would come through the door this instant.

He didn't.

Two hours later, he still hadn't arrived.

In the meantime, Callie had done her best to cleanse the ragged exit and entrance wounds with boiling water and soap, and covering them with strips of boiled linen she'd dried by the woodstove.

The preacher had been right. The bullet had gone clean through Luke's shoulder, missing bones but creating an awful-sized exit wound which she'd pinched the ragged edges together and expertly stitched up the tattered flesh with needle and thread.

Now he lay on what would have been their marriage bed, a gorgeous oak wood with thick beams as posts, which fit in perfectly with the décor of the rounded log walls.

He seemed agitated in his sleep, mumbling words she couldn't make out as he tossed his head restlessly back and forth on the pillow. Unwanted compassion ripped her apart as she watched the troubled expression twist his face.

She felt the urge to soothe him. Felt the urge to hold him in her arms and tell him everything would be okay.

But that gesture would only hurt his shoulder wounds.

Instead, she reached out and let her fingertips trail along the thick bands of his chest muscles, touching his hot flesh, tangling in the thick mat of downy brown chest hairs.

Immediately he calmed and she found herself relaxing, if only a little.

A question kept rolling around in her head. Why would the Barlows shoot Luke? She wished the preacher were here so she could ask him everything he knew. And question him as to why he'd brought Luke here instead of getting him directly to his own brother who was a doctor.

Speaking of the doctor, he should have been here by now.

Even if he had been out on a call or something, the preacher would have come back to tell her.

Something must have happened to him.

Something bad.

Whatever it was, she could only pray that he wouldn't give away her hideout.

Chapter Two

"Callie?" That one raspy whisper ripped Callie right out of the first nap she'd taken in two days.

Luke had been feverish and lay naked; his body drenched with perspiration while she'd tended to his every need. Finally, weariness had caught up to her and she'd dared to lay her head upon his hot chest.

Listening to the steady pattering of his heartbeat, she'd reassured herself she would wake up if, God forbid, his heart stopped.

Now after hearing his voice calling her name she blinked away the sleep from her eyes and her breath backed up into her throat as she noted there was very little signs left of the fever.

The flush of fever was almost gone from his face and his eyes sparkled clearly.

"You're awake?" The question slipped out before she could stop it. She needed to reassure herself this wasn't a dream.

He licked his chapped lips, prompting Callie into action. Sliding her hand beneath his head, she brought a cup filled with cool water to his lips.

"Easy, not too fast," she said as he started to gulp too quickly.

He frowned but heeded her warning.

After taking several more sips, his eyes fluttered closed. She thought he'd fallen asleep again when he whispered, "Where's...the preacher?"

Oh, darnit!

She'd been hoping he wouldn't remember their marriage vows.

"He…left." And he'd never come back with the doctor.

"So, he…wasn't…my imagination."

Clearly, he was offering her a way out, whether he knew it or not.

"No, he was here," she said slowly.

Luke's eyes flickered open again, a thoughtful smile on his lips.

"Strange…dream I had…about us."

She held her breath and waited anxiously for him to reveal what he remembered.

He didn't.

His eyes fluttered closed again and his chest rose and fell in sleep.

She sighed her relief.

Thank heavens. He didn't remember.

He'd always been an old-fashioned guy. There was no telling what he'd do if he remembered the hurried ceremony. Most likely claim his rights as her husband.

She couldn't stop the excited shiver from ripping through her at the thought of what it would be like on their wedding night. How his heavy cock would feel sliding into her eager and waiting pussy.

Although they had been engaged to marry before she'd gone to the experimental labs, they'd never made love. She'd wanted to, but he'd wanted her to remain a virgin until they were married.

And she was a virgin, although it had been difficult with the unwanted attentions of the scientist who had taken over her life at the lab a few weeks ago.

She shivered as she remembered the last encounter with the mad scientist. Her food had been drugged and she hadn't been able to stop herself from falling asleep.

When she'd awoken she discovered they'd done something to her.

She blew out a shaky breath and her hands slid over the still sensitive scars on both sides of her abdomen.

The bastard of a scientist! If she ever saw him again...

On the bed, Luke snored gently, and she forced her attentions back to him.

Now they were married and according to the preacher, it was legal.

Her gaze strayed to his well-muscled chest.

Despite being so weak from loss of blood, he looked so strong. So masculine. So sexy.

And for the moment, he was all hers to do with whatever she wanted.

Reaching out she lightly ran her fingers through the light dusting of soft chest curls.

In his sleep, his lips twitched.

Her hungry gaze followed the thatch of hair that arrowed down in a straight line over his belly and dipped downward to swaddle his cock and balls. For two days, she'd resisted the urge to touch his cock the way she'd touched him all those years ago when they'd been in love.

Now that his fever had diminished and she knew he'd be all right she couldn't resist the urge to re-explore his gorgeous body while he slept. Consider it a little something to get her by during the lonely nights ahead after she disappeared on Luke once again.

As she visually examined his enormous penis lying limp between those two swollen testicles, she could feel her empty vagina ache to be filled. His cock was much bigger than she remembered and a little sliver of jealously rippled through her when she recalled hearing about how sexual release with conscripted or volunteer women was mandatory during the Terrorist Wars.

How many women had made love to Luke while he'd been in the army? Had they been beautiful and gorgeous? Or plain everyday types like herself?

Holding her breath, she reached out and ran a finger along one of the blue veins that ran down each side of his thick shaft. Her eyes widened in surprise as his cock began to thicken and elongate right before her very eyes, the engorged head popped out from its sheath and a trickle of pre-come slid out from the slit.

Oh, my goodness!

She cast a quick glance at Luke.

Was he feigning sleep?

His eyes were closed. His chest heaved slowly up and down. Could he actually respond to her in his sleep?

She had limited sexual experience with men. Some heavy necking with guys in high school but when Luke had come along she'd only been with him. Aside from orally pleasing each other in a hurried, desperate way to gain sexual release, he'd never penetrated her vaginally. She noticed the sensual way his lips were tilted upwards into a sexy smile.

Maybe he was dreaming? About her?

A silly schoolgirl type giggle erupted from her and she shook her head at her silliness.

He wouldn't be dreaming about her.

While she'd been rotting away in the labs he'd been out there exploring life to the fullest.

Now maybe it was her turn to explore?

She cupped her fingers around his hot cock and felt it thickening further in her palms.

Callie's excitement grew.

Despite wanting to continue touching him she realized if he awoke and caught her fondling him it would only encourage him and give him false hope that they would pick up their engagement where they'd left off.

Obviously, that's what he'd had in mind by forcing the preacher to marry them. But Luke needed to know about what had really happened all those years ago. And what they'd done to her in the experimental labs.

She knew she wasn't brave enough to tell him the truth. If he found out, he would hate her forever.

Callie bit back a sob.

Reluctantly she let go of Luke's hard cock and lay her head on his muscular chest. The strong steady thump of his heartbeat eased away some of her pain.

He would get better and then she would leave him.

It had to be that way.

* * * * *

Luke had the sense that someone was nearby. He couldn't hear anyone but he just had the feeling someone was with him. From somewhere far off he heard the bone-chilling howl of a lonely coyote and nearby he could hear the distinct sounds of a fire crackling.

Was he on a campout?

They'd had trouble out in the west pasture with some of the cows being butchered. His brothers and he had spotted numerous tracks.

Not coyote tracks but human.

Women, not men.

It was bound to happen. Women who'd defied the new Claiming Law. Women who hid like animals in the woods evading capture from the numerous groups of men who were desperate for female company.

He himself was desperate. But forcing a woman to submit wasn't his way, nor was it the way of his brothers.

But still, the thought of going out there and finding a woman to ease the ache and erase the memory of Callie...

The thought of Callie made his heart pick up a mad pace. He'd had dreams about her while he'd been in the Wars and since he'd been back home.

Lots of dreams.

But these recent ones had been different.

So real.

And he'd had nightmares of getting shot by the Barlows. Hiding out in the church. The preacher finding him...

And then he'd seen Callie.

Of course she'd just been a dream, but she'd reassured him she wasn't.

Suddenly her sweet feminine scent swarmed around him like a teasing lover and along with it came a bitch of an ache in his shoulder.

What the hell had happened to him?

Visions swooped over him.

Naked bodies, the slurping sound of mouths on a woman.

Screams.

Overwhelming pain.

Luke's eyes snapped open and he blinked at a familiar ceiling filled with pine rafters.

It was the tiny log home he'd built for Callie.

After boarding it up years ago he'd purposely stayed away from here because it reminded him too much of her.

Yet here he was.

Why? How did he get here?

He tried to move his head but a dull throbbing erupted between his eyes making him stop.

He licked his lips.

So dry.

Man, he was thirsty.

He heard the rustle of someone moving and then he smelled her again.

A delicious combination of flowers and her own unique feminine scent. A scent he'd never been able to forget even when he'd been surrounded by the stench of dead soldiers.

Was he hallucinating about her now?

Conflicting emotions spiraled through him, threatening to sink him back into oblivion.

He fought against it and he began to remember more things.

Holding a gun on her, making sure she wouldn't disappear again. Ordering her to stand in front of the candlelight, so he could admire the outline of her long legs, the seductive silhouette of her shapely hips.

Where was she? She had to be somewhere nearby. Her scent was everywhere making him heady with desire. Making him scared, that maybe he'd somehow gone nuts.

"Callie?"

At least that's what he thought he'd said. The only thing that escaped was a groan. He could feel the disbelief sifting into his flesh and yet there was a wonderful hope simmering inside him, too.

She was here. She had to be.

He heard the rustle of clothing again.

And then she was there, a concerned smile on those luscious lips he'd been dying to kiss since she'd disappeared all those years ago.

"Welcome back," she said softly. "How do you feel?"

He tried to talk but nothing came out.

"Would you like some water?"

He nodded.

Momentary panic shot through him as she dropped out of his view but then he could hear the tinkling of water and suddenly she was back, pressing the cool cup to his parched lips.

He drank eagerly, relishing the liquid as it washed away the dryness and when she pulled the cup away, he groaned in protest.

"Not too much. I don't want you getting sick."

He nodded again.

Man, did she ever look good.

Her mid-back length auburn curls were gone in favor of a very short, basic cut that gave her a tomboy look.

A very sexy tomboy.

He couldn't help from grinning or stopping himself from exploring every inch of her flawless face. Her high forehead was barely concealed by wisps of short bangs that sat just above perfectly arched dark eyebrows. A dainty spattering of light freckles dusted her rosy cheeks and a perfect nose.

His eyes fluttered sleepily.

No! He couldn't go back to sleep. She wouldn't be here when he woke up.

She must have sensed his fear for her fingers intertwined with his and she held his hand to the generous swell of her left breast.

The hard pounding of her heart relaxed him. Reassured him that his fiancée was very much alive.

Before he drifted off, he thought he saw his wedding ring glittering on her ring finger.

But that wasn't possible.

They'd never gotten married.

* * * * *

The next time Luke awoke, he found Callie's hot fingers sliding a pleasant smelling ointment over the sensitive flesh surrounding the tattered exit wound in the front of his shoulder.

Immediately he remembered the ring he'd thought he'd seen earlier.

He looked down at her finger.

The ring wasn't there.

A dream.

Just a delirious dream. Like all the others must have been.

He hadn't held Callie at gunpoint. He hadn't savored her curvy silhouette as he'd made her stand in front of the candle glow with the preacher watching in the background.

But it had seemed so real.

Too real.

He lowered his lashes slightly so she wouldn't notice he was awake and allowed his hungry gaze to ravish her pretty features.

She was sleepy, he could tell by the way her eyelids fluttered as she softly massaged the ointment into his flesh.

Her eyes were just as he remembered them. Long black lashes that framed the prettiest pale blue eyes just like the color of the June sky at high noon.

He'd always loved looking into them.

Loved the way they'd flashed with laughter when he'd joked with her. It had always brought a gentle warmth coursing through him. And the way they darkened when he'd teased her had always made his breath back up into his lungs.

Most of all he'd loved the way they'd sparkled when he'd orally taken her clit into his mouth and later sucked her sweet feminine cream from her vagina.

Those familiar sparks in her eyes were gone now, replaced by a look of wariness.

A look of the hunted.

He frowned.

There were other things he hadn't noticed.

Like the dark circles beneath her eyes and the faint worry wrinkles lightly etched into her forehead.

He didn't know what horrors she'd gone through over the past five years but whatever they were he'd help her through her pain. They'd get through it together.

He lowered his gaze to where her breasts pressed tightly against the cotton material of the dark green blouse she wore. Every detail of her silky globes were etched in his memory forever, from the hot pink of her firm plump nipples, the darker pink of her areolas, to the darker blush on her face as she caught him watching her.

"Good morning," she said cheerfully, almost too cheerfully. As if she was forcing herself to be happy.

Immediately he knew something was amiss.

"What's wrong?" he whispered.

She shook her head and to his surprise, she laughed. It was a real laugh and it filled his heart with that wild happiness he'd always felt when she was joyful.

"You always did know when something was wrong."

"So? What...is it?"

"I think something happened to the preacher."

Luke's blood ran cold.

The preacher.

Yes, he had been here.

Something flickered in the back of his mind.

Pain. Confusion. The nervous preacher. An angry Callie.

The preacher reading wedding vows?

Luke blinked the silly thoughts away.

"It's been two days since I sent him for your brother," she explained. "Neither of them showed up."

Damn! She was right. Something had happened.

If Colter knew he was in trouble, he would have come.

"Can we trust the preacher not to give you away in case he's been stopped by the authorities?"

She seemed shocked at his question. "He's a man of the cloth. He won't betray me if that's what you mean."

"Are you sure?"

"He hasn't turned me in yet. He's reliable."

He became suddenly painfully aware of the sharp ache in his heart as he realized she'd gone to the preacher for help instead of him.

It hurt.

Bad.

A red-hot anger began to uncurl through him and he caught her gaze. "Exactly how long have you been here?"

She looked away, opting to concentrate on smearing more of that goopy stuff around his wound.

"Callie? I asked you a question." He tried hard to contain his anger but his rising voice gave him away. "And why the hell didn't you come straight to me? Which leads to my next question where have they been hiding you?"

Fear flashed in her eyes. Fear of him? Or fear of his questions?

Calm it down, Luke. You're scaring her.

She pulled away from him and slapped the lid onto the container holding the ointment.

"You weren't supposed to know I was here."

He wasn't supposed to know?

His gut twisted as if she'd just stabbed him. The pain felt worse than the bullet wound that scorched through his shoulder.

"Why not?" he forced himself to ask.

"It's too dangerous. I don't want you involved in my troubles."

She didn't want him involved? What the hell kind of answer was that from a fiancée?

His anger twisted tighter.

He tried to relax.

He couldn't.

His mind whirled with questions. Questions he needed answers to. Answers she obviously didn't want to give him.

"I asked you a question, Callie. Where have they been keeping you?"

Her face whitened in the candle glow.

"One of their top-secret labs. They have one in Bangor," she whispered as if she was afraid to say it too loud.

It was what the police department had told him when they'd located her car in a shopping mall in Bangor right after she'd disappeared. They'd said she'd most likely been taken against her will by the government. They'd said if that was the case there was nothing they could do. All records regarding X-virus-free women were sealed. They'd pretty much told him not to expect her to ever be released.

He hadn't stopped looking for her after hearing that news.

He'd mortgaged his piece of the Outlaw farm and used his entire life savings to hire a lawyer to cut through the bureaucratic red tape in his efforts to find her. In the end, the lawyer had gotten rich and Luke had nothing.

Despaired and depressed, and feeling utterly hopeless he'd followed his brothers overseas and taken his rage out by fighting the terrorists who'd ruined his life.

"Are you hungry?" she asked meekly. She was acting as if she was still scared of him.

Her sudden timid attitude toward him angered him more. Had they taken her spirit?

"What the hell did they do to you in there?" And why was she suddenly cowering away from him like she was some

submissive woman who was being berated by an overbearing husband?

Tears bubbled up in her eyes.

Oh, shit! He'd made her cry.

She'd never been able to handle anger very well, compliments of an angry mother who'd enjoyed yelling and beating her three daughters when she was drunk.

Man! He felt like a nasty son of a bitch.

"I'm sorry. I shouldn't have yelled at you. I'm just pissed off. I don't understand what the hell is going on here. They told me not to expect to see you again."

The burst of anger he'd just experienced had bitten away at his strength. Weariness washed over him.

She said nothing as she headed over to the cast-iron stove he'd installed after he'd built the cozy home for them. A home they hadn't been able to use.

He fought against the sleepiness but it was getting stronger, like a current trying to pull him under.

He closed his eyes and listened to the clattering of a spoon hitting the side of a pot.

She was preparing something for him.

He wasn't hungry.

He wanted answers.

As what happened whenever he was mad or upset he forced the visions of Callie to the forefront of his mind.

Visions of himself pinning her to the bed, removing her clothes piece by piece, until she lay naked before him. Her legs spread wide. Her pussy fully exposed to him, her juices making it easier for him to slide his engorged cock into her tight channel.

Luke's cock hardened painfully.

Well, at least that part of him wasn't tired or sick.

He gritted his teeth in annoyance.

He'd better get himself on the mend and pretty fast or she was going to slip away before he could show her that he wanted her more now than ever.

* * * * *

Callie turned from the stove with the cup of broth and saw his eyes fluttering sleepily. She didn't miss the breathtaking erection bulging against the sheets she'd covered him with before he'd awoken.

She trembled at the sensual sight.

Fear, excitement and a fierce sexual hunger shot through her all at the same time and suddenly all those old feelings of desire and lust she'd had for him, along with some new and mighty powerful feelings she couldn't quite put a name to, swarmed all over her leaving her hot and breathless.

By the way his cock was pushing up against the thin sheet Luke Outlaw was definitely on the mend.

Soon he'd start pursuing her.

Despite him being injured and weak, she knew Luke had a ferocious sexual appetite. He hadn't been able to go more than two days without asking her to go down on him.

Right now though wasn't the time to be feeling all hot and bothered. She needed to get some food into him so he could fight off the rest of the fever.

"Luke?" she said as she sat on the bed trying hard not to look at those bulging muscles in his arms or the way his chest muscles tensed magnificently at the sound of her voice.

His eyes snapped open and his gaze snared her.

Lust shone in his brown depths and the sensual sight of it whispered seductively over her skin, making her want to tear her clothes off and have his hot hands running all over her, touching her in the most intimate places, kissing her…

Callie swallowed tightly.

Oh, dear. Resisting Luke wasn't going to be half as easy as she'd thought.

"I've got some broth for you, open your mouth," she instructed trying to act as if his nearness wasn't affecting her.

"At the moment broth isn't what the doctor would order," his voice trailed dangerously over her and he watched her carefully for a reaction.

In response, she shoved the warm spoon against his sensually shaped mouth.

"Open."

The pink tip of his tongue snaked out and dabbed at the liquid and she couldn't help but remember all those times that same rough tongue had dabbed at her pussy opening or teased her clit with strong sensual strokes.

"Chicken soup, my second favorite type of liquid," he whispered softly.

Her breath caught at his words. His favorite being her pussy cream, if memory served her correctly.

He smiled, his white teeth stark against the flushed skin of his face.

She could hear the way she was breathing. Hard and shallow. Aroused.

"It's good," he whispered as he licked his lips in a sensual way that had her almost moaning with want.

"It's your mom's recipe. I had all the ingredients except the bullion cubes. Those are pretty hard to get these days in the store."

His heated look vanished, replaced by a dark anger that frightened her.

"You were in a store?"

"That was the preacher's job. Do you think just because I've been locked up in the labs that I didn't know what's been going on in the outside world...or in the Wars?"

A flash of guilt shot into his eyes and she knew instantly he'd been unfaithful to her during his tour of duty. As if she'd expected him to be true to her when sex was mandatory for a soldier.

Besides, Luke Outlaw had had no idea if she were alive or dead, so why should she care what he'd done with those women in the Wars?

"Callie…" The sound of his voice shot her back to the present. Instinctively she knew he wanted to explain his infidelities.

She didn't want to hear it.

At least not right now.

"Don't talk, Luke. I want you to save your strength and concentrate on drinking as much of this soup as you can. You still have a slight fever and I want you to sleep it off. We can talk later."

"Will you be here to answer my questions later?"

The dark undertones of his question made her frown.

She didn't answer. Couldn't guarantee she would be here when he got better. As if sensing her thoughts his eyes narrowed into dangerous slits.

"If you leave, I'll hunt you down until I find you and rest assured I'll make you mine in every sense of the word. Do you understand what I'm saying, Callie? You're mine."

Okay, so those words pretty much confirmed his intentions toward her.

She nodded, trying hard not to cave into the lusty excitement shooting through her at Luke's dark threat.

He opened his mouth and awaited the next spoon of broth.

His wet tongue was now lying dormant. Resting. Waiting for when he was strong enough to pleasure her again.

Callie's pussy trembled and creamed hot with anticipation.

Despite her need to walk away from him in order to keep him safe, she had a feeling she'd never be able to walk away from Luke Outlaw again.

Chapter Three

After she'd spoon-fed him Luke had fallen into a deep satisfied sleep filled with erotic dreams of Callie.

She arched against his mouth as he tunneled his tongue deeper into her wet pussy. Eagerly he sipped the warm, sweet cream sliding down her channel into his mouth.

Her whimpers of pleasure made his cock rock-hard. Made his whole body hum. Made him want to brand her his forever. Made him want to claim her legally, even if it meant asking his brothers to join him...

Delicate fingers slid sensuously over his injured shoulder making him open his eyes and he relaxed beneath her seductive touch as Callie smeared a thick greasy substance around the edges of the bullet hole.

To his surprise, his wound wasn't hurting near as bad as the last time he'd woke up. And he wasn't as tired either.

He smiled.

He was on the mend.

And that meant he could soon concentrate on seducing Callie back into his life.

"What is that stuff you're using?"

Her hand stilled for a moment. He'd surprised her. She hadn't realized he was awake.

"Comfrey plants and lard melted together. Promotes healing," she shrugged her thin shoulders and smeared more of the thick greasy substance around the angry, red-ragged hole. "It's the best I can do."

"It's working." He could literally feel the soothing balm extinguish the throbbing pain.

"Good. Do you think you can get onto your side? I need to check the other wound."

He nodded.

It wasn't a feat he wanted to do anytime soon as with her help he managed to get into the position she wanted him in.

When he was on his side, he breathed through the pain that lanced his shoulder and when the pain became less intense he became very aware of the mild air slapping against his ass.

His very bare ass.

It was at that moment he realized he was totally naked and the sheets had slipped down over his hips.

An odd excitement rippled through him as he looked over his shoulder and caught her gazing at his butt.

"You like what you see?"

"Nothing I haven't seen before," she answered quickly as a pretty pink blush swept across her cheeks.

Gingerly she removed the tape that held the bandage in place and soon he was sighing his relief as she smoothed more of that goopy stuff onto his injured flesh.

"Why did the Barlows shoot you?"

The question caught him quite off-guard. How could he tell her he'd walked in on the Barlow brothers having sex with their new wife, her youngest half-sister?

"Why the hell didn't you tell me you were hiding here?" he snapped trying to take focus off the question she'd just asked.

Her fingers stilled on his flesh.

Immediately he wished he hadn't asked. For years, he'd wondered and worried about her. For years, he'd fought the terrorists with a burning rage inside him. It was because of them that his fiancée was gone from his life.

As far as he was concerned, all terrorists were in the same barrel, rotten to the core.

Especially the DogMarX, a group focused against women's rights. A group of men who believed a woman should be subservient to men in every aspect. The bastards had released the X-virus into an unsuspecting women's rights convention. The virus had targeted estrogen-rich women, turning them into virtual zombies. Mindless women who did whatever they were told to do by men.

The X-virus had spread like wildfire. Unfortunately, while it had spread, it had mutated into many forms. Most of them deadly to women.

Callie had been exposed over and over again. When her mother and half-sisters had gotten sick, she'd taken care of them. When his mother and sister had gotten sick, she'd taken care of them, too.

He'd been pissed off at her for exposing herself.

She'd done it anyway.

They'd fought about it all the time.

In the end both their mothers and his sister had died.

Her sisters had lived and now required the daily doses of expensive medicines to keep them alive.

Nothing had happened to Callie.

It seemed she was immune, as were a minority of other women around the world.

And then the government had started up the experimental labs, looking for unaffected women to volunteer themselves as guinea pigs in the name of womankind.

Callie had come to him telling him she'd wanted to volunteer to give them some blood samples. He'd vehemently told her no.

And then she'd disappeared without a trace.

Luke's guts crunched as he remembered waiting anxiously on their newly built porch for her to return from grocery shopping.

He never should have let her go alone.

Men were already getting crazy at the prospect of so few women available to them.

He'd waited until he could wait no more then he'd hopped into the truck and rode into town. He hadn't been able to find her and no one, not even the grocery cashiers or the mall's security video had seen her inside.

Immediately he'd gone to the cops. A day later, they'd found her car at a shopping mall in Bangor, Maine. She'd disappeared without a trace.

Deep inside he'd known the government had taken her. He'd heard horror stories of what happened to the X-virus-resistant women in those labs. About how they eventually snapped under the loss of their freedom as the government scientists housed them in isolation units for weeks even years in a mad attempt to find a vaccine to help the girls who would ultimately turn into women and get the deadly virus.

"Are you hungry?"

Obviously, she was changing the subject. He'd let her. For now.

He took a moment to see if maybe he had an appetite and to his surprise discovered his stomach felt quite empty.

"I think I could manage something," he admitted.

He watched her ladle more of that chicken broth from the steaming pot she had on the stove into a tin cup.

A concerned frown marred her luscious lips and fear for her safety rammed into his stomach.

"Maybe you should go to the Outlaw farm. See what happened. It might be better if you don't stay here. Someone might see the smoke from the stove..." *and come here to claim you*, he added silently.

Her head snapped up. A look of insult twisted her face. Her blue eyes flashed with anger.

"I don't need anyone to protect me. I can take care of myself."

Her confidence was unnerving. It angered him.

"You didn't do so good when I showed up."

"You surprised me, that's all."

"And you think a group of sex-starved men, won't?"

"If it hadn't been you, I would have handled the situation."

"Oh, yeah? How?"

Her eyes strayed to the kitchen area where he noted the long gleaming knife on the counter.

"I don't think a knife against a horde of men would do much damage."

"It wouldn't be for them."

Shock sucker-punched him.

Sweet shit! She would have killed herself?

She came toward him, a grim smile on her face confirming that yes indeed she would have committed suicide. "Like I said — I would have handled the situation."

He found himself nodding numbly and realized exactly how close he'd been to losing her yet again.

* * * * *

It was a full bladder that prompted Luke to awaken the next time.

Immediately he realized he felt stronger, his thoughts less foggy.

It was night.

He could tell because the front door of the cabin was wide open and bright moonlight spilled inside.

Bullfrogs croaked in the pond outside the cabin. It was windy, too. Refreshing gusts of it blew into the room splashing all around Luke's naked flesh. He knew Callie loved to take walks when a stiff wind was blowing. She'd said she liked the way it caressed her face. A direct contrast to the hard fists of her mother when she got drunk, and beat her and her half-sisters.

He'd taken a few windy walks with her himself in the past but never in the middle of the night.

A sliver of uneasiness coursed through him.

Had someone broken in and taken her? Surely, he would have heard. He wasn't a light sleeper but he wasn't a heavy one either.

Instantly his fears were put to rest. From somewhere in the distance he could hear her humming. It was a delicate mournful song he couldn't put a name to. Nonetheless, it tugged at his heart and made him feel sad.

He lay on the bed for a few minutes listening to her gentle voice and tried to will himself to go back to sleep.

But he couldn't.

The bathroom wouldn't wait too much longer.

Either he could call out to her for some help or he could do the deed on his own.

He opted for the latter.

Making a sudden move to sit up, a brief swirl of dizziness assaulted him. Thankfully it quickly subsided.

The pain in his left shoulder however was another story. It felt like a fiery arrow had lodged itself right through him but with a few controlled inhales and exhales, and instinctively holding his arm close to his body in order to prevent any unexpected jarring motions which would shoot more dreaded pain into him, he sat up.

Moving his legs to the edge of the bed, he swung them over the side.

Managing to push himself off the mattress, he cursed at the tremors weakening his knees.

The urge to call out to Callie for help almost overwhelmed him, but pride and independence urged him to step forward. The mere movement sent agony shooting into his wounded shoulder.

But he persevered.

One wobbly step at a time.

One bolt of pain after the other.

Using first the night table beside the bed and then a couple of chairs and the couch, he managed to make it to the door. With trembling legs, he stepped outside. The mildness of the refreshing wind felt absolutely fantastic against his skin as he quickly went about his business and listened to the rustling of the trees swaying wildly in the breeze and smelled the musty scent of damp earth.

When he was finished, he stood there for a few moments, his fingers curling tightly around the porch railing for support as he slowly inhaled the fresh air trying hard to ignore the weakness in his knees and the throbbing pain shooting through his shoulder.

Callie's humming grew louder and then she was there right in front of him ready to come up the stairs. In the moonlight he noticed her short hair was stringy, her face wet. Obviously, she'd taken a dip in the pond.

When she saw him, she stopped cold and stared wide-eyed with surprise, the surprise quickly flashing to unmistakable lust.

He suddenly remembered he was naked and thoroughly enjoyed the way her hungry gaze immediately lowered to his cock and her tongue erotically darted out to lick at her full upper lip.

Plump lips meant for sucking.

His cock stirred to life at the thought.

She was almost naked.

The skimpy T-shirt she wore did little to conceal her delicious curves. Her breasts hung heavy and full, her large nipples vivid pinpoints against the white clothing.

Her bikini underwear hid practically nothing. Her pubic hair shadowed most of the front and he swore he could see the fleshy outline of her clit in the moonlight as it pressed against the cloth.

His cock thickened and lifted at the delicious sight.

Oh, boy. He was definitely getting better.

He continued to stare at her, admiring how her hips had filled out.

They were wider.

Perfect for grabbing her so he could impale her from behind.

His balls grew tighter at the thought.

Her legs were long and shapely. Just right for curling around his thighs as he plunged his cock deep into her warm and waiting slit.

"What are you doing out of bed?" her whisper sounded soft and sultry.

"Answering the call of nature."

She swallowed and he heard her breath catch at his answer. Obviously, she'd mistaken his meaning.

He held her gaze, his cock sending her blatant signals he hoped she'd react to.

Heck! Did he even have the strength to perform? His rock-hard cock said yes.

The rest of him said no.

His legs trembled. Pain gnawed at his shoulder and a cool perspiration popped out over his skin.

She shook her head slightly and his hopes were dashed.

"You're in no condition for anything but resting. Those wounds won't mend if you're..." she hesitated, obviously searching for appropriate words.

"Making love to you?"

She looked away but not before he saw the cutest little blush sweep across her cheeks.

Hot damn! He needed to get better, pronto!

"Get back into bed," she said again.

"Just give me a minute." He didn't know if he could even walk on his own now that he had a massive hard-on to contend with.

"Okay, but just a minute." Biting her lip, she slipped past him and went into the cabin.

His cock reacted more violently this time around when her feminine scent drifted into his lungs. Fresh and clean. No flowery aromas clinging to her skin, just her own sensual odor of arousal.

From the doorway, he watched as she headed toward his bed and gave him a great view of her rounded ass as she bent over the bed and quickly rearranged the rumpled sheets.

He stifled an aroused groan at the erotic sight of the dark outline of the crack in her ass. The thought of impaling her in the rear end smothered his senses.

Swallowing against the tightness in his throat, he grabbed onto the doorjamb and stumbled back inside.

She heard him and turned around. She watched him with hungry eyes as he headed toward her, his stiff cock bobbing painfully up and down with every lurched step.

Damn! He wished she wouldn't look at him like that, with a ferocious sexual hunger in her eyes and large nipples poking against her top. He could feel his cock elongate even more and it flushed with a wild heat demanding satisfaction from her. He inhaled sharply as he imagined her taking his shaft into her mouth in a desperate effort to soothe him. At that thought, he almost stumbled and fell.

"Do you need some help?" she said taking a step toward him.

"No," he said defiantly.

The sooner his legs got used to walking the faster he could mend.

A touch of anger gnawed at him for wanting to fuck her so bad that his entire body literally ached with the need for release.

He didn't remember his attraction to her being so intense. So forceful. Surely if it had been this way in the past he wouldn't have wanted to wait for them to get married before he made love to her.

He could only believe that he'd waited due to his sexual inexperience at the time. Or perhaps the sexual attraction he felt for her had grown over the years of being apart.

When he reached the bed, she moved out of the way and he sat heavily upon the mattress, grimacing at the pain shooting into his shoulder.

The walk had been tiring to say the least.

Unfortunately, his cock wasn't tired in the least.

It pulsed with heat and throbbed with need, demanding relief, but he was too weak to bring himself off.

"Luke?"

Her voice dripped with seduction capturing his immediate attention.

He hadn't realized she was still standing there. His weariness forgotten, he looked up and caught the sexual yearning shining in her eyes. She stared directly at his cock, the tip of her pretty pink tongue sticking out of her mouth.

He could read the hunger in her eyes. Could sense her feminine desire to satisfy him.

Excitement roared through him and he moved his ass closer to the edge of the bed and spread his legs wide giving her full access.

She hesitated as if unsure if she should do this.

"For old time's sake," he whispered hotly. It wasn't as if they'd never taken each other orally before. They had. Many times.

She sank to her knees on a cry, her face still flushed, her eyes twinkling up at him with passion, her mind waiting for his instruction.

"Open your mouth, Callie."

She wiggled in between his legs, leaned real close and parted her curvy lips.

Her ragged breath brushed across the bulging head of his engorged penis and he almost climaxed on the spot.

Without making him suffer any longer, she took his mushroom-shaped cockhead into her moist mouth making him groan as the hot flesh of her plump lips wrapped tightly around his aching flesh.

Sweet mercy! That felt absolutely fantastic.

Her small hands reached up and she cupped each of his balls like he'd taught her to do years ago. Her fingers dug painfully into his tender scrotum and she began a slow erotic massage that had him blinking back tears of arousal.

Damned he'd missed this. Missed having her between his legs. Missed tasting her sweetness.

His cockhead twitched and jerked in her mouth as she took more of him all the way to the back of her throat.

"Yes, Callie! That's it!" he cried out as his gut clenched tighter.

He winced when her teeth raked against his hard flesh and then alternated with a fierce sucking motion that almost blew his mind.

Oh, man! She hadn't forgotten a thing he'd taught her.

Slurping sounds mixed with his strangled gasps as her lips caressed seductively one moment and then her teeth nipped at his hard shaft the next.

With his good arm, he leaned forward grabbing her shoulder making sure he didn't fall over from all the pleasure slamming through his cock and searing into his swollen balls.

Agonized groans spilled from his lips while he watched with fascination as her eyes closed dreamily and her head bobbed faster.

In the past she'd told him many times that she enjoyed sucking his penis. Told him how she loved the velvety feel of his

rigid shaft sliding in and out of her mouth. Had told him she enjoyed the taste of his cum on her lips.

He could feel his body tense.

Could feel the orgasm coming.

His grip around her shoulder tightened and his head swam.

As if sensing his impending climax her head bobbed quicker, her hot lips sucked his stiff shaft deeper until he was literally going down her throat.

He gyrated his hips harder in a delicious dance of desire, searching madly for the relief he so craved.

He found it.

"I'm coming," he warned as the delicious blade of lightning sliced up his cock almost lifting him off his bed.

The wild explosion slammed into him like a tidal wave, jerking him so violently he would have toppled backward if his fingers hadn't been clenched tightly over Callie's shoulder.

He closed his eyes and allowed the release.

She whimpered as his sperm spewed into her mouth and down her throat.

God! There was nothing like the sound of a beautiful woman between a man's legs as she serviced him.

She continued to suck hard, draining him of every drop and then the erotic rush was over, leaving him spent and gasping like a fish out of water.

He barely felt her warm lips release him. Barely felt her fingers pry his hand off her shoulder.

When her hands curled over his shoulders, his eyes popped open.

"Let's get you further back onto the bed, Luke," she whispered, a satisfied smile on her face. Her lips glistened in the flickering candle glow from his arousal and perspiration dotted her forehead.

He nodded weakly and allowed her to guide his body back. She swung his legs up and left him in a seated position.

Damned if she didn't waste any time in covering him up to his waist with the sheet.

"What's the matter? You don't like looking at my cock, anymore?" he teased fighting the sexual fatigue flooding his body.

She ignored his remark and hustled away. "You think you can handle a few minutes of sitting up while I change your bandages?"

"Avoiding my question. A very good sign."

She said nothing as she washed her hands at the sink then returned with a makeshift shoebox containing rolled up white bandages and that comfrey ointment she'd been using on him.

It took her only a moment to unwrap the bandages.

"Tell me if anything hurts."

"Not anymore, thanks to you."

She smiled shyly, a direct contrast to the bold way she'd taken his cock into her eager mouth only moments earlier, and prodded gently the sensitive areas around the entrance wound at the back of his shoulder.

"What were you doing out at this hour anyway?"

"Couldn't sleep, so I went outside."

Her soft scent was doing a number on him again. Making his balls tighten once again into hard eggs. Urging his cock to press harder against the sheets.

Shoot! Was he horny or what?

She cocked a puzzled eyebrow at him. "What? No arguments that I went outside alone?"

"Would it help if I did argue?"

"No."

"We'll argue when I have my strength back." There was no way he would let her wander around aimlessly on her own. He

didn't care if it was in the middle of the night. These days there was no telling what strange men might be lurking around out there looking for the women who hid in the woods.

He winced as she pressed some ointment into the fiery wound, and then quickly taped a thick patch over it.

"Things are healing quite quickly back here. You can lie back now."

He did and she repeated the gentle poking around the ugly, ragged edges of the wound in the front of his shoulder then quickly followed up with a healthy dose of that salve.

A sudden stab of pain shifted through his shoulder and it was quickly accompanied by déjà vu.

Visions bombarded him.

Pain claimed his senses.

He saw guns in his hands. One pointed at a terrified preacher. One pointed at a rather nervous Callie.

He saw her standing beside a candle. The buttery lighting gave him an eyeful of her long legs, curvy hips and those luscious nipples as they poked proudly against her tight shirt.

Then she was sitting next to him on this bed.

The preacher's words rang in his ears.

"You may kiss the bride."

"You're looking too pale. Are you feeling sick?" Callie's voice slashed through his vision.

"No," he managed to croak.

"I shouldn't have done what I did. It was too early. I'll just put a patch onto the front here and then you can sleep."

Her voice drifted away as he closed his eyes and tried to conjure up more images.

He remembered sliding the wedding ring onto her finger.

His eyes popped open. His heart crashed wickedly against his chest as he gazed at Callie's ring finger.

It was still empty.

His hopes plummeted.

Surely, he'd been delirious. He would remember if the preacher had married them, wouldn't he?

Sure he would.

He forced himself to relax.

The urge to marry her burned anew. The craving to fuck her senseless, to have babies with her, to love her until his dying day tangled together with his overwhelming need to know what had happened to her over the past five years.

"Callie?"

"Hmm."

She put the last piece of tape over the bandage.

"What happened to you in the government labs?"

She stiffened visibly and stood.

"I could ask you the same thing about what happened to you in the Terrorist Wars, but I won't because I don't wish to know."

Guilt assailed him and this time it was his turn to tense up.

He got her point.

She didn't want to talk about it. At least, not yet.

"Go to sleep, Luke. You need your rest."

"We'll have to talk about it sometime. Five years is a long time."

"No. We won't," she said firmly. "It's my private business. It's none of your concern."

"None of my concern? You were my whole life back then, Callie. We were supposed to get married in a week and then they came and got you...they ripped our lives apart. Don't you think I want to know what happened to you? Don't you think I always feared you were dead?"

"Well, I'm not dead."

"Sometimes, you look like you are."

Her head snapped up. "What's that supposed to mean?"

"Something's different about you, Callie. That spark of life is gone from your eyes. You have the look of a caged animal…"

"They kept me locked up like a lab rat, Luke. Five years. Every day they came and took my blood and anything else they wanted. Not just once but several times a day until I was so weak I could barely pace the room I was stuck in. They took skin samples, saliva samples, nail clippings." She grabbed a tuft of her short hair and smirked angrily. "They cut off my hair. They did everything and anything they could think of to find out why I wasn't affected by the X-virus. In the end…I escaped."

That explained the hunted look.

And at least she was talking.

"And they want you back."

"They want me back, yes."

"Well, you're going back over my dead body."

"They won't hesitate to kill you to get me. I'm not prepared to put your life in jeopardy for me."

"That's why you didn't come to me for help. That's why you went to the preacher. Because you were afraid to put my life in danger?"

She didn't say anything.

But he understood now.

My God!

She still cared enough for him to protect him. And the way she'd devoured his cock earlier made him realize she was still physically attracted to him.

It was a darned good start to rekindling their relationship.

"Close your eyes, Luke. We're finished talking. I want you to rest."

He nodded in agreement.

Rest. That was the ticket.

He'd rest and when he felt strong enough he'd show her exactly how much he'd missed her.

Chapter Four

Callie blew out a long breath as she settled onto the lone sofa and tried to fall asleep.

She knew she was in for a long night especially now that she'd gotten a taste of Luke's cock again.

Oh, dear.

When she'd first spied him in the doorway she'd thought he'd followed her out of her dream. The one that had made her go outside into the wind and masturbate while she'd taken a dip in the nearby pond.

She'd been dreaming of him. Dreaming he'd take her back even after she'd told him her secrets. Dreamed of his thick rod stretching her vaginal muscles as he rode her hard and fast, plunging deeper into her pussy with every wild thrust.

When she'd realized he wasn't a dream but reality and she'd noticed the way his cock had thickened and elongated under her hungry gaze, she'd wanted that rigid piece of flesh in her mouth.

Just like old times. Just like he'd said.

She'd wanted to taste him so bad her pussy had creamed while she'd made his bed.

When he'd returned from outside and she'd seen how red and engorged his penis had become she knew he wouldn't rest. Not until she'd brought him relief.

He'd felt so hot in her mouth.

As if his cock had been on fire.

Just like her pussy was now on fire.

She hadn't been prepared for the agonizing ache of unfulfillment when she realized he would be too weak to return the favor. She would have preferred his volunteering to slide his long tongue between her pussy lips and nibble on her clitoris bringing her to the orgasm.

An orgasm she now craved so desperately.

But the thought of masturbating right here on the couch with Luke sleeping on the bed a few feet away didn't make her feel too comfortable.

She loved the man with all her heart but she didn't feel right about masturbating in front of him, even if he was asleep.

She could go back outside and do it.

That thought didn't appeal to her either.

She wanted Luke, darnit!

And she wanted him real bad.

* * * * *

The cackling sounds of chickens was like music to Callie's ears as she quietly pried apart the bushes that surrounded the Barlow Ranch's screened henhouse and hen yard. All she had to do was open the screen door and slip inside the coop.

It wouldn't be the first time she'd walked miles to this ranch. Barlow eggs were the best in Rackety Valley not to mention the closest to their cabin where she'd been hiding over the past several weeks.

The creaking sound as she opened the screen door split the silent evening air making shards of slivers rip up her spine. When the chickens saw her enter their domain they let out monstrous cackles of alarm that had her almost backing out. But she stood still and the birds lowered their white feathers and went back to their business of eating the seeds spread about the ground and chattering amongst themselves.

Passing the feathered creatures, she quickly dodged into the humid henhouse. Wrinkling her nose at the offending odor of too many birds cooped up without a thorough cleaning of their quarters, she began filling her sack with eggs.

She had about a dozen or so when she heard the sound of approaching voices.

Men's voices.

Oh, shit!

Had the Barlow brothers been alerted by the commotion and were now coming to check?

No, they wouldn't be talking. They'd be coming in quiet.

The voices drew closer.

Callie tensed as she made out what they were saying.

"She'll do what I tell her to do, Zeb. And she'll like it." It was Seth Barlow's voice. He sounded mad. But that was his character. He was always mad about something.

"We agreed with her she'd have no piercings, especially there."

"I don't care. I want her clit pierced. She has no say in the matter."

Clit piercing? Callie shivered with anxiety despite the heat inside the coop.

They must be talking about the woman they'd claimed.

From the sound of their voices, the men had stopped just outside the henhouse. She dared a look out the dirt smeared, chicken-wired window.

She was right.

It was Zeb and Seth Barlow, the two eldest of the four brothers.

They were big men, as were all the Barlows. All stood over six feet. All of them weighed over two hundred and fifty pounds. But all of it was pure muscle.

She had to admit they were good to look at. All of them possessing the traditional deep blond hair of their German-born father, and the deep blue eyes of their Swedish mother.

They bordered on being almost too pretty. For men.

Unfortunately, they all had vile tempers.

At one time or another she'd seen all of them, more than once explode at the slightest provocation, their fists flying in anger against some poor fool who'd dared to defy them something during their high school years.

It was natural that they'd be wild and unruly because they were never disciplined by their meek mother or overbearing father.

No one controlled a Barlow.

The Barlows owned the ocean-side town of Rackety Valley and the one and only bank. In this tight-knit community, they held pretty much everyone's mortgages. If anyone lifted a hand against a Barlow, they were seen leaving town by sundown or being buried in the local cemetery the next day.

It was like a spaghetti western. Unfortunately, it was reality in Rackety Valley.

In the gym locker room or over lunch she'd heard from the other girls about the sexual appetites of the Barlow brothers. Had heard the rumors of sexual bondage, the sharing of their women at orgy parties and how small their dicks were and how they couldn't make a woman orgasm.

If those rumors were true whomever they'd claimed was in for a rough, unfilled sex life with these guys.

Callie felt sorry for the woman. Real sorry.

The woman would probably never experience love or sexual pleasure.

"If you insist on the clit piercing she'll be out of commission for days while it heals, and I for one can't go a day without fucking her cute little ass," Zeb argued.

Seth frowned and ran a hand over his chin as he thought about what his brother said.

"You're right. I still have a few things I want to try out on her. But then we'll get her clit pierced."

"Fine, but you'll have one tough fight on your hands with Laurie, she sure doesn't like to be told what to do. C'mon, let's get back inside."

Callie's blood froze at the mention of the woman's name.

Laurie?

Her ears buzzed with an odd white noise as the men chuckled and walked away.

Not her sister, Laurie?

It couldn't be. The one and only time she'd seen Laurie, she'd been reassured by her that she was going into hiding with a group of women who planned to start a resistance against the Claiming Law. She'd asked Callie to come along with her but Callie hadn't wanted to put the resistance into danger by joining. Laurie had been the one who'd directed her to the preacher, the only man for miles around who'd been secretly helping with the fledgling resistance.

Suddenly she remembered the night Luke had shown up. How angry he'd been when the preacher had mentioned the Barlows.

Oh — my — God!

Had Luke known all this time that her sister was the woman the Barlows had claimed?

Dizziness washed over her and she almost dropped the sack of eggs. Reaching out she grabbed onto the windowsill for support.

Sweet Jesus! Don't let this be true.

Not her baby sister.

It had to be another Laurie. But there weren't any other ones in Rackety Valley.

A cold clammy perspiration broke out all over her.

If Laurie was the woman they were talking about, so help her God, she'd kill every last one of those Barlows with her bare hands.

* * * * *

Luke was just waking up when Callie burst into the cabin, her face flushed with anger.

"You son of a bitch!" she spat at him, as she hoisted a sack onto a table and rushed over to him. Her fists were knotted, her chest heaved and her face was as pale as a white sheet.

Alarm sifted through him brushing away the cobwebs of sleep. "Whoa there, what's happened?"

"My sister! That's what happened."

Oh, shit!

"By the way you're looking at me it's quite obvious you know what I'm talking about. Why the hell didn't you tell me, Luke? Why didn't you tell me they had claimed my sister?"

"I didn't know how."

"You just spit it out instead of keeping it a secret from me. I don't like secrets, Luke!"

She had a wild-eyed look that made him uneasy and a tinge of hysteria laced her voice. Somehow, he got the feeling she wasn't only talking about this secret he'd kept from her.

"C'mon calm down, Callie."

"Calm down? Don't tell me to calm down," she ground out as she came toward him, her finger jabbing forcefully into his chest, making him wince at the pain. "I have every right to freak out about my little sister getting clit rings and nipple rings and who knows what else they're doing to her."

"Where'd you hear this?"

"At the Barlow ranch. I heard them talking while I was stuck in the chicken coop getting eggs for you! Imagine my surprise when I heard them mention my sister's name. It hurt, Luke," her voice cracked. "It hurt like hell to hear those men talk about my sister as if she were just a piece of property."

Fat tears began to roll down her cheeks.

"I'm sorry, baby. I should have told you."

"Darned straight you should have told me. You had no right to keep that information from me."

He reached out and wiped away the wet tears from her hot cheeks, quite surprised that she wasn't pulling away from him in her anger. In fact, she slumped down on the bed and melted against him. She trembled violently as he hugged her.

"I feel so helpless," she shook her head. "I can't believe all this has happened. This Claiming Law. Laurie forced into having sex with the Barlows. It's just sickening."

"She wasn't forced."

"W…What?" The look of surprise in her eyes had him cursing himself for not explaining everything to her right from the beginning.

"There was a deal on the table."

"What? What are you talking about? What kind of deal?"

"Originally they wanted Cate."

"The Barlows wanted my older sister? What the hell is it with those bastards? I know they've been pursuing her since high school but she belongs to Jude and he belongs to her. They love each other and nothing will keep them apart."

"I know." He smoothed his hands over her hair, cupping her ears. "And they aren't apart. They're together. Jude made it happen. He and Cate took our boat, the *Outlaw Lover* and they sailed away."

The look of anguish on her face slowly disappeared.

"Cate's gone? She's with Jude?"

He nodded. "Laurie stepped in for Cate."

"Why? It's insanity."

"I don't know the whole story. Only Laurie, the Barlows and the government know the agreement. But from what I've heard, Laurie volunteered to take Cate's place. I've never had a chance to verify the story. It was why I went to the Barlow ranch that night and…she didn't look like she was there against her will."

There was more to it than that. He should tell her the rest.

"And you found them together?"

He nodded.

"I know there isn't any good blood between you and the Barlows, but why would they shoot you?"

"They thought I was an intruder. They didn't know who I was until after Seth pulled the trigger."

"My God, why did she do this? I thought she'd gotten over Tyler being MIA. She must have snapped or something."

At the mention of his youngest brother, Luke couldn't stop himself from tensing. She immediately noticed his reaction and started to shake her head in denial.

"What? There's more to this, isn't there?"

He'd promised his brothers and the Barlows he wouldn't tell anyone about Ty. But keeping secrets from Callie wasn't a good thing. If he ever expected her to trust him then he would have to trust her with this delicate information.

"Tyler is alive."

"No." Callie closed her eyes and he could feel her sway against him.

"You okay?"

"I thought he was dead? The preacher told me he was dead."

"The Barlows know different. They know where he is but they aren't saying."

"What do you mean they aren't saying? Force it out of them. And Laurie knows this? She can't know. She'd never in a million years go near a Barlow if she knew Ty was alive."

"As far as we know she knows nothing about Tyler."

Suddenly Callie ripped herself away from him, wildly brushing away her tears from hope-crazed eyes.

"Well then, we'll just have to tell her, won't we? She has to leave them. She can't stay with them."

"And how do you propose we do that? The Barlows know where my brother is. If you go and tell Laurie, then Ty's as good as dead, isn't he? They wouldn't have any reason to dangle his life over our heads anymore. We're stuck, Callie. After the deal with Cate fell through, the Barlows told me they would think of something else for us to do in order to free Tyler. They also said if anyone breathed a word to Laurie, Ty was a dead man."

Callie swore under her breath and pressed her fingers to her temples.

"I'm getting a headache."

"Join the club."

She gazed up at him and his heart clenched at the helpless look shining in her eyes.

He knew how she felt. Helpless. Alone. Angry. Scared.

"What do we do?" she whispered.

"I don't know," he admitted, and curled his arms around her waist, holding her tight. "I don't know."

* * * * *

The confirmation that her baby sister was the woman who'd been claimed by the Barlow bastards had hit her like a Mack truck.

And now with the news that Tyler was alive and the Barlows knew where he was, it felt like a double whammy.

She'd wanted to ask Luke more questions about her sister and about his brother but their fight, if that's what she could call it, had worn him out.

After she'd checked his wounds and tucked the sheet around him he'd lain silent, staring up at the ceiling with his hands clenching and unclenching in anger.

She understood his frustration. She was just as helpless when it came to her sister.

That night the nightmare that had been haunting her since she'd escaped the government labs swooped over like a vulture,

tearing her mind apart. Only this time there was a new twist. Instead of the mad scientist coming to her secluded compartment to ask her the familiar questions of how she was feeling after the latest experiment and all the other redundant crap that followed, Luke had replaced him in her dream.

He looked dashing in a white lab coat as he settled down on the bed where she was lying.

"How are you feeling today, Callie?" his husky voice shimmered over her in seductive waves making her tremble with want.

"Horny," she admitted.

He grinned. "I knew you'd be. That's why…" He unbuttoned his lab coat and pulled the sides apart revealing his nakedness beneath. His cock was thick and long, and so unbelievably huge it made her nipples harden and her pussy so wet she could feel the stickiness coming down the insides of her thighs.

"You look beautiful when you're horny," he whispered, as his head descended and his moist lips slid seductively over hers. "I'm going to fuck you so long and so hard you'll be spoiled for any other man who wants to claim you."

Callie's body hummed with approval at his words.

"You're the only one I've ever wanted, Luke," she murmured against his hot mouth.

"Luke? Who is Luke?"

Callie gasped as Luke's face transformed into the mad scientist who'd tormented her the last few weeks she'd been in the labs.

His thin lips twisted in a snarl. "I'll never let you go, Callie Callahan. You're going to be my bitch, always. You'll never escape this lab."

His laughter rang evilly in her ears.

No! It wasn't true. She wasn't in the labs.

Please, don't let me be back in the lab!

Callie awoke on a strangled gasp, her heart pounding violently against her chest. In the holder beside the sofa, the lone candle she allowed herself during the night flickered, casting eerie shadows over Luke.

He lay quietly on the bed, his eyes closed, his hands clasped together over his bare chest in a peaceful sleep.

She heaved a sigh of relief.

She wasn't in the lab.

She was here with Luke. Here at their tiny ranch cabin. Safe and sound.

Throwing away the remnants of the nightmare, she smiled as she got up and remembered the part of the dream where Luke had shown up in the white lab coat and she'd confessed she was horny.

Tiptoeing she walked over to where Luke lay sleeping. Temptation was great to slide the sheet aside and fondle his cock until it was lusciously long and thick. His hard flesh would soothe the constant throb she'd had between her legs since she'd caught him out of bed.

His hard, red cock swollen with a need just as great as hers.

What would he do if she woke him up? Asked him to have sex with her?

Or, better yet, simply whipped the sheet off him, climbed on top and sank herself onto his hard shaft?

She took a step toward him and stopped, reality sinking in.

Despite her horniness, she couldn't fuck him. She couldn't risk ripping open the bullet wounds.

It was too soon.

She inhaled a deep breath and steadied herself.

If the electricity hadn't been disconnected she could have taken the edge off with a cold shower.

An alternative idea swiftly came to mind.

She'd masturbated many times over the past several weeks since escaping the labs. She could do it again, but not here.

Outside. In the pond.

Grabbing a bar of soap from the kitchen, she headed outside, leaving the door wide open to allow fresh air inside for Luke.

As she headed down to the nearby pond, she cast peeks over her shoulder at the log cabin. It looked eerily beautiful illuminated beneath the blue-gray moon-glow with the tall rocky cliffs as the backdrop.

The boarded windows, made the cabin look deserted, as if no one had been here for years, and that's exactly what she wanted to portray should any unwelcome visitors be wandering around.

She sighed her relief when she reached the pond.

No need to test if the water was too cold. She knew it would be blessedly cool because she'd done all her bathing and her masturbating here.

Striping off her sticky shirt, she slid her damp panties down her legs then stepped into the water, her toes sinking into the wonderfully cool mud.

Perfect.

She waded further, relishing the refreshing liquid as it washed around her hot legs and thighs. When it tickled against her aching clit, she gasped at the pleasant sensations.

Immediately she drew Luke back into her thoughts.

She wondered if he knew how much she needed him, and how hard it had been keeping her feelings and the truth buried deep inside over the past few days.

According to the preacher, they were married. She had every right to seek sexual gratification from her husband. Unfortunately, he'd been so drunk that night he obviously couldn't remember what had happened.

She could simply tell him. Or produce the wedding ring she'd slid off her finger and stashed in the underwear drawer with the other ring.

Or she could wait until he got better, and leave like she'd originally planned. And go where?

Maybe go to Laurie and beg her to come with her to join the resistance. But if Laurie ran from the Barlows, it would mean Tyler's life. She didn't know if she could live with herself if she caused the death of her sister's one true love.

Besides, running away with Laurie would mean both of them would be looking over their shoulders every minute of the day.

Perhaps it was selfish of her, but it wasn't something she really wanted to do.

Unfortunately, she had no choice in the matter, did she?

She was an unclaimed woman. Free for the taking by any group of men who caught her.

And it was all legal.

Callie shivered in the cool night air.

Getting claimed by strange men would be the death of her, literally. She would kill herself before she'd let a man she didn't want touch her. Of that she was sure.

But if Luke decided he wanted her, with the help of his brothers...

Callie blew out a sharp breath at the unexpected thought.

To her surprise, a zip of arousal coursed through her.

From the strong way Luke's cock had reacted when he'd seen her clothing clinging to her every curve the other night it proved he was on the mend faster than she'd ever expected.

And if his brothers were built like Luke...

Her nipples tightened at that thought.

How would it feel to have several men's hands all over her or their cocks plunging inside her?

Callie shook her head and splashed some water against her hot pussy.

She had to stop thinking like this.

She couldn't give into this newly evoked Claiming Law no matter how much she wanted to stop running and no matter how much she craved protection and safety from the mad scientist who was after her.

Staying here put Luke in grave danger.

And yet...how could she part with him now that he'd found her?

She gazed longingly at the open doorway of the cabin wishing he would walk out of there right now. Walk naked in the moon-glow toward her, his large cock swollen with need, his balls hard and full. He'd drag her from the pond throw her onto the ground and ruthlessly fuck her until she was screaming her love for him.

She shivered as she remembered the way he'd looked at her that night he'd first arrived at the cabin. His hot gaze had awakened long dormant desires that had only gotten worse over the past few days.

If you leave, I'll hunt you down until I find you and rest assured I'll make you mine in every sense of the word. Do you understand what I'm saying, Callie? You're mine.

His hot promise rang in her ears and she suddenly found herself imagining that she was running through the woods, Luke hot on her heels.

She could hear his aroused breaths, the pounding sound of his feet hitting the ground as his powerful legs carried him closer.

Deep in her heart, she knew she couldn't outrun him. Knew she wanted him to catch her.

To claim her.

His hot hands wrapped around her naked waist, grabbing her, pulling her to the cool ground.

"I'm going to claim you, Callie. I'm going to slide my cock into you and spoil you for any man who dares to try to claim you."

Shivering at his words, she whimpered as his long fingers slid her pussy lips apart. A calloused thumb grated perfectly against the tense bundle of nerves making her cry out.

Her vaginal muscles clenched and she slid a finger between her labia and began a slow torturous massage of her clit.

Oh, yes, this feels so good.

Throwing her head back, she gasped into the mild night air.

Her thighs tightened as she imagined wrapping her legs around Luke's waist.

Her belly quivered as she pushed her stomach against his.

Water splashed around her as her finger quickened upon the swollen bundle of nerves.

The familiar stirrings of lust deepened.

And then Luke's cock would slide into her.

One deep thrust was all she would need. He'd bury himself to the hilt, his hard balls slapping against her flesh.

Callie whimpered at the vision of Luke's thick penis disappearing into her tiny slit.

She could feel the climax coming.

Oh, yes! Luke! Yes!

Her fingers were slick with the warmth of her pussy juices making it easier to slide over and over her aching clit.

Quickly slipping her other hand between her legs, she thrust two fingers inside her wet vagina.

The climax was instantaneous.

Washing over her in a brutal wave of lust, making her cry out at the sudden violent impact.

When it was over, Callie's breath burst harshly from her lungs.

Masturbating had taken off the edge.

But she knew it wouldn't last. Already she could feel the familiar ache beginning to build deep inside her womb.

Soon she'd want Luke.

And she knew she wouldn't be able to stop him if he wanted her back.

* * * * *

Luke groaned his frustration as he watched Callie masturbating in the pond. Something had awakened him earlier and he'd opened his eyes just in time to see her open the door and slip outside.

He'd cursed his slowness as he'd struggled out of bed and had managed to get to the doorway just in time to see her slipping naked into the pond.

Her body had glowed like a goddess in the moonlight.

His abdomen had clenched tightly as he'd watched her hand slip between her legs. Watched her head move back as she cried out her release.

She needed to be fucked good and hard. That would put an end to her midnight escapades to the pond.

But all he could do was watch helplessly as she brought herself off.

Soon though. Soon he would be strong enough to have her.

* * * * *

Callie noticed immediately that Luke was acting strangely the next morning.

As she checked his bandages, he watched her more intensely than usual. And when she brought him breakfast in bed, he struggled into a seated position and fed himself as if he hadn't been seriously injured only a short time ago.

Strength was definitely returning to him faster than she'd anticipated.

"Heard you get up in the middle of the night," he said after he polished off the feathery scrambled eggs and two fat slices of her homemade bread.

"I was hot."

He grinned with amusement.

Oh, shoot—bad choice of words.

"Did you go for a swim?"

She felt her eyes widen in surprise.

Easy girl, don't panic. He's just asking you a simple question.

"Actually, yes."

He nodded and helped himself to a third slice of bread, which she'd liberally spread with the last of the butter and sprinkled with sugar.

"Was it nice?"

"What?"

"The swim. What did you think I was talking about?" His grin widened and she held her breath, as his eyes suddenly seemed a lusty black.

"You know, I was just thinking," he continued, his gaze capturing hers. "I never realized what a wonderful view we have from the door of our cabin."

Oh, my God! He knew!

He'd watched her masturbate last night!

Heat fused through her veins and suddenly she felt so hot she wanted to rip her clothes off and straddle Luke.

"And those night noises sound awesome."

Callie cleared her throat trying hard to break his mesmerizing gaze upon her. She couldn't.

"I...I hadn't noticed."

Liar!

"Maybe tonight I can join you...for a swim."

Oh. My. God. Now that was an invitation if she ever heard one.

"It's too soon."

Too soon to fuck? His eyes seemed to question.

Desire roared inside her. The desire to kiss him. The desire to make love to him and tell him they were married.

Only she couldn't tell him. He'd never believe her. He'd laugh at her and think it was a cheap trick to get him to have sex with her.

"I...I have to go and get some more water. You rest."

Rest for tonight? A tiny voice whispered in her ear.

Before he could say anything else, she grabbed the tray with the breakfast dishes, practically threw them onto the counter, seized a couple of empty pails and rushed outside.

Shutting the door behind her, she dropped the pails and wiped away the perspiration beading her forehead.

Gosh! Was she reading too much into things? Had he in fact seen her masturbating in the pond?

He hadn't said so, but the way he'd looked at her and the way he'd talked insinuated that he had.

Oh, boy.

And he'd said he wanted to go for a swim tonight.

What exactly did that mean?

That he wanted to swim? Or, to fuck?

Her pussy burned with the idea of finally having Luke between her legs. Her mind however screamed it was too soon.

There were secrets between them. Secrets she needed to explain.

In the end, she growled her frustration, grabbed her pails and headed to the nearby stream.

Chapter Five

Luke chuckled and leaned back against the pillows, trying hard to ignore the twist of pain lancing through his shoulder.

He enjoyed teasing Callie. Enjoyed getting her all hot and bothered.

It seemed as if they were rediscovering themselves all over again after the years of being apart.

And tonight he meant to do a whole hell of a lot more exploring.

A scorching fire began to build inside him at that idea, a fire that could be extinguished only in one way.

Making love to Callie.

* * * * *

As it turned out, they couldn't go for a swim that night for it began to drizzle in the early evening.

An easy truce had been formed between them when Callie had returned with the buckets of water. For the rest of the day they played cards, laughed carefree and forgot all about their troubles.

By late evening, Luke's eyelids were drooping with sleep and Callie silently cursed herself for taking advantage of him. She should have made him take a few naps during the day, but she'd enjoyed his easygoing company so much. He hadn't so much as mentioned the years they'd lost between them and hadn't asked any more questions about her stay at the government labs or the fact she was now a hunted woman.

Nighttime quickly draped over their tiny cabin and with it came a thunderstorm that had Callie shaking on the couch with every thunderous crash.

He must have seen her shivering in the candle glow because suddenly he called out from the bed, "You still afraid of storms?"

"No," she lied and flipped through an old romance she'd found on the bookshelf.

"Come hop into bed with me. I'll protect you from the storm."

Yeah, but who will protect me from you? she wanted to call back.

Another ear-splitting crash had her scrambling from the couch and diving into bed with him so fast, she hadn't even realized she'd done it until his warm, hard body curled along her entire backside.

Lust shot through her like a beautiful blade as he covered the sheet over both of them and felt the impressive length of his thick cock pressing between her panty-covered ass cheeks.

"You okay?"

"Yes," her voice sounded so sultry. Too sultry.

He chuckled against the back of her head.

"What's so funny?"

"The lab hasn't changed you much. You're still the same woman I fell in love with, baby."

His endearment had her heart picking up a mad pace.

She found herself sighing as his fingers sifted through her short hair and his warm breath whispered against the nape of her neck igniting a torturous burn deep inside her pussy.

Oh, boy, she was so ready for his cock to sink into her, it wasn't even funny.

"Try to sleep, Callie."

Her eyes popped open.

Sleep? Was he serious?

How could she sleep with him lying beside her?

She didn't want to sleep. She wanted action.

Thunder crackled ominously overhead making the bed shiver beneath them. She burrowed deeper against him.

Darnit! Not that kind of action!

He groaned softly into her ear. His hips shifted slightly and his cock lodged harder against the crack of her ass cheeks.

Oh, my! Now we're talking.

Suddenly the storm outside didn't seem so bad anymore. Not with Luke here with her.

"Luke?"

"Mmmm?"

"Make love to me." It came out as a primitive whisper she herself barely heard. But he must have heard it. Surely, he must have.

She waited for a response, half expecting a hand to slide over her breast. But nothing happened.

"Luke? Did...did you hear me?"

A soft snore came back as her answer.

Oh, crud! He'd fallen asleep.

"Son of a bitch," she whispered, and whimpered her frustration into the pillow.

"What's the matter?" he chuckled. "You think I didn't hear you?"

Oh, my gosh!

He wasn't asleep after all.

"Luke. I..." She wanted to tell him she'd understand if he was too weak but he cut her off.

"Shh. I was giving you an out. A moment to see if you wanted to change your mind."

Change her mind? Was he serious? A flicker of anger zipped through her.

"I don't want an out. I want you to fuck me."

Silence followed for what seemed like endless moments.

Had she gone too far? Had she misread all the signals? Was she being too bold? Maybe he wasn't ready? Maybe he was the one who wanted an out.

Gosh, she was starting to feel like an idiot.

"I wanted to wait a little longer, 'til I could use my arm."

"I don't need your arm, I need your cock."

"That's all I am to you? A cock?"

By the way his chest heaved against her back she knew he was laughing at her.

Oh!

This was not how she imagined he'd be with her. She'd expected something more intense. Like him throwing her onto the bed, and taking her hard and fast.

She sighed her annoyance, and cursed the thunder crackling overhead.

"Oh, go away!"

"I hope you don't mean that," he whispered, his breath oh so hot against her neck.

"Not you! The storm! Oh, this is going all wrong."

And this was so embarrassing!

She made a move to get up, but his hand snapped around her elbow holding her hostage in the bed.

"You going somewhere?" She shivered as his warm lips whispered over the nape of her neck.

"You want something from me. So take it."

Her eyes widened at his words.

It had never occurred to her to be the one to make the first move with their first time together.

She'd always thought that since she was a virgin he'd want her to be...submissive?

Silly girl! She chastised herself for being so stupid.

She was a woman. She had needs. Sexual needs and she wanted to get fucked by the man she loved.

Now!

A surge of power zipped through her.

He was injured. At her mercy.

She could do with him what she wanted...well, up to a certain extent. She didn't want to reopen his bullet wounds.

"Callie?"

Oh, this was going to be so much fun.

Turning herself over, she came face-to-face with Luke.

The ever-present shadow of bristle on his face made him look even sexier than usual. The candle glow was reflected in his dark, lusty gaze, sending a primitive excitement through her.

He was hers.

All hers.

That thought made her feel even bolder than usual.

The tips of his hot fingers whispered teasingly along the edge of her mouth sparking an ache to be kissed. "I've been waiting for my shoulder to get better so I could make love to you the way a woman I love should be made love to. I've been selfish. I hadn't even considered your needs."

Oh, boy. Did she have needs!

His fingers trailed down the length of her neck, over her shoulder and down her side, brushing against the side curve of her breast leaving a blazing trail of desire.

"When you masturbated down in the pond, I knew you needed a proper fucking but I ignored the warning signs."

She inhaled sharply as his hand slid over her waist and dived beneath her panties.

Hunger, deep and raw rushed through her veins. All kinds of emotions were swirling around inside her. From "let's forgo the foreplay and let me fuck you now" to, "oh no, let's go slow and make this pleasure last forever".

She reached out and slid her hands around his hot neck, feeling the fierce heat as she tunneled her fingertips through his velvety hair cupping the back of his head. His sexy masculine scent seeped into her lungs. Erotic heat shimmered through her. She felt her breasts swell against the trappings of her T-shirt while her pussy grew hot and damp as his hand nudged at the apex of her closed legs.

"Spread your legs a little."

She did as he instructed, hoisting a leg upward over his muscular thigh, creating perfect access for him. He slid his hand between her legs and groaned against her neck, "Man, you're soaked down here."

She cried out when his hard thumb flayed erotically against her vulnerable clitoris and his mouth descended upon hers, cutting her off.

Eagerly she kissed him back, re-igniting the fire that had blazed between them since the first night he'd come here. Since that wedding kiss.

Only this time there would be no stopping from going all the way.

Come hell or high water, tonight would be her first time with him.

His velvety tongue slammed into her mouth, making her head spin wonderfully, and making her moan at the erotic invasion.

Gosh, the man sure knew how to kiss.

Already she could feel herself hum with arousal from head to toe.

Suddenly he ripped his mouth away and whispered hoarsely, "Take off your top, Callie."

Oh, yes! Now we're really talking!

Uncurling her arms, she quickly struggled out of the garment and whipped it away. She made a grab to pull down her underwear but he stopped her.

"Not yet. Your panties are keeping my hand nicely in place."

As if to prove his point, he slid a finger inside her drenched channel.

The storm roared outside.

And inside her pussy.

Rain pelted the tin roof of the cabin. Lightning flickered between the wooden slats on the windows. Thunder shook the bed.

To her surprise, she wasn't afraid anymore.

How could she be? With a strong man lying beside her, his hand doing wonderful things to her cunt, his wet mouth kissing its way toward her now exposed breasts.

She could literally feel her nipples hardening into glass pebbles. Pleasure flared deep inside her womb and spread outward.

Suddenly, his breath was hot against her right nipple.

When he popped it between his lips, she couldn't stop herself from arching closer to him, pressing her breast into his face.

Her heart beat hard and fast.

Her breath came in sharp gasps.

Perspiration blossomed over her exposed flesh.

Oh, yes! This closeness is exactly what she'd missed over the years.

She cried out as he gently bit her nipple.

His thumb massaged her drenched cunt, sliding sensuously over her pulsing clit and long masculine fingers slid in and out of her slippery vagina rushing her toward a climax.

She trembled with need.

Needed to have his cock inside her.

"Luke!" she groaned as he speared a third finger into her tiny hole and a scorching fire raced through her veins.

With his three fingers impaling her, her vagina felt so stuffed.

How would she ever take Luke's cock inside her?

Her doubts vanished momentarily as his mouth let her nipple go with a pop. She moved her upper body a little to allow him access to her other breast. He latched onto it like a starving man.

His tongue poked and jabbed at her sensitive nipple and she moaned her pleasure.

He tasted her. Sucked her. Bit her until her breast felt so swollen she thought it would burst.

Breathing in ragged bursts, she felt the hard length of his cock outlined against her thigh.

He was so hard.

So hot.

And she was so ready.

Reaching down she grabbed him by the hair and tugged him away from her breast.

"I have to have you now," she hissed. "On your back!"

To her irritation, he chuckled.

He didn't move fast enough, so she yanked his hand from between her legs.

Desperate for release she slipped off her soaked panties, scrambled onto her knees and ripped the sheets from his body.

"Oh, sweet mercy," she cried out as she spied his rock-solid cock pulsing at full mast.

Perfectly huge.

Perfectly engorged.

But was he perfectly too big for her?

She'd find out soon enough.

His eyes danced with lusty amusement as she lifted herself over him, her legs positioning themselves on each side of his torso.

She grabbed onto the base of his cock with both hands making sure the aim was good.

"You look so beautiful," his voice sounded raw and so sexy it made her tremble with need.

She came down upon his solid length slowly, allowing his mushroom-shaped head to nudge at her tiny pussy opening. He groaned as she slid his cockhead into her cunt about an inch and then lifted herself slightly so his rigid flesh broke free of her, then swiveled her hips in order to feel his penis slide sensuously against her clitoris.

She did that several times until the aching fire in her pussy burned so torturously hot she thought she would climax right on the spot.

She heard Luke cursing beneath her.

"I'm going to explode soon, Callie," he warned.

"So am I," she said between gritted teeth.

He reached up and palmed her breasts.

"Come for me, Callie. Come for me, now." His fingers slid over her hard nipples in a seductive massage and she felt the line of need snowball deep inside her pussy.

He was obviously weakening her resolve to take her time pleasuring herself. "You bastard!" she cried out.

"Make love to me, sweetheart. Make love to me."

His hot gaze seared straight to her very soul encouraging Callie to sink her hips. She gasped and whimpered as his thick erection split into her vagina, spreading her vaginal muscles wider than they'd ever been spread before.

His hands tightened erotically over her breasts making her lower her body faster.

His cock penetrated her like a long, thick piece of velvet-encased molten steel. Impaling her so fully—so wonderfully—she couldn't stop the tremors of arousal from taking hold of her.

When his cock was fully inserted inside her, she ground her hips into his pelvis, loving the way his shaft pulsed and enjoying the agonizing sensations ripping through her.

He twisted and groaned beneath her.

Lifting herself, she allowed his shaft to almost withdraw from her soaked pussy then impaled herself on him again.

His fingers plucked at her breasts dragging harsh breaths of arousal from her lungs.

She felt her thighs tighten.

Felt her whole body go tense.

Then she exploded. The orgasm splintering through her like the lightning bolts outside.

Her mind shattered.

She ground herself harder on his thick cock. Riding the agonizing waves of ecstasy. Focusing on the shards of sensations pummeling her.

Beneath her, Luke growled his own pleasure.

She gave him no mercy, and rode him so hard and so fast that he cried out.

Whether it was from pain or pleasure, she didn't care anymore.

She wanted this pleasure to last and instinctively realized a wild, carnal side of her had been unleashed forever.

Now that she'd had the brand of Luke Outlaw's engorged penis deep inside her pussy she knew her heart would never let him go.

* * * * *

Late the next morning the clouds hung low over the valley as Callie sat on the cliffs overlooking their tiny log cabin, her pussy aching and sore from last night's sex.

Five years she'd waited for last night.

Five long years she'd craved for something that should have happened on their wedding night like they'd planned.

Now she felt the pang of guilt at having their original plans ruined, but at least she was now sexually branded by the man she loved.

Yet, there were still secrets that she needed to confess.

Secrets she had to tell him before this went any further. She had to give him the opportunity to learn the truth so he could walk away. Before it was too late.

For her though, it was already too late. She realized that now. Had realized it deep down inside her heart the minute she'd seen his shadowy silhouette in the cabin doorway the first night he'd arrived injured.

She bit her bottom lip and nodded.

The time had come for her to tell Luke her secrets.

* * * * *

You may kiss the bride.

Those words echoed in Luke's ears so clearly that his eyes popped wide open and he immediately reached for the chain necklace he'd seen on the nearby night table.

Shit!

The tags were there but the rings were gone.

Why hadn't he noticed it before?

Luke grinned and ran a thoughtful hand over his bristly face.

He hadn't noticed because he'd been too busy getting reacquainted with Callie.

At the thought of her, his cock roared to life.

Hardening. Pulsing. Readying itself to make love to her again.

Man! Last night had been awesome.

The frantic way she'd rode him. Her wild cries as she'd climaxed over and over again.

She hadn't been able to get enough of fucking him.

He hadn't been able to get enough of getting fucked by her.

And by the way his cock was swelling and his balls were getting so rigid it was beginning to hurt he couldn't wait to find her and start fucking her.

Screw his bum shoulder. He'd put up with the pain.

He whipped aside the sheet and got out of bed.

A quick glance around made him frown.

Where the hell were his clothes?

Those were the only clothes he had here, having removed the rest years ago when he'd cleaned out the place before heading off to the Wars.

If he was lucky, he might have at least a pair of old underwear stashed in one of the drawers.

Opening the top drawer, he smiled when he saw a few pairs of Callie's skimpy underwear.

Before the government had abducted her, she'd moved some of her clothes into the cabin. He hadn't had the heart to get rid of them. Instead, he'd taken his stuff and simply boarded up the windows and walked away.

He was about to shut the drawer when a golden glitter peeking out from beneath one of her panties caught his eye. Lifting it, he gasped with surprise.

The wedding rings were nestled in her panties.

You may kiss the bride.

Those words echoed in his ears again.

Weird.

Turning, he spied two pails sitting in the middle of the room.

A drop came down and splashed noisily into the bucket.

Looking up, Luke saw two bullet holes in the ceiling.

What the hell?

Chapter Six

Callie hesitated at the door.

Luke was already up. She could hear him whistling happily inside the cabin.

Dare she tell him her secrets?

Dare she break his heart?

But she had to. If they were ever going to have a future, she needed to tell him.

Do it now, Callie! her mind urged. *Do it now, before he finds out on his own and never forgives you.*

Her heart clenched painfully.

She had to tell him. Tell him everything or she would slowly go insane with these lies between them.

Biting her bottom lip, she turned the doorknob and shakily stepped inside the cabin.

Her mouth dropped open at the erotic sight.

Luke stood in front of the woodstove, frying some scrambled eggs in a frying pan.

And he was totally naked.

Oh. My. Gosh.

His ass cheeks were wonderfully plump and she resisted the urge to lave her tongue over those masculine cheeks.

He must have heard her come in for he turned around and smiled sweetly. Almost too sweetly.

Uneasiness slipped through her and her breath backed up in her lungs.

"Oh, look what the cat dragged in," he said.

"What are you doing?"

"Cooking you breakfast."

"Without any clothes?"

"When a woman makes a man's clothes disappear, he gets some interesting ideas and has certain expectations."

Certain expectations? Her pussy throbbed wildly.

"I did the laundry down in the pond this morning. I have your clothes hanging out on the line. They should be dry soon," she explained.

"The laundry. What a lovely wifely duty."

Her heart picked up speed at his remark.

He continued stirring the eggs and she couldn't help but notice the golden glint on his finger.

Oh, my!

He'd found the wedding rings in the underwear drawer.

He settled the frying pan on the nearby countertop and turned around. A dark fire of lust ignited inside her pussy as she got a full frontal view of his massive erection.

She could only stare as he drew closer, holding out his hand. Her wedding ring glittered in his palm.

"I think you forgot to tell me something."

"You remembered?"

"Bits and pieces. The holes in the ceiling kind of prodded me into the right direction."

Thank goodness, one of the secrets was finally out in the open.

"Please, let me explain."

"I'm all ears." He took another step toward her.

"Um…well, when you woke up and didn't say anything I thought you'd been too drunk to remember."

"You could have told me."

"I didn't think you'd believe me. I thought…you might think I was looking for an excuse for us to be together," she said, quite aware that he was now standing right in front of her in all his naked glory, pure masculine heat radiating off his body and slamming into her in erotic waves.

His eyes darkened, whether it was with lust or anger, or a combination of both she wasn't sure. Whatever it was he'd never looked at her quite this way before.

It made her flesh burn with want and at the same time, it made fear shimmy through her.

She took a step backward and her butt smacked against the closed door.

"Give me your left hand," he growled.

She held out her hand and watched breathlessly as he slid the smooth ring onto her finger.

"With this ring I thee wed," he said.

Quickly, he let go of her hand.

Muscles bulged in his arms as he raised them and placed his hands on the wall on each side of her, effectively trapping her.

He lowered his head and his warm lips touched her neck.

The sensual touch almost had her knees buckling.

"We haven't had our wedding night yet," he whispered.

"We…last night."

"Not the same. I didn't know we were married then. I want a proper consummation of our wedding night and I want it my way, and I want it now."

His teeth nipped sharply at her neck.

She yelped at the erotic pain.

He kissed the area where he'd just bitten, taking away the hurt.

"But first, I'm going to give you a dose of punishment for lying to me."

"I...I didn't lie about us...I...simply avoided telling you."

She cried out as he planted a teasing nibble against a sensitive spot between her shoulder blade and neck.

"Avoiding the truth is just as good as lying, Callie. Lift up your arms, sweetheart. We're going to start the punishment phase."

Excitement roared through her at his whispered command. She did as he asked and raised her arms into the air.

His hot hands slid against her belly and he began to lift up her shirt.

"I want you naked, Callie. I want to hear your wild cries as I make love to you like a man makes love to his wife."

Her shirt pushed up higher and her braless breasts spilled free.

A split second later, her shirt was off and Luke was staring at her breasts.

His eyes sparked with lusty heat.

His breathing sounded heavy and tortured.

His skin smelled of perspiration and wild sex.

"My wife has the most beautiful breasts I've ever seen. Not too big. Not too small. Nice and plump with nipples so large I can nibble on them all day. But first I have to punish you for lying to me."

His hands intertwined with hers and he pulled her toward the bed. His eyes were darker than she'd ever seen them before. The exotic sight made intense sensations flood her.

When they reached the bed, he dropped her hands. "Take off your pants and your underwear. I want you on the bed, on your hands and knees so I can administer your punishment."

Callie blinked at his instruction.

On the bed? On her hands and knees?

What in the world did he have in store for her?

He moved over to the kitchen area and busied himself with something. The thought of going over to see what he was up to was so great she almost did it but at that instant he looked at her over his shoulder, sexual hunger blazing in his eyes.

"Do it now, Callie. Hands and knees on the bed, ass facing me."

His voice dripped with lust and Callie hurried to do his bidding.

What was he planning to do to her? Spank her like she was some bad little girl?

Oh, please. If he did that she'd burst out laughing.

When she was totally naked she climbed onto the bed and did as he asked.

No sooner had she gotten into the required position she felt his warm hands smooth a sensual caress that literally seared the curves of her ass cheeks.

"That feels wonderful," she hissed. "Yet it seems an unusual form of punishment."

"More to come."

His strong hands settled over both sides of her hips and he held tight. His hot breath whispered against the crack of her ass and a new urgency raced through her.

Was he going to go down on her?

His next words answered her thoughts.

"Your pussy lips are so pink and you smell so sweet, I could just devour you in one sitting."

The instant the burning tip of his tongue parted her labia she jerked in response, crying out her need.

"You're already soaked," he chuckled against her pussy. "I've always loved the way you creamed so easily."

"That's because my pussy loves you."

He gave her cunt another slow teasing lick, expertly missing her engorged clitoris. The roughness of his long tongue

lapping against her flesh in that one long stroke had her spreading her legs wider and her quivering cunt begging for more.

"Your pussy loves my cock and my tongue, and my fingers," he whispered, "But what about the rest of you? Do you love me?"

"Of course I do."

"Then show me with your body. Say that you love me. Say you love me with your very soul. That you'll do anything so we can stay together."

She wanted to say all those things, but his tongue was working its dark magic against her engorged clitoris making her moan instead. His breath seared hot against her swollen flesh, his moist lips sucking at her drenched labia with strong, powerful motions that left her literally speechless.

He circled her rigid clit, dabbing at it playfully and alternately pulling her blistering labia into his mouth one at a time, fondling each pink lip until they burned with fire. His dangerous torture had her arching her butt desperately against his mouth, had her thighs trembling with sexual tension. A tension that was building so quickly she could only cry out in frustration with her need to climax.

"Luke!" she managed to moan.

"Tell me, my sweet. Tell me how much you love me."

"I...oh, God!" His tongue dipped into her cavern driving her to the brink of begging him to stick his cock inside her.

The sounds of suckling split the air. Her cunt muscles clenched around his welcome invasion. She could literally feel her juices traveling down her vagina and into his mouth.

Soon her vagina felt like an inferno begging to be doused.

"Luke, please fuck me," she begged.

"Not yet," he said as he pulled his mouth away from her trembling pussy. "I've got a surprise for you. Something I

wanted to introduce you to on our wedding night. And since we're married now…" his words trailed off.

Her heart swelled painfully at his words. Made a tingle of guilt seep into her pleasure. She pushed it aside.

Later! She'd tell him the truth later!

For now, she needed to enjoy this. Needed to enjoy Luke's torturous attention. For it could very well be their last time together.

The gentle scent of her comfrey salve drifted to her nostrils and she heard him rubbing his hands together.

"What…what are you doing?"

"Don't look. I want this to be a surprise."

His hands were on her ass now. Generously smoothing the greasy salve over the curves of her ass cheeks, his palms leaving a trail of slippery fire wherever he touched. Her eyes widened and she almost mounted a protest when a finger suddenly lodged at her tight little nether hole.

But she changed her mind the instant he gently dipped inside.

He'd lubed his finger and it slid in easily.

She groaned as her tight anal muscles clenched wickedly around his digit.

It was an awesome feeling having him where no one had gone before. A feeling she rather enjoyed.

Was this what he meant by punishment? Was he going to finger-fuck her ass? She was virgin down there. She'd never even thought about having him do her there with his finger, until now.

He moved slowly, dipping in and out. Filling her deeper with his lubed finger each time.

"You like?"

"Oh, my!" she gasped as he inserted a second finger. "It's different."

"Enjoyable?"

She nodded quickly as her asshole tensed, and then relaxed and quickly accepted the second intrusion.

Tears of pleasure-pain zipped into her eyes. She could feel an oddly sensual tingle slither up her neck, too.

His two fingers continued a slow erotic thrust and Callie closed her eyes and relaxed into the sensual rhythm.

The sucking sounds of her ass protesting his exit split the air and intermingled with the whimpers of her arousal as he slid his lubed fingers deeper and deeper with each thrust.

Then suddenly something cool and smooth, and foreign lodged at her rear hole.

Her eyes popped wide open in surprise as he began to insert something.

"Luke? What is it?"

"A butt plug," his voice sounded darkly aroused.

"Where…oh, sweet mercy." She could feel the plug going in deep. It was larger than his two fingers. Much larger. Her muscles constricted against the erotic invasion and she forced herself to relax, allowing it to seep into her.

"Where did you get it?" she managed to ask.

"Bought it years ago for us. Forgot about it until I was searching for something to wear. Remembered I'd stashed it in a bottom drawer. There are other things I bought, too."

"Like?" Pleasure-pain burned her ass now as the butt plug finally stopped and her anal ring trapped it inside her.

"You'll find out soon enough." He gave her ass a sharp swat and she yelped from the burn. "Stay here for a minute. Don't remove the butt plug and don't peek."

"What have you got in mind for me, Luke Outlaw?" she mumbled beneath her breath as she kept her eyes glued straight to the wall and listened to him doing something else in the kitchen.

She could feel the sticky essence of wet vaginal juices staining her inner thighs. Her legs continued to tremble from sexual tension and her vagina felt so distressed at not having been penetrated by his cock that she could just scream bloody murder.

But her ass?

Now that was a different story.

Her ass hummed.

Clenched with arousal.

Simmered with such an exquisite ache that she could literally feel every muscle stretched around the butt plug.

A butt plug that seemed so big she wondered if he'd shoved a bat up her ass.

Not to mention she wanted to come so bad she was nearly in tears, and ready to start masturbating if he didn't hurry the hell up with what he was doing.

Her clit felt engorged. On fire.

The knot of nerves in her clit were raw and pounding, full of blood as a result of his velvety-rough tongue's seductive ministrations.

Her labia felt puffed and swollen.

The only thing that felt neglected were her breasts.

She pouted.

Perhaps if she sat on her haunches and played with her nipples?

A sharp smack to her rear made her straighten to attention.

"Don't even think about it, sweet stuff."

"Oh, come on, Luke, I'm in agony here."

"The punishment should fit the crime," he soothed.

The mattress moved as he climbed onto the bed beside her.

Without warning, his finger flicked against her nipple.

"Ouch! That hurts." But she loved the fiery pain and there was a similar sensation that zipped through her pussy at the same time.

She looked over at him and her heart thumped out of control at the sensual way he looked at her.

He grinned back and flicked her other dangling nipple.

"Do you love me?"

"I love you," she breathed.

"Show me. Show me how much you love me, Callie."

"What…what do you mean?"

"Keep your eyes straight ahead and just go with the pleasure-pain. Enjoy what else I'm going to do."

"What else are you going to do?"

He didn't answer but his head tilted slightly as if he was telling her to follow his instructions.

She breathed out a frustrated breath and kept her eyes glued to the wall.

He began an intense flicking at her nipples, the pressure got harder and harder until they were two painful tips of raw agony.

Fire raced through her breasts.

She could actually feel them swelling and hardening with desire.

And then he did something wonderful.

Gently smearing some warm comfrey salve onto her burning nubs, his fingers massaged her aching points so erotically that his sensual touch turned the fiery pain into something else, something electrical and fiercely arousing.

She dipped her shoulders back allowing her breasts to dangle even more freely.

"That feels so wonderful."

He grunted in response.

She could hear that he was breathing harshly now.

And her breaths were just as harsh and matching his.

Then suddenly she felt a sharp pinch and a heaviness hanging off one of her nipples.

Then her nipple began a slow erotic burn.

She resisted looking.

She knew exactly what he was doing. Placing nipple clamps on her.

A moment later, the same thing happened to her other nipple.

A sharp pinch, a heaviness and then a slow erotic burn.

"You like your wedding presents?" he said as he climbed away from her and returned to her backend.

"I love my wedding presents," she said and breathed into the pleasure-pain engulfing both breasts.

They sure didn't feel neglected anymore.

"I want to fuck you now, Callie. I want to fuck your pretty little cunt, but first I have to do one more thing."

A sharp sting smacked across her ass.

He was spanking her?

The bastard!

"Your punishment for not telling me about our marriage."

He smacked her ass harder and her eyes widened in shock as a strange arousal shifted through her lower abdomen and straight into her vagina.

My God! Earlier she thought she'd laugh if he spanked her.

This erotic pleasure was nothing to laugh at.

What followed had Callie gasping and crying out as each sharp smack of his palm landed against her sensitive ass cheeks. With every slap, she could feel her ass muscles clench erotically around the butt plug. With each smack, more juices dripped between her thighs.

When he finally stopped, she was gasping at both the sweet, hot pain flaming her ass and the erotic pleasure screaming through the rest of her.

Her arms were weakening and perspiration dotted her flushed skin.

"Sweet heavens, Luke, I love you, but I can't take anymore of this punishment."

"Did it hurt to say it?"

She felt his rigid cockhead lodge at her pussy entrance.

"Say what?" she growled, sexual frustration building.

He entered her in one swift plunge.

She sucked in her breath through her teeth, and bucked against his hard impalement.

"You know what," he ground out, withdrawing his shaft and thrusting hard into her.

His fingers were at her clit, massaging quickly, rubbing hard, rapidly bringing back her pleasure.

An agony of sensations ripped through her. She grew anxious at the raw intensity of it. Grew frustrated at the perfectly timed rhythm, as if he wouldn't bring her release until she told him what he wanted to hear.

Frantically, she thought back to what she'd said and then it clicked.

She smiled.

Son of a bitch.

"I love you, Luke Outlaw!" she cried out.

Those were the magic words.

His control disintegrated.

He plunged deeper than he'd ever thrust before and she shattered.

Waves of ecstasy overloaded her.

She bucked against him as she exploded.

The sultry sensations making her cry out, making her dig her fingers into the mattress while he rammed her good and hard.

Agonized groans spilled from him followed by a gurgled cry.

And then she felt the hot jets of his sperm spurt deep into her womb.

When they both had finished climaxing, he kept his thick cock buried deep inside her cunt and guided her down onto the bed where they remained joined and lay gasping.

"I want you to say it to me every day for the rest of our lives," he breathed.

The rest of their lives. That's all she ever wanted. All she'd ever dreamed.

* * * * *

"Callie?" His fingers wiped the tangles of her damp hair off her perspiring face.

They'd made love again and again.

And now they were both spent.

His shoulder was aching like a bitch, but Luke's mind was racing.

He was getting stronger. Fucking her senseless over and over again proved it.

Soon they would have to leave their little love nest.

They needed to decide what to do and where they would go.

"You awake?" he prodded.

She moaned and then her eyes blinked open.

"We have to talk, sweetie."

Confusion etched her flushed face. "Talk? About what?"

"We can't live here forever. It isn't safe for you. I've been thinking that we should maybe go back to the main farm and get a truck and try to escape to Canada."

She tensed against him, a deep sadness washing into her blue eyes.

"Canada?"

"I've been there on several fishing trips when I was younger. We could find a way to cross the border. My brother Cade, he'd have some contacts with the authorities. He's a bounty hunter now. He could get us some false papers. We could head north into the Canadian wilderness. There's not much of a population deep in the northern woods. We could live off the land. We could build our own log cabin, just like this one."

The more he talked the more he liked his plan.

"But what about your brothers? You all are so close. What about Tyler? We have to find a way to help him. And I can't leave Laurie to those Barlow bastards. And the Outlaw farm? Who will help Colter and Mac and Cade run it, if you take off? And what about our ranch? What will happen to our house?"

Shit! He hadn't thought about all that stuff.

"It's too dangerous for you here with this new Claiming Law, Callie. We can't hide you forever out at the farm. People come and go all the time. It's a business. And you can't hide in the house all the time. You'll go nuts. Someone will see you. The government will take you away. I can't fight them. I'm broke, and the farm and this land is mortgaged to the hilt. I won't lose you, Callie. I won't lose you again."

Anxiety at losing her again only made his heart beat frantically. Made his wounded shoulder tense with pain.

She reached up and stroked his chin. The sadness in her eyes only deepened, and it sent shards of alarm racing through him.

"Luke...we... I have to tell you something. I..."

He brushed his lips against her mouth stopping her cold. From the anguish twisting her face, he instinctively knew he didn't want to hear what she wanted to tell him.

"Don't, Callie. Don't say a word. I don't want to know."

Desperation slammed into him.

Maybe he should tell her about his alternative plan. It had been kicking around at the back of his head. It was something dark and yet oddly exciting, too. Something he'd never actually thought he'd ever hear himself say.

"There might be another way to keep you protected. I could ask my brothers to help me to claim you."

He held his breath, cursing silently for bringing up the subject.

She stared back at him. Emotions brewing in her eyes he just couldn't put a name to.

Maybe he'd just lost her with that suggestion. Maybe he was idiot for even considering giving into the Claiming Law.

"I'm sorry, I shouldn't have said that."

She touched trembling fingertips to his lips. A look of utter devastation flooded her eyes.

"I can't...not until..."

His fingers quickly found her engorged clitoris and his lips breezed across her mouth again.

"Just relax and enjoy this," he whispered.

He didn't want to hear it. Not now. Not ever.

She closed her eyes and nodded.

It took him very little time to put a sensuous smile back onto her face.

Chapter Seven

Their last lovemaking session had been even more beautiful than the ones they'd shared earlier in the day and last night, Luke thought as he dipped the bucket into the cool stream then hauled it out, wincing as a wicked pain nudged through his wounded shoulder reminding him he still had a long way to go before his shoulder was healed.

Fucking Callie hadn't helped his wound, but it sure had helped his aching cock.

He grinned despite the pain in his shoulder and focused his thoughts onto Callie. There was a primitive wildness in her.

A carnal eroticism he'd unleashed inside her.

And there was something troubling her, too. Something she wanted to tell him.

He didn't want to hear it.

He wanted them to be happy.

He'd give her a little time to get used to the idea of a possible Claiming. Of course, there was that major drawback of a one-month waiting period where any other groups of available men could fuck her, but that wouldn't happen.

If she agreed to the Claiming, he had a plan to get rid of that one-month waiting period, and keep her safe from the government's clutches.

The water washing against his hand as he allowed the bucket to fill reminded him of her pussy juices.

The way it always gushed down her channel and onto his tongue and into his mouth was unbelievable. She had so much pleasure juices to give him. And the taste of her cream was even sweeter than he'd remembered from years back.

She tasted as sweet and as thick as honey.

No, she tasted better than honey.

His brothers would be very pleased.

That is, only if she agreed to a Claiming.

He remembered the soft velvety feel of her pussy lips as he'd sucked the throbbing flesh into his mouth. Loved the way she'd whimpered and moaned when he'd attached those nipple clamps to her rock-hard tips. Most of all he loved the erotic tightness of her cunt due to the butt plug buried in her luscious ass.

After making love to her for the rest of the day, he'd left her tangled in the sheets, whispering to her to keep that butt plug buried in her ass until he told her to remove it. It would keep her muscles wide, stretched and prepared for him.

And for the Claiming.

Hoisting the heavy bucket from the stream, he began to head back to the cabin when he saw it.

Behind the cabin.

On the top of the cliffs.

A metallic glint.

His blood froze.

Someone was up there.

* * * * *

Callie wrapped the sheets around her nakedness and stumbled out of the bed to pick up her clothing.

She couldn't believe she'd actually been able to keep the two one-inch scars on her abdomen hidden from Luke. He'd tried touching her abdomen a couple of times but she'd managed to distract him. He'd even pulled the sheets off of her.

She thought he'd see them but thankfully he hadn't.

But it was only a matter of time before he did.

Then the questions would follow.

And the devastating betrayal he'd feel.

Callie sighed heavily.

She didn't want to tell him what happened to her in the lab. But she had to.

If she agreed to the Claiming, the government would probably have records about what the scientist had done to her during that last experiment.

Luke would find out.

She had to tell him.

When he came back from the creek, she'd confess.

She'd confess everything.

If he still wanted her then she'd agree to the Claiming.

A shiver of excitement nudged away her fear.

Being fucked by Luke and his brothers had been something she'd never thought about doing.

Sure, she'd imagined a ménage à trois.

But it had only been fantasy.

She'd never taken it seriously.

Until now.

Luke's sharp curse as he burst through the door made shards of fear slice up her spine.

"We've got company," he said as he stomped over to the back door they'd opened earlier to let some cool air inside the cabin.

"What do you mean, company?" Callie gasped as she rushed over to join him.

"Stay to the side. I don't want him to see you."

Sweet Lord, please let Luke be wrong.

She took a peek out the door and immediately relaxed.

"I don't see anyone."

"He's there. I saw a glint off a rifle."

"Are you sure?"

"Seen enough glints off metal when I've been out hunting with my brothers."

"You think it might be one of your brothers?"

"Can't think of a reason they'd be up on the cliffs. They'd be coming in from the front. Most likely by the road."

"How many do you think are up there?" She braved another look at the gray cliffs and still saw nothing.

"Just one… I hope."

Terror washed over her. All she could think of doing was running. Getting as far away from here as possible.

"Should we leave? Maybe head for your brothers' farm?"

"From that vantage point he's got the perfect layout of the cabin, the yard and the surrounding meadows. If we run, he'd pick me off as if I was a turkey at a turkey shoot. And you… Where's your gun?"

Callie frowned. Her knees started to shake.

Shoot! Where had she put her gun?

God! She'd been so involved with their lovemaking she hadn't even given her gun a second thought.

Quickly she gazed around the room and spotted it on the night table.

"I see it."

He nodded, and then looked back up at the cliffs.

"Where's your gun?" she asked.

He lifted up the back of his shirt and she saw it pressed against his lower back, the gun handle sticking out from where he'd jammed it into the waistband of his pants.

Thank goodness, he wasn't as careless as she was in leaving it lying around.

"So, what should we do? Sit here and wait for him or them to come and get us?" Callie gripped the sheet tighter around her nakedness. "That plan won't work for me. I'd rather chance us getting shot. Go to the Outlaw farm."

She knew she wasn't thinking straight, but she couldn't stay trapped in here not knowing who was up there.

"If we got away, they'd hunt us down within hours. We'd never be able to make it to the farm." His voice sounded so cool and calm. It made her even more nervous. "We stay put, Callie. We don't know how long he's been there. Could be minutes. Maybe I saw him before he could get a glimpse of me. If that's the case and we go out there, or if we close this back door he'll know we're here for sure, and he'll know we know he's here. It'll be dark soon. Then I'll slip out—"

"You're not going out there!"

"I have to see what we're up against. It could just be a hunter."

"That's what I'm afraid of," she admitted.

He reached out and slid his arm around her waist pulling her close.

"Let's not jump to conclusions."

Despite his words, she read the worry in his eyes. He was thinking the same thing she was thinking. More than one man could be up there. And if they were, they wouldn't waste too much time in coming down to claim her.

* * * * *

It seemed to take forever for the sun to set as Luke peered out the back door watching for any sign of movement. He hadn't seen a thing since that one metallic glint earlier.

Maybe he'd been mistaken?

Maybe it had just been a reflection off an old pop can or something.

Or maybe someone really was up there.

"Check how many bullets we have for the guns, would you?" he said to Callie who'd quickly gotten dressed and now looked as if she might bolt at a moment's notice.

"There's two packages of bullets for my gun buried in the flour canister," she said quietly.

"Hmm, I guess that's what I must have sunk my teeth into the last time I ate some of your home-baked bread."

His attempt at humor rewarded him with a stony smile. His gut clenched as he realized that god-awful hunted look was back in her eyes.

"Sorry—just trying to see that pretty smile of yours again. I kind of got used to it over the past few days."

"That's because I let my guard down. It won't happen again," the steeliness in her voice rattled him.

He didn't want her to be this way. Cold and bitter. Looking over her shoulder for the rest of her life. It was no way to live. When they got out of this mess he needed to think of something to bring back the old, carefree Callie, and if she didn't agree to the Claiming, he needed to find another way to keep her safe and protected.

"How are we for food?" he asked.

He'd expected her to go look through the cupboards and do an inventory. It was a desperate attempt to keep her occupied.

His attempt didn't work. She didn't move from his side.

"Aside from a few days worth of canned food in here, I've got one week of cans that the preacher brought me. I buried it in a hole in the backyard."

The backyard which was in full view of whoever might be up there. He sighed wearily and glanced back up at the quickly darkening cliffs, half expecting movement.

He saw nothing.

Impatience gnawed at him.

If they knew there was a woman down here, they wouldn't wait long. They would come in tonight.

"It's dark enough now. I'm going up there," he said and reached for the gun he kept nestled against the small of his back.

"We discussed this already," Callie hissed.

"No, you discussed it. I didn't agree."

"Luke, no." She grabbed a hold of his arm and held on so tight he grimaced at the pain of her fingernails digging into his flesh.

Fear flashed brightly in her eyes and his heart ached for her.

"Callie, listen to me. I just want to go up and scout around. Maybe I didn't see what I thought I saw. If that's the case it'll save us a lot of anguish. We can't sit around here and wait for help. My brothers are obviously not coming. The preacher isn't coming either. I have to go and see what we're up against. In the meantime I want you to lock yourself inside the cabin and keep both guns."

He made an attempt to hand her his gun and she pushed it away.

"No! You're not going up there unarmed. If you go. I go with you."

"C'mon, Callie. Don't make this hard for me."

"Screw you," she spat and raced over to the kitchen counter.

Lifting the lid to the flour canister, she dug out two flour-covered boxes of bullets and shoved one box in each of her back jean pockets.

When she reached his side again, she had her gun firmly in one hand and a butcher knife clenched in the other.

His gut twisted at the sight. It was the same knife she'd said she would have used on herself the night he'd first come to the cabin and taken away her gun.

"Ready?" she asked him, determination flaring in her blue eyes.

"Can we argue about this?"

"No."

Shit!

"Okay, just stay close to me and do as I say."

She tilted her head slightly in a most endearing way. "Don't I always?"

He almost laughed but stifled the urge. There were more important things to do right now than to afford himself the luxury of laughing.

* * * * *

The cabin and the surroundings were in almost complete darkness when they sprinted to the cliffs. She half expected to hear the zing of a bullet and see Luke fall to the ground, but nothing happened. As they reached the rocks, pure adrenalin raced through her making her want to sprint up the trail and come out on top shooting at anything that moved. She would have, too, if Luke hadn't been here with her.

Luke pointed to the eastern horizon where she noted the full moon shining through the trees.

"We're going to have to move fast before that moon clears the trees and catches us in the open," Luke whispered.

She nodded and followed closely behind him as they began to ascend the dark track that would ultimately lead to the lookout where she'd enjoyed her time alone just this morning.

Gosh, it had been a close call.

What if the person or persons had come along this morning while she'd been up there?

She would have been in big trouble as she'd sat there debating whether to tell Luke her secrets. Anyone could have snuck up on her. As she'd told Luke earlier, she'd let her guard down over the past days. She couldn't allow that to happen again.

Her fingers tightened around the gun and the knife, and she trudged silently through the cool darkness.

They were almost to the top when she noted Luke's pace had slowed significantly. It was a good thing they hadn't tried to make a run for it. Obviously, he was hurting more than he'd let on, and she wished she could call a halt to this insanity of

coming up here. But the moon was rising steadily and it wouldn't be too long before everything became illuminated.

The urge to grab him and pull him back down to the safety of the cabin was so great she almost did it. But then they hit the crest of the cliff and Luke halted.

A cool breeze blew against her making her shiver as she looked around. Up here the moon-glow had already arrived. Everything was illuminated in an eerie blue glaze that sent shivers rippling up her spine.

"Look," Luke whispered.

She followed his pointing finger and barely made out the lone silhouette of someone sitting with his back against a gnarled pine tree, about thirty feet away. The intruder was facing the area where their cabin was located but his baseball cap was pulled over his eyes as if he were asleep. She didn't miss the rifle cradled in his arms.

Luke had been right. Someone was up here.

"I'm going over to pay our friend a visit," he whispered. "You stay here and cover me. If he moves...shoot him."

Before Callie could mount a protest, Luke had disappeared into the shadows.

* * * * *

Luke gently placed the open end of his pistol against the stranger's neck.

"Not one move, mister," he hissed.

The stranger didn't so much as flinch, and for a heart-stopping moment Luke thought he might be dead.

And then he spoke.

"How's the shoulder doing?"

Luke tensed as he recognized the voice of Seth Barlow, the man who'd shot him.

"What are you doing here, Barlow? This is Outlaw land."

Barlow tilted the brim of his baseball hat off his forehead and smirked, "Noticed you've shacked yourself up with an unclaimed woman. Callie Callahan, if memory serves me correctly."

Dread ripped through him. He'd seen Callie.

"Hand over the rifle."

Barlow hesitated a moment, and Luke prepared himself for a fight. Then the man lifted the butt-end of the rifle and Luke quickly snatched it away.

He pressed his gun harder against Barlow's head.

"I asked you a question, Barlow. What do you want?"

"Been scouting around."

"Why?"

"We're considering expanding our empire. We've got plans for your land, and your brother Tyler's land."

Barlow's blue eyes gleamed with amusement as he waited for Luke's reaction.

"Our contract says no foreclosure unless we miss two payments. We haven't missed any. You have no rights to our land. Get out of here. Don't come back."

"There's talk about an offer. You want to hear it?"

"No."

"Even if we considered telling you where your brother Tyler is?"

Son of a bitch!

"You tell me where he is right now and I'll sign over my land when I have him back here safe and sound. You'll have to talk to Tyler about acquiring his property. If I remember correctly it's paid for."

Barlow pursed his lips thoughtfully. "Your brother is one tough nut to crack. He's already refused any deal regarding his land."

"Can't say I blame him."

The urge to strangle the whereabouts of his brother out of Barlow was so great that he almost did it, but Barlow didn't give him a chance.

Before Luke could so much as blink, Seth knocked the rifle out of Luke's hands and crashed shoulder first into his injured shoulder.

Pain exploded through him.

His legs gave out and he careened to the rocky ground.

The barrel of the Barlow's rifle kissed his forehead.

"You should know by now no one says no to a Barlow. Not even an Outlaw. When we want something, we always get it. And right now I want that pretty little lady you got stashed away down in that cabin. Once I'm finished with you, I'll be paying her a visit."

A gunshot blast shattered the night and Barlow's eyes widened in the moonlight.

A split second later he toppled over, hitting the ground with a dull thud.

"Luke? Are you all right?" Callie called shakily as she raced toward him.

"I'm fine."

"Is he dead? Who is he? I saw him grab the rifle away from you..." She stopped mid-sentence and recognition rolled into her eyes.

"Oh, my God. It's a Barlow."

"Don't be frightened, Callie."

She didn't say anything as she stared down at the body. With a bullet hole in his upper left back and barely any blood spewing, he'd have to say Callie shot him square through the heart.

The pain in his shoulder was almost unbearable as he struggled to stand. Reaching over, he grabbed the rifle from the dead man's hand and searched through his pockets.

He came up empty.

But there was a sack beneath the tree where Barlow had sat.

He seized the sack and the rifle, and grabbed Callie's arm ushering her away from the body. In the moonlight, her face glowed a sickening white and she was shaking like a leaf.

"I...I've never killed anyone before, Luke," she whispered, as she cast quick glances at the dead body.

At this point, he would have done anything so that she hadn't been the one to pull the trigger.

"I know, sweetie, but you did right. Or else it would have been me lying there instead of Barlow." He shoved his pistol into his waistband, and pried her gun from her cold fingers before throwing it into the sack. Pain rippled through his shoulder as he intertwined Callie's cold, stiff fingers with his and pulled her toward the trail.

"Don't worry. Everything will be fine." He hoped he was telling her the truth. And he hoped there weren't any more Barlow brothers lurking around up here.

"C'mon, let's get down to the cabin."

* * * * *

By the time they reached the cabin, the pain in his shoulder had turned to barely a dull throb. But it wasn't himself he was concerned about it was Callie.

Anxiety ripped across her features, and she'd vomited twice on the way down.

She wasn't taking her first kill very well. And he didn't have the heart to tell her there might be more deaths on both their hands if things kept going the way they were.

"Here, take a swig of this."

He uncapped a half-full bottle he'd found in the Barlow sack, rubbed the rim clean and handed it to her. Right now, he didn't care if a dead man had been drinking from it; his first priority was to get her warm.

"Whiskey?" she blinked at him with tear-filled eyes.

"It'll warm you up."

She nodded meekly, tilted the bottle, took a giant gulp and made a sour face.

Grabbing a comforter from a nearby shelf, he wrapped it around her shivering body then began massaging her tight shoulders.

"No one kills a Barlow and gets away with it," she whispered then took another gulp.

"We will. At first light, I'll go up and bury the body."

"They'll come looking for him. They'll find him. They'll figure it all out."

Panic laced her voice. She took another long swig of the whiskey.

"They'll only figure it out if we tell them, sweetie. And we aren't telling them. Do you hear me?"

She nodded and smiled wryly. "More secrets to keep. When will they all stop?"

"This is a secret we have to keep, Callie. Okay? Are you listening to me? Tonight never happened. We don't know anything."

"The Barlows own the town. They own the cops. They own the judges."

Luke didn't have the heart to disagree. He knew she spoke the truth.

The Barlows would come looking. They'd come asking questions.

He needed to get Callie out of here.

They'd leave for the Outlaw farm tomorrow.

* * * * *

That night there was no incentive to make love, no reason to be happy as Luke urged her to climb into bed with him so they could rest. The whiskey had done the trick by taking the

edge off her panic and calming her enough so she could relax in his arms.

In spite of her best efforts not to fall asleep, she did. With sleep came the familiar nightmare memory. Like always she was helpless to stop it...

Even with her sudden grogginess, her heart picked up a frantic pace, and she clutched the sheets tightly around her as she always did when she heard the footsteps pause at her isolation unit. No one had come to take any samples from her for several days now. That was highly unusual considering not one day had gone by in the five years since she'd been locked up in this facility that a nurse or a doctor hadn't come to jab needles into her body parts or told her to pee in a cup, or something.

What would they want from her this time? Blood samples? Urine? Maybe her fingernail clippings like the last time? Or maybe they'd shave off skin samples from her thighs like the time before?

She shuddered. That was one of the worst things they'd done to her so far and she wasn't eager to repeat it anytime soon.

The door clicked open, and a strange pockmark-faced man in a white lab coat walked inside.

Instantly she didn't like him. Whether it was because of the creepy satisfied way he looked at her from beneath his black, handlebar moustache as if she were some prized guinea pig, or because of the odd tray filled with empty test tubes that he held in his hand, she didn't know. But instantly she did not like this guy.

She blinked away the sleepiness that was tugging down her eyelids and sat up in bed.

"Hello, Callie," he said casually.

"Hi." The palms of her hands grew damp with a sudden nervousness. Who was he? She'd never seen him before.

"I've heard you've been in here for quite a few years."

"That's right."

He sat down on the lone steel chair, and lifted out a thick file from the tray he'd brought in. He flipped it open and read the contents for a

moment, the sound of his heavy breathing split the sterile air of her isolation cell.

He looked at her with coal-black, frosty eyes that made her shiver, and cocked a dark eyebrow in puzzlement. "You never acquired the X-virus?"

"You sound surprised?" What a stupid question. Why else would she be locked in here?

He glared at her and she shifted uneasily.

"I am surprised, considering I'm the one who created it."

Her mouth opened in shock. Her thoughts whirled.

This was Blakely? The scientist who'd sold the X-virus to the DogmarX terrorist group. What the heck was he doing here?

"I gather by the expression on your face you've heard of me."

"Hasn't everyone?" she snarled as raw anger sifted through her.

The monster had single-handedly almost wiped out womankind. And he was walking around scot-free! As if he'd done nothing wrong.

He shrugged coolly. "Well then, let's get down to business. I've been hired by the US government to find a vaccine for the mutated versions of my virus. And I can do it by any means necessary."

The US government hired him? That couldn't be possible.

"The first business at hand is to try and infect you with the X-virus."

Her blood literally froze in her veins. Infect her?

"I don't think so," she snapped blinking away the odd sleepiness that was claiming her senses despite her growing fear.

He frowned obviously not liking her defiance.

"I should tell you that the government has allowed me free rein over you, Callie. You belong to me now. I can do whatever I want with you. Anything."

Callie shivered at his chilling words.

"But before that, I'll be extracting samples from you, so I can analyze your DNA."

"Like hell you will."

"Unfortunately, my dear, you have no choice in the matter. By now you should be feeling a little sleepy."

Sleepy? How the hell did he know?

"Drugs in your food, Callie."

No!

She tried to push aside the sheets covering her so she could stand up, but her hands didn't cooperate.

Oh, my God!

He chuckled, the horrid sound slicing blades of terror through her.

"Don't worry. You'll survive this operation."

"Operation? I'm not having any operation," her words were beginning to slur.

Fight it, Callie! Fight it!

"We're just going do a little internal exam on you, among other things."

"No fucking way are you touching me!" Callie made another move to get up, but her limbs wouldn't cooperate and she sprawled helplessly onto the bed.

Above her Blakely hovered like a grinning vulture, drenching her in a sickening scent of tobacco that made her stomach churn, and showing off a set of yellow stained teeth that made her cringe.

Raw terror washed through her veins as his cool finger trailed up along the side of her neck and settled beneath her chin.

"Easy, Callie. It'll all be over before you know it."

She wanted to scream but darkness swooped over her, freezing her cries for help deep in her throat.

Chapter Eight

It was a strangled cry that broke Luke from a deep sleep. A noise that sounded oddly similar to that of a trapped animal.

For a moment, he thought it was, but when he squinted through the darkness and saw Callie, his heart nearly froze at the shocking sight.

She was still fast asleep and in the grips of a nightmare.

Her face was so pale in the candle glow it sent a shiver of fear through him that had him bolting upright to find her fingers knotted in the bedsheets as if she were preventing someone from ripping them off her.

My God!

"Callie," he whispered, trying to keep his voice low so as to not alarm her.

She didn't respond.

"Callie, c'mon baby, you're having a nightmare."

He gently shook her shoulder. It was a big mistake.

She turned on him like a wildcat.

"Get away from me! You bastard!" Her fists shot out blindsiding him. Hard knuckles smashed into his eye, a knotted fist made impact with his sore shoulder, sending renewed shards of pain ripping through him and making him cry out.

She must have heard him because suddenly her fists went slack.

Terror-filled eyes blinked back at him.

For a moment, she didn't recognize him, and it took every ounce of strength for him not to cuddle her into his arms and

soothe away her horror, but that look of fear on her face led him to believe the last thing she wanted right now was to be touched.

Tears washed over her rounded cheeks and she quickly wiped them away, as if trying to erase the evidence that she was distraught.

Instinctively, he knew it was finally time for her to tell him what was bothering her.

"I think we'd better talk about your nightmare, Callie."

A new kind of terror flashed in her eyes. A fear of telling him?

She reached out and brushed soothing fingertips against the bandage covering his shoulder.

"Did I hurt you?"

His eye smarted from where she'd struck him, and his shoulder ached like the dickens, but right now Callie was top priority.

"I'll live, but you have to tell me what's been bothering you."

She shook her head. "It was nothing. Just a dream."

"Don't be afraid to trust me, Callie. Just talk to me. Did someone hurt you in the labs?"

Despite his need to know, he dreaded asking that question. The thought of anyone laying his or her hands on her…

She nodded and her shoulders started to shake.

Shit!

The knot in his gut twisted harder.

He reached out to comfort her, but she pulled away, sitting up beside him in the bed. She drew her gaze to her fists that were once again knotted in the bedsheets, as if she didn't want anyone to touch her body.

"I should have told you right from the beginning. Should have had the courage to tell you what he did to me."

My God!

Awful, cold chills slithered over his flesh.

"Who? What…happened?"

"His name was Blakely, the scientist who created the X-virus…"

"Blakely?" Disbelief gnawed at him.

She nodded and she began to explain how he'd shown up in her isolation chamber, how she'd been drugged.

A few minutes later Luke sat in stunned disbelief as Callie lowered the sheets, lifting her top and pushing down her underwear just enough to expose her abdomen.

To expose the two little scars.

Scars he hadn't even noticed before! Why hadn't he seen them?

"When I woke up after he'd drugged me, I found these. I knew they'd cut me, but I didn't know why or what he'd done to me. Later, when he came back, he told me."

She hesitated and closed her eyes tightly.

"What did he do to you?"

"He…cut out my eggs."

It was as if he'd heard what she'd said from somewhere far away, as if she were talking to him through a tunnel.

Her eggs?

"He said I could still have children, that he left some eggs, but I don't know if he was lying because I was hysterical…" She raised her face; her eyes glistened with fresh tears. "I know how much you wanted to have children."

A mad scientist had cut out Callie's eggs? The shock was almost unbearable.

For a few moments, he thought maybe he was dreaming. Maybe this was a nightmare?

"I'm so sorry. It's all my fault," she whispered.

"No, no, no, baby, it has nothing to do with you, Callie. You had no say in the matter. They took you against your will. You're innocent."

"I'm not innocent."

"You are. Someone invaded your body. You had nothing to do with it."

She shook her head slowly, and instinctively he knew there was more.

"You don't understand. I...wasn't taken against my will. I...volunteered to go to the labs."

It was as if her confession sucked the life right out of him. He felt faint. Stunned.

This time it was his turn to shake his head in denial of what he was hearing.

She'd volunteered?

He couldn't be hearing right.

"It was only supposed to be for a couple of days. Just enough to give them some samples so they could run some experiments on those samples...but when they had me, they wouldn't let me go."

"Sweet Jesus!"

She flinched at his outburst, but he didn't care.

"I know we discussed it," she whispered with desperation. "That I'd said I wanted to volunteer to help them out, and you'd said absolutely not. But I had to. Don't you understand? I had to do it for the other women who were suffering. Other women like our mothers and our sisters."

"Fuck the other women!" Luke snapped. "We'd agreed to keep you out of it."

Anger bit deep into his heart, and he whipped aside the sheets, scrambling out of bed.

"I can't believe this! Because you defied me, we lost five fucking years. Even lost our chance at having kids."

The Claiming

"I'm sorry."

Despite his wanting to throw his arms around her and wipe away the fresh tears streaming down her face, he forced himself to harden his heart. "Sorry doesn't cut it, babe."

Man, he couldn't look at her. Couldn't stand to see the pain in her eyes. He just couldn't stay there. He would explode if he did. He would say something he'd later regret.

He needed to think this through.

He made a quick grab for his pants.

"Where are you going?" she sobbed, clutching the sheets to her in desperation.

"I need some air." He needed some time to digest this news.

Oh, man! He couldn't believe what he'd just heard. She'd volunteered to go to the labs? She'd gone against his wishes.

He scrambled into his jeans and made a mad dash for the door.

Behind him, he could hear her ragged sobs. Each and every one of those brutal sounds pierced a hole into his heart.

He wished he could stay. Wished to hell he had the guts to comfort her.

But he knew he was going to be sick.

Nausea splashed through his stomach as he rushed outside, slamming the door shut behind him.

The bitter bile climbed into his throat. A cold sweat peppered his flesh.

My God! She'd allowed herself to be taken in by the government. How could she have been so naïve? How could he have been so stupid to not realize how passionate she'd been about wanting to help other women?

He stumbled down to the road in the hopes she wouldn't hear what came next.

185

When he was far enough away from the cabin, he allowed himself to lose the contents of his stomach, and then let the harsh curses of what that mad scientist had done to their future break free from his soul.

* * * * *

The distinct sound of a branch snapping near the tree line made Callie's heart pick up speed. Automatically she slid the gun off the nearby rock, the cool metal seared against the palm of her trembling hand and her finger tightened on the trigger.

She scanned the surrounding forest but saw nothing.

Luke had been gone all morning.

She'd cried all morning.

Cried over the guilt of taking a man's life and of the devastated look on Luke's face when she'd told him they might not be able to have kids.

About an hour ago she'd finally dragged herself out of bed and come down to the pond to wash her face, and where she'd then stayed, watching the tiny ripples of water as the fish jumped in desperate efforts to catch their afternoon meal of flies.

The sight had had a somewhat soothing effect on her jangled nerves.

But now as the eerie shades of an impending rainstorm swooped in around her, she wanted nothing more than to go back into the cabin and throw herself onto the bed, allowing herself the luxury of crying for the rest of the day.

But she couldn't.

She needed to face reality.

Luke might not come back.

Allowing him to fall in love with her all over again without telling him the truth was unforgivable.

The tiny hairs on the back of her neck prickled a warning, and Callie nervously bit her bottom lip forcing herself to keep calm.

Had that sound of a branch breaking been just an animal?

God, she hoped so.

She blew out a slow breath thinking that maybe she had imagined the noise.

But then she saw it.

A shadowy movement skirting just the other side of the tree line, near the road.

The distinct figure of a man jogging.

At first, her heart soared.

Luke had come back. She almost called out to him. But caution whispered to be careful.

She waited for another glimpse and saw him.

Her hopes deflated.

The newcomer didn't have Luke's brown hair, and he seemed much taller.

Thankfully, he hadn't seen her yet.

Quietly, Callie blended into the nearby bushes and watched as the stranger headed directly for her ranch.

* * * * *

The woods were just as noisy as the inside of his head, as Luke made his way through the forest adjoining his property. He'd gone back up to the cliffs with a shovel, found the dead Barlow and buried him.

Surprisingly, he felt no guilt at Barlow's death. If Callie hadn't done what she'd done then Luke would be dead, and who knows what they'd be doing to her. There was no need to tell the authorities what had happened up here. Due to the economic collapse, the law belonged to whoever had the most money. In this case, it was the Barlows. When their brother didn't return, they'd come looking for him.

They'd find Callie.

They'd take her to the authorities or worse…sell her as a sex slave on the ever-growing black market.

Luke swore beneath his breath and winced as he hoisted the shovel over his good shoulder.

The task of burying the body had been hard, but the manual labor had been more than welcome as he fought with what Callie had told him.

She'd innocently gone to the government lab to give blood samples.

She'd planned on telling him what she'd done when she came back.

But they'd kept her against her will.

Why in the world had she gone against his wishes when he'd been so adamant about her keeping a low profile? She'd mentioned to him she wanted to help the government find a cure. Had even approached him with the idea that she would give them samples.

That's when he'd exploded telling her he'd never allow it.

He hadn't given her a chance to explain why she wanted to risk exposure, even when they had heard unconfirmed rumors that the government was sanctioning the kidnapping of some of the women who came forward to help.

She'd gone to them like a lamb to the slaughter.

Now that he looked back at it, this whole nightmare had been his fault.

Guilt washed over him, slicing through his every nerve and fiber.

If he'd only listened to her. If he had, he would have realized how passionate she'd been about helping to find a cure.

He could have gone with her to the lab and protected her.

He could have avoided this whole mess.

How in the world would he ever be able to face her again? How could he apologize to her for them losing five years of their life? For possibly losing the chance of having children?

Perhaps staying out of her life would be the best thing he ever did for Callie.

* * * * *

"Looking for someone?" Callie hissed as she stuck the gun barrel into the back of the blond-haired intruder she'd found peeking through the boarded slats to the window of her home.

The man stiffened, and his shoulder muscles bulged wonderfully against his tight, black shirt as he slowly raised his arms and clasped his large hands on top of his head.

She knew she should have kept herself hidden. Should have waited for the man to clear out.

But she was in a very bad mood. Fed up with hiding, upset because Luke had walked out on her and ready to murder anyone who dared to intrude upon her home.

And call her stupid, but he looked oddly familiar when she'd seen his shadowy figure in the woods.

If he was whom she suspected, then she didn't have to fear him. "Who are you?" she asked.

His low amused chuckle breathed through the air. "Have I changed that much in five years?"

His voice sounded familiar and Callie closed her eyes, and silently thanked God.

But these days caution was her best friend, and she needed to make sure he was who she thought he was before she let down her guard.

Taking a few steps back, she kept the gun trained on him.

"Keep your hands raised and turn around. Slowly. No funny moves or I'll plug a bullet into you."

The amused chuckle came again as he turned around.

Instantly all her fears melted away, as the carbon copy of Luke smiled back at her.

"Colter Outlaw! You son of a bitch! I've never been so happy to see anyone in my life!" she laughed at the doctor.

Colter was a year younger than Luke and just as cute. Where Luke had dark-brown hair, his brother's hair was longer and a dirty blond, his eyes a twinkling soft blue, characteristics of the Outlaws' mother. Bless her soul.

"You're protecting my brother like you're some kind of she-wolf," he nodded to the gun in her hand.

She lowered the weapon and flushed.

"Shouldn't have done that." His smile disappeared, and his eyes suddenly turned cold, sending a fissure of alarm racing through her.

In one quick swoop, he grabbed the gun from her.

Stunned at his unexpected behavior she could only stand helplessly.

He nodded to the woods behind him where she spotted two men standing there with their guns drawn and pointed at her.

Oh, my God! No!

"Never trust a man these days, Callie. Not even an Outlaw. We could claim you right here and now. With Luke, there are enough of us."

A wave of dizziness twisted around her.

Never in a million years had she thought she couldn't trust an Outlaw. For a split second, she thought about making a grab for her gun and killing herself.

That thought spun away rather quickly.

Oddly enough, Luke's suggestion whispered in her ear about her being claimed by him and his brothers.

It wouldn't be such a bad thing, and if Luke was included...

Callie shook the crazy thought from her mind.

Sweet heavens! She hadn't escaped the government labs just so she could become some sexual slave and servant to a bunch of men.

"Where's Luke?" Colter asked.

Before she could answer and explain that Luke was gone, she heard his voice snap through the air.

"Right here."

She blinked at the gun barrel that poked out between the slats of the plank-covered window, and found herself sighing with relief. Found herself wanting to burst into the cabin and fling herself into his arms, and beg him to forgive her for not telling him everything right from the beginning.

"How'd you find me?" Luke growled from inside. Anger laced his words.

Obviously, he was still very upset with her. But he was back.

At least that was something.

"I went to visit the preacher in jail. He told me."

"He's in jail? What happened?" Callie asked. Concern for the man who'd been helping her overrode Colter's threat of claiming her.

"Don't worry—he'll be out soon enough. Unfortunately for him, in the government's haste to install the Claiming Law they forgot that men of the cloth had powers higher than theirs...some government officials and judges were actually allowing some couples to remain married after the preachers united them. The government has done a harsh crackdown placing those judges, officials and all preachers in jail. All marriages in the eyes of God have been revoked."

Luke cursed from the other side of the window.

A hollow feeling zipped through her.

They weren't legally married after all.

"Well, it is nice to see you both alive." Colter nodded to her, his gaze dark and somewhat sensual. "Especially you. We all had you figured as good as dead."

"As you can see she's very much alive, now give her back her gun," Luke growled.

Thank God! At least she could trust one Outlaw.

"She needed to be taught a lesson, Luke. She should know not to trust a man. Any man."

"Your point is well taken," Callie said, relief pouring through her as she extended her hand for the gun.

Yet Colter hesitated.

He stared hard at where Luke's gun barrel poked through the slat.

She could literally feel the tension bursting through the air between the two brothers. She wondered what was going through Colter's head. Would he defy his brother? Would he do as he threatened, and instruct his brothers to claim her here and now?

"Give her back the gun, Colter. The last thing we need is to have more bullets flying around. One bullet through me is quite enough."

What was Luke insinuating? Would he fight his brothers to protect her?

The thought both pleased her and scared her.

Would the Outlaw brothers actually try to claim her? Without Luke? Or did it go much deeper? Did Luke still want her? Even after her secrets were now in the open?

She burst from her thoughts when she felt the smooth handle of the gun slap into her palm.

"Don't let that gun out of your sight," Colter said in a menacing tone that made shivers of fear run up her back.

"Get your asses in here," Luke said from inside. "Callie, could you put some food up for our guests?" Without waiting for an answer, the gun barrel disappeared from the crack in the window.

When she looked back at Colter, her grip tightened around her gun, as she found his appreciative gaze sliding sensuously up and down the full length of her body finally settling upon the swell of her breasts.

She knew the look in the eyes of a man who was interested in a woman and Colter Outlaw was definitely interested.

His eyes, no longer soft, were now so dark and so captivating that to her shock, she could feel the heat of sexual awareness shimmer deep inside her womb.

"I apologize for scaring you, Callie. But you have to know what'll happen to you if you let down your guard. Men know there is a good possibility they can't have a woman in their lifetime. They can get quite...desperate."

Callie nodded suddenly understanding why he'd been looking at her the way he had.

He probably hadn't had sex in quite some time.

And his brothers standing by the tree line were in the same boat.

She tried to ignore the strangely sensual stirrings that began to consume her at the erotic visions of having the Outlaw brothers making love to her in order to claim her.

All those men.

All that sexual energy saved up for her.

She felt her face begin to flush with embarrassment at what she was thinking...or maybe what she felt was excitement?

"I'll go get my brothers. Back in a minute."

She watched the tall Outlaw saunter off, his long legs clad in a pair of tight jeans that showed off the fine curves of a nicely shaped tush, his wide shoulders and arms were covered by a tight, black shirt that prominently showed the curves of some mighty nice-sized muscles.

In the past, she'd met all of the Outlaw brothers.

They'd been very kind to her. Very sweet.

She remembered thinking how sexy they all were, but to her, Luke was the sexiest of them all.

Sexy or not, unfortunately Colter was right. These days no man could be trusted. She'd do well to remember that.

Chapter Nine

"What the hell happened? The preacher said the Barlows shot you," Colter asked the instant he and his other brothers Cade and Mac stomped into the cabin.

Luke hadn't even had a chance to apologize to Callie for running out on her. He'd tried but she'd stopped him by saying she had to cook, and they'd talk later.

He wished he hadn't run away. Wished like hell he hadn't left when she'd needed him the most.

It had been selfish of him to hide his anger, his anxiety and his sickness as to what had happened to her.

Just like it had been self-centered of him to instantly explode when she'd told him she'd wanted to help the government all those years ago. Just like he'd been selfish to suggest his brothers and himself claim her.

He needed to stop being such an asshole and start being a man, and put Callie's needs before his own.

He had to protect his woman.

Despite his renewed vows, he couldn't help but grin as he watched Callie frying up some eggs at the woodstove, and throwing nervous glances at his brothers as they sauntered in.

Being nervous would be the last thing on Callie's mind if his brothers followed through on claiming her.

During the Terrorist Wars having sex at least once a week with the conscripted women or lady volunteers who came to service the men was mandatory R&R. Luke and his brothers had had plenty of opportunities to learn the ways to pleasure women.

"I asked you a damn question, Luke! What happened? Is it true? Did a Barlow shoot you?" Colter snapped, as he stood in front of Luke eyeing the bandages covering his wounds.

"It's true."

A round of protests ripped free from his other brothers who circled around him with concern.

"Shit, Luke! What the hell did you do to piss them off?" his brother Mac asked.

"He heard rumors...about my sister, Laurie, being claimed by the Barlows." Callie explained.

Colter's eyes widened in surprise. Mac and Cade gasped in shock.

He'd forgotten that his brothers didn't know about Laurie.

"Laurie? As in Tyler's woman? She's the one who volunteered to get claimed by the Barlows?" Colter hissed.

Luke nodded.

"That traitorous bitch!" he spat.

"She has no idea Tyler is alive, Colter. I know she wouldn't have done it if she'd known," Callie said, coming to her sister's rescue.

Colter ignored her and threw Luke an anguished look.

"You told Callie about Tyler, too? We agreed we wouldn't tell anyone until we had him out."

"She had a right to know."

Colter swore and shook his head in disappointment. "So, now Laurie knows?"

"I never told her," Callie said coldly. "Although I wanted to. She has every right to know."

Colter whirled on her, his eyes sparking anger.

"She's a Barlow now! She has no rights to my brother anymore. Not after what she's done. When he finds out, he'll kill her."

"When he finds out, he'll be the man I know he is and get her out of there," Callie snapped back.

To Luke's surprise, Colter said nothing. But he glared at Callie with a fierce anger Luke had seen him use many times with fellow officers who gave him trouble in the army. It was a look that would have made any man twice Luke's size back down from him.

But Callie stood her ground, staring right back at his brother with open defiance.

The silence in the room was stifling and Luke's other two brothers Mac and Cade shifted uncomfortably.

Luke couldn't stop from grinning.

She looked gorgeous when she was mad. Her face all flushed pink like she always looked like when he was making love to her. Her fists were knotted with boldness, and her breasts heaved wonderfully against that tight shirt she wore.

The muscles in Colter's jaws twitched with anger, and for a moment, Luke thought he'd continue the argument.

He didn't.

Instead, he turned to him, his eyes narrowed with irritation.

"So, why'd they shoot you?"

Luke explained how he'd knocked on the front door, found the ménage in progress, and how they'd shot him because they thought he was an intruder.

"Better let me take a look at your wounds. There's blood seeping through the bandage in front."

Luke held up his hand in protest, but Colter was already untying the bandages.

"Who did the stitch job?" he asked, as he firmly poked and prodded around the ragged edges of the wounds, making Luke curse at the renewed pain shooting through his shoulder.

"I did." Callie said, anger still evident in her voice as she hovered in the background watching what Colter was doing.

"You did a real good job. Just like an expert."

Luke noticed Callie's eyes widen in surprise at his brother's comment.

"My mom taught me how to sew before I could even talk. I'm glad it came in handy."

Colter nodded, and continued with his poking and prodding.

"The Barlows are pressing charges against you. They've got a warrant out for your arrest. Trespassing. Peeping Tom," Colter explained. "We're going to have to keep you under wraps here until we can get everything sorted out."

"Do you think he's safe here? One of the Barlows came over here and almost killed Luke," she interjected.

Luke swore softly. He'd told her not to say anything to anyone.

Callie turned on him. "I know you said to keep quiet, but we can trust your brothers. They can help us."

"What the hell happened?" Colter and his brothers swooped in around him, armed with curses and an arsenal of questions.

"Don't worry he's dead." Luke explained.

"I killed him," Callie said coolly as she hustled back to the eggs on the stove. "Just before he was about to shoot Luke."

"She saved my life."

Cade and Mac immediately thanked her, swooping around her like a couple of starry-eyed teenagers who had their first crush on a girl. The angry flush that had flooded her face darkened now with obvious embarrassment as they asked her if she needed some help in the kitchen.

Colter's angry glare softened a little as he watched Callie delegate duties of setting the table.

"That's not all." His brother turned back to him and lowered his voice, obviously not wanting Callie to hear what else was going on. "They say you tried to talk to Laurie without

their permission. That's virtually a hanging offence, talking to an unrelated woman these days."

"I figured I was a goner. I wasn't thinking straight. I tried to tell her Ty was alive, but they dragged me out of the house before I could do it. I heard one of them mention they should kill me. I thought it a bit odd they'd want to kill me for trespassing, so the first chance I got I escaped. Then last night I met up with Barlow. He said something about wanting Tyler's and my land because they were expanding. We're going to have to look into that, see what they're up to, and I think you should get Callie over to the main farm before the Barlows come looking for their brother." Luke said.

"I'm staying with Luke," Callie said sternly as she came up behind them.

"I'm not willing to chance it," Luke said. "Take her with you and keep her safe."

"Well, I'm not going!" Callie's fists were clenched in defiance as she glared at Colter. "You're a doctor. You know he needs someone here to take care of him and make sure he doesn't do something stupid and re-injure himself. I'm staying with him."

"One of my brothers can stay here. I'll heal faster when I know you're safe."

Her eyes blazed with fury, and he sensed she was about to explode in protest when Colter broke in, "You'll heal faster with Callie staying here. I'll keep a watch outside. You won't even know I'm here. Cade's got contacts with the authorities. He and Mac can snoop around in town to find out why the Barlows want a slice of Outlaw land."

"That's it? I have no say in this?" Luke complained, as Colter popped some clean bandages and ointment out of his black doctor's bag, and efficiently patched up his wounds.

Colter shrugged his shoulders and threw him an amused grin. "Not unless you want to argue with her. I know I sure don't."

Callie smiled smugly at his brother. "Good. Then let's eat. The food is ready," she said as she headed back to the stove. "I'm sorry, it's not much… I haven't been able to go to the grocery store lately." The sarcasm in her voice made the brothers' heads hang in shame as they all headed to the table.

No woman was allowed to go anywhere alone unless accompanied by one of her husbands. And no woman was allowed to speak to a man in public unless she was given verbal permission by one of them.

Luke swallowed the tight knot scrambling into his throat.

The laws passed down by their government were all still so new, so crazy that sometimes he couldn't believe the life dreams he and Callie had discussed over five years ago were gone, along with their specially planned wedding, their plan of having one boy and one girl, their idea of just the two of them farming this section of land.

It was too dangerous now for a man and woman to live alone. These days, men had to live in groups in order to protect their wives from being taken by other groups of desperate men. "These eggs are damned good," Mac's thrilled voice rescued Luke from his sad thoughts.

"If I might ask where you got them? So I can whip up a batch when I get back home?"

"I got them from the Barlows."

Luke heard Colter drop his fork. His other two brothers watched her with suspicion.

"You went to the Barlow ranch? Alone?" Anger flared in his brother's eyes.

"She did." Luke interjected quickly. "And she didn't say anything to Laurie about Tyler. She already told you that, so let's drop the subject."

Colter turned his anger on Luke. "I know what she said! That's not what's pissing me off. What's the matter with you? Don't you know what'll happen to her if she's caught out on her own?"

"She can take care of herself."

Pride swelled as Callie threw him a surprised look. Obviously, she hadn't expected him to stick up for her.

Well, from now on, he would do whatever it took to make the woman he loved safe and happy.

"Oh, she can, can she? Just like she was taking care of herself today? Maybe she takes these chances because she wants to get caught. Did that occur to you? Maybe she wants a group of men fucking her brains out!"

"Oh, I don't know, maybe that's what she wants. Maybe she'd enjoy a ménage? Maybe she wants to be claimed?" Luke said casually, as he noted Callie's face flame pink.

He may as well start dropping hints now to see if his brothers were receptive to the idea of claiming Callie, even if she hadn't told him yes.

Colter's mouth dropped open in apparent shock.

Then his reaction slowly changed and Luke saw the realization of what he was implying wash over all of his brothers' faces.

Their faces grew flushed, whether it was from embarrassment or excitement he wasn't sure, but after that, Luke noticed they wouldn't look Callie's way.

Perhaps they were embarrassed. More than likely, they were unsure of what was going on. Sooner or later, he would have to ask them, but first he needed to talk some more about it with Callie. He needed to be sure this was what she wanted and he needed to tell her how sorry he was, and to ask her forgiveness for the way he'd behaved today.

"We'll be leaving now," Colter said the instant their plates were empty. "Thanks, Callie, for the grub. It was really good."

Mac and Cade echoed their brother's compliments.

She shrugged her shoulders and seemed somewhat embarrassed by all their compliments.

"Cade and Mac will go and find out about the Barlows' plans. Maybe then we can see if we can square a deal for them to drop the charges against you. I'll be stationed up on the cliffs," Colter said. "You won't even know I'm there."

Both Luke and Callie thanked them, and the rush of feet was like a stampede as all his brothers raced to get to the door. When it shut behind them, Luke couldn't stop himself from laughing at their uneasiness. The sound of a gun cocking made his heart stop.

His amusement disintegrated.

His breath locked in his throat at the sight of a gun in Callie's hand.

It was aimed directly at his groin area.

Oh, shit! He'd pushed her too far by hinting that his brothers might be able to claim her.

He swore beneath his breath.

"Your brother Colter made one big mistake," she said quietly, as she came closer.

"He insinuated I needed protection…from them. What they didn't know is you're the one who needs protection…from me."

He swore he saw her finger tighten on the trigger.

"Callie, I'm sorry. I didn't mean to drop the hints in front of my brothers without discussing it with you first. It's just I wanted to see…"

"Drop your pants, Luke."

"What?" He blinked in surprise.

"You heard me. I want to see how aroused you are. Don't think I didn't notice that bulge getting bigger when you were watching how your brothers were eyeing me."

She was toying with him?

"Do as I say Luke Outlaw, and maybe I won't shoot off one of your balls."

Oh, boy.

She swooped her gun off the chair were she'd placed it earlier. Now she had both guns trained on him.

Damned if the thought of being forced to show his cock to her without his permission wasn't turning him on even more.

The pink tip of her tongue peeked out of her mouth and a thick wave of desire rammed into him.

"Do it, now." Her voice was barely a whisper.

The pain in his shoulder throbbed wickedly, as he used both hands and quickly unbuttoned the stud at his waist and lowered the zipper.

Curling his fingers beneath the waistband of his jeans, he slowly pulled them over his hips.

His rigid cock sprang free.

Her eyes widened with appreciation and he noticed a slight tremor move through her.

"Keep going," she sounded breathless, aroused.

He did as she instructed, lowering his jeans, and then stepping out of them, giving her a perfect view of his full-blown arousal and swollen balls.

He saw her long slender throat move as she swallowed.

Lust shone brightly in her eyes.

His cock twitched.

"The thought of your brothers claiming me arouses you, doesn't it?"

He didn't answer.

Instead, his cock did the talking for him. Pulsing and growing red with a wild eagerness, it thickened and lengthened, readying itself for whatever she had planned for him.

"I bet you'd like to see me in all my naked glory between two of their rock-hard bodies, writhing and moaning while your brothers double-penetrate me."

His cock grew harder.

Have mercy! The woman sure did have a way with words.

"Maybe you could suck on my nipples before they fucked me? Maybe you could do it...now."

His breath locked in his throat as she placed one of the guns back down on the dresser, and began to unbutton her blouse with somewhat trembling fingers.

Luke blew off a stiff breath at the sight of her creamy curves, the deep valley and finally he was given a perfect view of her luscious breasts in their full beauty.

His breathing picked up speed as she drew closer.

She allowed the blouse to slip off her shoulders and it fell to the floor in a whisper.

"You think I don't fantasize about getting caught by some men?"

He held his breath as she leaned over, her silky-looking breasts bobbing as she stroked the length of his red cock with the barrel of her gun. The cool, smooth metal did nothing to douse the raging heat claiming his shaft, or the god-awful tightness squeezing his rock-hard balls.

"You think I don't wonder what it would feel like to have several men claim me? Lots of woman fantasize about that...it doesn't mean they want it forced upon them, though."

With the open barrel of the gun, she kissed his pulsing cockhead.

"You think I don't fantasize about forcing you to have sex with me at gunpoint?" she asked.

Luke swallowed at his excitement. "Seems like you had a lot of time to come up with fantasies while you were...incarcerated."

She stiffened momentarily, the cool barrel of the gun hesitating ever so slightly.

He hadn't meant to break the mood.

Thankfully, he hadn't.

The gun barrel dipped between his balls. At the same time, she bent over, her bare breasts brushing teasingly against the

length of his massive erection. He almost exploded at the velvety feel of her flesh caressing him.

His hands ached to palm those luscious globes, to feel their heavy weight in his palms, to pinch those elongated, pink-colored nipples or rub his tongue around the slightly raised areolas.

But he dare not break her fantasy, especially when she kept the gun barrel poked firmly between his balls.

His heart beat against his chest as she got down on her knees, between his legs, and her red lips parted.

The instant her hot tongue laved against the tip of his cock, he felt as if he might explode.

He gritted his teeth against his arousal and forced himself to rein in his urges.

"I've wanted to do this to you for a long time, Luke. I've missed doing it. And I've missed seeing the way you clench your teeth while I suck your cock," she whispered against his pulsing flesh. "And I've wanted to taste your cum in my mouth for a long time."

"I've wanted to taste your pussy again, too," Luke whispered. "You don't know how many times I wished…how I pretended they were you…" He stopped himself. She'd already said she didn't want to hear about what he'd had to do during the Wars.

She smiled with reassurance. "It's okay. I know all about those women in the army. About sex being mandatory."

"At first, I didn't want to—"

She stopped him cold when her mouth opened and she slid her lips over his cock, taking him halfway into her hot cavern.

He gave a strangled cry as the wild pleasure threatened to blow his balls apart.

Her moist lips clamped over his shaft, and she began a hard suck that left him helpless beneath the pleasurable onslaught.

Sharp teeth nipped at the skin encasing his shaft and he cried out at the pain, and without warning, he came hard into her mouth.

After orgasming, all he could do was slump onto the bed and lie there panting.

His eyes fluttered, and he watched her wipe away his cum from her passion-bruised lips.

"I want to make love to you, Callie..." he said softly. "I want to show you how much I love you. I need to apologize for how I behaved earlier. I shouldn't have left you all alone. Shouldn't have been such an asshole. We don't need any babies..."

She sat on the bed beside him and placed a tender finger to his lips. "Shh. You've overtaxed yourself today, Luke. I can tell you're tired. Rest, my Outlaw lover," she murmured softly. "You can fuck me as much as you like when you wake up."

He grinned and nodded.

He could hardly wait until he awoke.

* * * * *

"How about a moonlight skinny-dip?" Luke's soft whisper curled through the layers of sleep, prompting Callie to open her eyes.

He stood beside the bed, buttery candle glow splashing across his features. Clad only in a long, thick erection that popped straight out from between his widespread legs, he held his engorged cock at the base with one hand while the fingers from his other hand brushed along the length of his swollen vein-riddled shaft.

Oh, boy! The man was ready to make love!

His eyes glittered with excitement and lust.

"Take out your butt plug, wife of mine, and join me at the pond. I've got everything ready. Last one down gets the sex toy."

Take out her butt plug? An erotic shiver zipped through her as she imagined what he had in store for her. And did he mention a sex toy?

Suddenly he was laughing and running for the open doorway, the muscles in his magnificent naked ass quivering with every step.

Instantly the cobwebs of sleep dissolved.

She didn't even bother to throw something on as she scrambled from the bed, carefully removed the plug, and then raced outside just in time to catch another glimpse of his cute ass as he slid into the dark waters of the pond.

The mild night air gently brushed along her naked flesh as with mounting excitement she hurried along the walkway, marveling at the croaking sounds of bullfrogs and relishing the coolness of dew beneath her hot feet.

"Come on in! The water is absolutely great!" he called out as she came to the water's edge.

He stood near the middle of the pond, blinking fireflies flickering all around him.

Moonlight splashed over the hard planes of his upper body. The white patch taped over his shoulder wound blazed in sharp contrast to the dark water rippling low over his hips, hiding his cock from her view. His biceps bulged wonderfully as his hands moved beneath the surface.

She assumed he was touching himself, pleasuring himself as his long fingers glided up and down the swollen length of his velvet-encased steel rod. A rod she wanted impaled deep inside her moistening vagina.

Her breath quickened at the dark lust shining in his eyes as he stared at her.

"God, Callie, you look so damn beautiful when you're naked," he said as his gaze wandered over her body. His voice sounded strangled, filled with longing.

She trembled at his words and stepped into the pond.

"Are you saying I don't look good when I wear clothes?" she giggled.

The mild water wrapped around her knees, urging her to move quickly toward him.

"You're my beautiful princess no matter what you wear or don't wear," he grinned widely.

When she was waist-high, she suddenly looked up at the dark cliffs wondering if his brother was there, watching them frolicking naked in the water. From up there Colter would have the perfect view of them skinny-dipping.

She blew out an aroused breath.

Her heart picked up speed and a strange elation zipped through her as she realized he'd be watching them. Watching everything Luke did to her.

Oh, boy. It was a strange excitement, thinking they were being watched. It was something new and it felt pretty intense.

"What's wrong?" He wiggled his eyebrows with mischief. "You afraid of what your present might be?"

"Your brother can see us."

Luke's eyes darkened, and he held out one hand to her.

She reached out and his fingers intertwined with hers. Immediately, he pulled her against him.

His strong body felt hot with passion as his flesh met hers. The hard tip of his cockhead poked proudly against her belly, and his hand slid between her legs heading toward her eager and waiting pussy.

"Doesn't it give you an odd thrill to have another man watching us? Watching what I'm about to do to you?" he asked, his head lowering to kiss the sudden hot blush of excitement sweeping across her cheeks.

Her vaginal muscles contracted wonderfully at his question. Or maybe she was excited because of the way his calloused, wet finger smoothed back and forth over her ultra-sensitive clit. She could feel the pleasure uncoiling deep in her

belly. Could feel the heat of her cream sliding down her vagina, preparing for penetration.

"I could ask you the same question?" she hedged, reaching out to curl her hands around his hard waist, spreading her legs to allow him easier access.

His moist lips teased the edge of her mouth. Desire shot through her, hot and intense. "I asked you first. Tell me the truth, Callie. I'll take you inside the cabin, away from his eyes if you want me to. I don't want to do something you don't like. Does it bother you having one of my brothers watching us?"

"No," she said softly. Truthfully. "It's kind of thrilling. Let him watch."

The pressure of his finger intensified, the roughness of the hot pad creating an enticing friction that made her whimper at the delicious sensations.

"Yes, that's it. That feels so good," she moaned.

His head dipped toward her heaving breasts, and he sucked a nipple into his hot mouth.

"Oh!" she cried out, as he bit sharply against her sensitive flesh, unleashing a searing trail of fire that led straight from her breast down to her pussy.

He suckled roughly. Teeth nipping. Tongue licking until her tip hardened into an aching peak, and the sexual tension made her shiver.

He released her nipple and moved to the other one.

She watched with wondrous desire as her plump nipple disappeared into his perfectly shaped mouth. He repeated the erotic sucking motions. Twirling his wet tongue around her areola, biting her nipple with sharp, yet gentle, tugs.

When she thought she could stand the pleasure-pain no longer, he lifted his head and grinned widely.

"Your nipples feel as big as cherries and taste as good as lollipops."

"Screw the cherries and the lollipops, I want you to make love to me," she breathed, pressing her lips against his hard mouth, kissing him solidly until he groaned.

"How about something else first?" he whispered hoarsely as he broke the delicious kiss.

His finger slid away from where he'd been massaging her slick clit beneath the dark water. Instantly it was replaced by something soft, round-tipped and ultra-warm.

At first, she thought it was Luke's cockhead sliding against her clit-hood but it felt different.

"Luke? What are you doing?"

"Your present. A waterproof vibrator and the batteries are still good."

Delicious!

"Am I hitting the right spot?"

"Just a bit lower, lover." Her hand curled around his warm fingers leading him directly to where she wanted it. She jolted and gritted her teeth as the wicked vibrations played with her clit, unleashing a rapid-fire burst of pleasure deep into her vagina.

Oh, baby! These sensations felt awesome.

She wanted it pulsing deep inside her.

Guiding his hand, she led the tip of the vibrator to her vaginal opening.

He stopped her there, holding firmly, not allowing the new toy to enter her eager channel.

"Luke? What?" she ground out in frustration.

"It has a clit stimulator."

"Okay, I'll find it." She tugged at his hand. He didn't budge.

"What?"

He chuckled. "Did you take out your butt plug?"

"Yes." She swallowed at the intense way he was looking at her.

"I'm going to take you in the ass first."

She sucked in a sharp breath as she remembered how tight she'd been when he'd slid that big butt plug into her the other day.

She'd done like he'd asked. Kept it buried inside her. Had felt it lodged inside her with her every moment. Removing it only to clean it and when she went to the washroom. It had been smaller than his large cock and she'd wondered how it would feel to have his rigid piece of hot flesh impale her ass.

It looked like tonight she was going to find out.

"Play with yourself," he whispered and turned her around.

She was facing the cliffs now. Whether Luke had done it on purpose, having her facing those cliffs or not, she didn't know, but just the idea that his brother was up there somewhere, most likely seeing her bared breasts, watching Luke taking her in the ass…

Whew!

Was she weird, getting all hot and bothered at the thought of someone watching them?

Oh! Who cared!

She was free to do what she wanted.

Physically free. Sexually free.

And she wanted Luke.

She wanted safety and protection.

If she decided to go along with Luke's idea of her getting claimed by his brothers and him so she could live protected and happy, then she'd best get used to being watched while her number one man made love to her.

From behind her, she felt Luke's hot, wet palms smooth over her ass cheeks. He caressed her flesh gently, massaging her mounds lovingly with long fingers.

"Play with your clit," he instructed. "But don't fuck yourself just yet."

She nodded, and slid the vibrator against her clit again, sighing at the heavenly raw vibrations pounding her.

He spread her ass cheeks apart.

She inhaled sharply as his finger slipped into her anus.

Her anal muscles clenched tightly around him, but she could tell right away the insertion was easier than the first time he'd inserted the butt plug. He must have felt it too, because with each delicious thrust he went deeper and deeper, stretching her easily, making her grit her teeth against the odd carnal sensations rippling through her ass.

The combination of his searching finger in her butt and the vibrator pummeling her aroused clit made her bite her lip to keep from crying out from this wondrous arousal.

"The butt plug has done its job well, spreading you wider," he said a few moments later.

Her pussy clenched as he slid another finger into her anus.

Mercy! This was actually a beautiful kind of sexual torture she could learn to love.

She wanted to thrust the vibrator into her pussy now. Wanted to push her ass against him and let his fingers sink even deeper.

She needed to tell him what she wanted.

"Luke—"

"Easy," he calmed, sensing her sudden intense need to be fucked. "Let me prepare you just a little more."

Oh, my gosh!

A third finger sank inside her ass and she sucked in a sharp breath at the pleasure-pain rocking her.

Her legs were trembling now.

And she couldn't stop gyrating her hips.

Luke chuckled in her ear. His breath hot against her neck.

She blinked against the sexual haze as halfway down the cliff she thought she spotted a movement.

Was it Colter?

Sweet mercy! What if he came down and asked to join them?

Her heart pounded wildly at the thought of having two Outlaw men making love to her.

"He's up there, watching us. Wanting you," Luke breathed.

Oh, my goodness!

Her pussy heated with longing.

"Your ass is ready to be fucked, sweetheart. Are you ready?"

"Yes," she hissed. "Fuck my ass. Make love to me."

He withdrew his fingers one by one, leaving an odd burning, empty sensation in its wake which left her gasping, her body trembling.

"I've lubed my cock nicely with waterproof oil. It'll sink in easier. You okay?"

She nodded, the excitement making her unable to speak.

An instant later, the hot, round tip of his thick, wet cock touched her anal hole.

"Here goes."

She heard him groan as his solid, lubed cock invaded her ass.

Callie whimpered at the sensations washing over her, and Luke groaned into her ear, his mouth intimately nibbling on her earlobe.

He slid deeper, the pleasure-pain burning, making her gasp, urging her to cry out.

His large hands came around her and intimately cupped her breasts.

Oh, yes! That feels wonderful.

Her anal muscles clenched tight around his thick intrusion. She could feel every heated inch of his thick flesh burn deeper and deeper. A wild pleasure-pain zipped through her.

Oh, his cock felt so big!

So wonderfully big!

Her vision grew blurred from the sexual haze.

Just before she closed her eyes, she saw Colter standing there, not on the cliffs, but at the edge of the pond. Mere feet away.

Moon-glow bathed his tall figure. Washing over his clothed silhouette.

He was watching them.

Lust glazed his heavy-lidded eyes.

She shuddered at the intensity of dreamy pleasure that contorted his face. His jeans' fly was open, and he held his swollen, vein-riddled cock at the base and eagerly stroked his massive length with the other.

But she didn't care that he was watching. Didn't care that maybe Luke might have set the whole thing up.

She just closed her eyes against the pleasure-pain. Gasped as Luke's expert fingers massaged her swollen breasts, teasing and drawing out her nipples.

And soon, his entire cock was buried inside her.

This feeling of a man's thick flesh buried in her ass was like nothing she'd ever felt before.

Awesome.

It was something beyond words.

"So beautifully tight, Callie," he ground out, and started a seductively slow thrusting that had her ass and pussy burning alive.

She stiffened as the climax gathered speed.

Pleasure loomed.

Oh, God!

Luke moved faster. Pistoning in and out of her ass with long smooth strokes that had her on fire—had her racing toward something wild and untamed.

From somewhere in her sexual haze, she realized the vibrator was still pummeling her clit keeping her hot and bothered.

He seemed to know she was nearing the precipice of pleasure, and whispered softly against her ear, "Fuck your pussy with the vibrator. Let him hear your cries of pleasure. Don't hold back. Let him hear what he'll be missing if we decide there will be no Claiming."

She stiffened momentarily, wanting to tell him she hadn't agreed to anything, but she also wanted to tell him to keep fucking her so she could go over the edge into the carnal bliss that awaited her.

The tension of needing to have something deep inside her vagina along with her ass was now so overwhelming, she slammed the pulsing hot vibrator into her tight, soaked pussy with one swift plunge.

And climaxed on the spot.

An incredible explosion of fiery convulsions ripped her mind and body apart, making her cries of arousal split the moonlit air.

The orgasm went on forever.

Wicked sensations mingled with Luke's every plunge into her vulnerable ass and with every thrust of the pulsing vibrator deep into her vagina, the clit stimulator brushing wonderfully against her engorged clit.

She thrust her hips back at him, welcoming every delicious impalement. Welcoming the sounds of his erotic grunts and groans, as his cock made love to her ass.

Her body jerked in a primitive dance and perspiration peppered her hot skin.

Luke's hands kept massaging her swollen breasts and pulling at her aching nipples; sometimes he even used her

breasts as handles as he bucked harder against her backside, plunging deeper and deeper into her.

The walls of her vagina were convulsing wildly. Her ass burned wonderfully.

And Callie knew this was an experience she wanted to try again and again.

* * * * *

Every muscle in Colter's body was tense with primal lust as he watched his brother making love to Callie in the dark water.

The erotic sight of Luke's hands massaging her small breasts, drawing out her hard nipples, right there in front of him, tormented him. It reminded him of another woman he'd love to exact the same sexual pleasure upon.

Callie's mouth was open in a silent cry as Luke's cock tunneled in and out her snug ass. Soon her gasps and wild cries of pleasure sifted around him like an erotic blanket, making his breath escalate, making him want to shove his cock into her pretty little mouth, to feel her luscious lips smooth over his heated flesh as she sucked him hard and brought him to orgasm.

He thought of the *other* woman. Thought of Ashley.

He'd enjoy tying Ashley down, enjoy sexually torturing her for days, fucking her sweet ass and her tight little cunt until he was sure she would never forget him.

Never leave him again.

But that was only a hungry dream of revenge.

A dream that probably would never come true.

Luke's words from earlier today sifted into his erotic thoughts.

He'd hinted about the Outlaw brothers claiming Callie.

Maybe he should go along with a Claiming if they asked him.

It might make him forget Ashley.

Make him forget the lusty revenge that burned through his cock every time he thought of that sweet, viperous woman.

He clenched his teeth as Callie's climatic screams wound tighter around him. He felt his balls swell to an awful ache, felt himself sear closer to a climax.

His cock hardened painfully at her carnal sounds and at the pleasure groans of his brother.

The sexy noises built the tension inside him until he suddenly exploded, unleashing the lusty blades of lightning through his cock and into his balls, blanking his mind and making him join the carnal world of erotic bliss.

* * * * *

Luke made love to Callie for the rest of the night and off and on for the next day, and the following night.

Taking her in the mouth, in her ass and her pussy.

He loved the powerful orgasms that ripped her apart. Loved the way her velvety vaginal muscles tightened and contracted around his cock, prized her erotic whimpers, her sensual cries.

Colter didn't show again, and Luke wasn't upset that he'd come down to watch him make love to Callie.

All his brothers were hurting for a woman.

They'd been back from the Terrorist Wars for a few months now, and there wasn't an unclaimed woman around for miles to fuck, except for the ones hiding in the woods and they weren't easy to find.

Although the hunted look had finally disappeared from Callie's eyes, replaced by a look of love and happiness, his heart still ached over how he should keep her safe.

The more he thought about it, the more it seemed that the Claiming Law was the best solution to protect her from the government and other men. He just didn't know how to bring up the subject again and mar their happiness.

In the afternoon of the second day as they lay in bed snuggled in each other's arms, Callie finally opened her heart to him.

"I've been thinking about what you said. About your brothers claiming me."

It took all his strength not to stiffen against her. He thought he'd be prepared to talk about the subject.

Surprisingly he wasn't.

"And?" he asked with hesitation.

"I don't want to run anymore, Luke. I'm not made for it. I've always been a stay-at-home kind of gal."

"That's one of the reasons why I fell in love with you, Callie. You're a homebody. Like me."

He hugged her closer, inhaling the sweet scent of her feminine flesh, tracing a finger over one of the raised welts where the mad scientist had cut into her abdomen. He tried hard not to show his anger, tried hard not to feel the pain of them maybe not being able to have their own kids.

Years ago they'd chatted about two kids. A boy and a girl. But now that he knew there might not be a chance at all, he suddenly wanted a dozen of them.

"Like I mentioned before I can't leave Laurie, and we need to figure out some way to find Tyler."

She was still considering everyone's needs before her own.

"What do you want, Callie?"

She took a deep breath, her luscious breasts jiggling. She looked him straight in the eye, and said rather nervously, "I want to stay with you. If you still want me."

"I'll always want you, sweetheart. Please never doubt that again."

She smiled, and her gaze sparkled with something new. Excitement? Desire? Contentment? Maybe all of those emotions. He couldn't be sure.

"And I've decided I want you and your brothers to claim me."

Now that she'd said it out loud, he didn't know how to react. It was his turn for mixed emotions to run through him.

Fear.

Excitement.

Maybe a little bit of jealousy.

Most of all—confusion.

"Luke?"

"Are you sure? I mean…we need more time to think about this."

Her eyes flashed with amusement. "We?"

"Okay, so I mean me."

"You've changed your mind?"

"It's not every day a man asks the woman he loves to share herself with his brothers."

A puzzled frown marred her pretty forehead. "If you'd rather I not…"

"I want you to be perfectly sure, Callie. Above all, I want you safe and protected, and the Claiming Law is the best way to ensure you get what you want, but if you don't want to…"

"You're so sweet, Luke. That's the main reason I fell in love with you. You're sweet and so caring."

"If I were so caring I wouldn't have left you alone the other morning when you told me about them kidnapping you. I wouldn't have blown it five years ago by giving you no other option but to go behind my back and—"

A sharp rap on the door made Callie scramble for her gun.

"Relax," Luke soothed. "That's Colter's knock."

A flitter of horror shifted through her face, and she reached up to smooth her tangled tresses.

"I must look awful."

"You look beautiful after two straight days of getting fucked."

She blushed sweetly, and Luke resisted the urge to kiss her.

Instead, he scrambled out of bed and slipped into his pants. Callie quickly followed suit.

"Hey! Anyone home? I've got news!" Colter's excited voice came from the other side of the door.

"You ready?" he asked Callie, as she finished buttoning up her blouse.

She nodded, a pretty pink blush sweeping across her cheeks.

Luke smiled.

Although they hadn't discussed it, he knew she'd been turned on when she'd seen Colter at the edge of the pond while Luke had made love to her ass.

After the fact, she was embarrassed. It was only natural.

But if they were going to go ahead with the Claiming, she was going to have to get used to his brothers seeing him making love to her, and he was going to have to get used to seeing his brothers making love to her, too.

She'd already decided on a Claiming. With her decision firmly in her heart, it would be easier for her to accept his brothers into their sexual life. He just hoped he could accept it, too.

A moment later, Luke unlocked the door.

Chapter Ten

When Colter walked into the cabin, Callie's heart couldn't help but speed up at the sight of the good-looking Outlaw man. Lean and muscular, he walked with a careful, confident grace, seemingly on edge, ready to fight…or maybe ready to fuck?

The intense way his hungry gaze caressed her certain intimate parts made her tingle with a charming sexual awareness. Made her remember the other night in the pond when Luke's swollen erection had slid into her ass while Colter stood by and watched the whole thing.

"Hi Callie," he said, as he nodded politely to her, a gorgeous smile beamed across his lips. "You're looking a whole lot better than the last time I saw you. Callie must be tending to your needs," Colter said to Luke.

She noticed the underlying meaning in his words, the sexual frustration in his voice. Perhaps even a touch of jealousy?

No. Not jealousy.

Envy.

"We've found out what the Barlows are up to. You aren't going to like it."

Luke's eyes narrowed with curiosity.

"They've agreed to drop all the charges against you if you agree not to tell Laurie about Tyler being alive…and you give them…your ranch."

"No way!" Callie spat. "We have to tell Laurie sometime, and there's no way we're giving away our land. Luke didn't do anything wrong. He simply went to visit the Barlows and got shot for his troubles. We'll bring them to court for attempted murder and—"

She suddenly noticed two sets of gorgeous Outlaw smiles aimed at her. Her body trembled in sexual awareness.

Frustration at her reaction angered her.

"What?" she snapped.

"Anyone tell you that you'd make a fine lawyer?" Colter grinned.

She couldn't stop the warmth from caressing her cheeks at his compliment.

Luke threw her a wink, and returned his attention to his brother.

"You heard the lady." Luke replied.

Colter nodded. "Didn't think you'd take the deal, but I thought I'd put it onto the table anyway. They said if you wanted to talk to them directly, they would be willing to make certain adjustments and that you're welcome to go over and talk to them."

Luke didn't comment, but Callie could tell he was considering what Colter had said. Anger that he would even think about going over to the Barlows and discussing this farce almost made her explode.

However, she opted to remain silent.

She could talk sense into Luke about this newest development later.

"Something else you should know," Colter continued. "The Barlows aren't only interested buying up Ty's and your land. They're buying up parcels of land throughout the entire Rackety Valley as fast as they can get the money out of their bank accounts."

"Any ideas as to why?" Luke asked.

Callie noted the muscles in Colter's cheeks jump with tension. She got the feeling he was trying hard to contain his anger.

"Pleasure Palace, a legal bordello. They're going into partnership with the US government, and bringing in some of the conscripted women from the War."

Luke didn't say anything and Colter continued, "With the government backing them, we don't have much of a chance of protecting our pieces of property. They want your place and Tyler's spread, plus the western quarter section of the main farm, which is a few hundred acres, and the land of a few close neighbors. They say if we don't hand it over, they can expropriate it in the name of progress. They're looking at the entire western part of Rackety Valley. Can't say that I blame them. It's an ideal location. Picturesque. Untouched by man. Not to mention hundreds of acres bordering the ocean. Inland it's private…away from prying eyes."

A lump of frustration clogged Callie's throat.

The Barlows were powerful, rich and very influential in the court systems. They also owned the mortgages on their ranch and the Outlaw farm. Suddenly her earlier show of defiance, of going up against them in a court of law, made her realize why Colter and Luke had been smiling at her.

They'd thought her outburst amusing.

Was it any wonder they hadn't simply burst out laughing?

Maybe Colter was being kind to her for a reason. The intense way he'd looked at her when he'd first entered the cabin. His hungry gaze roaming all over her.

She swallowed against the mixed emotions coursing through her.

Fear.

Excitement.

Loss.

Tangled emotions, all fighting for recognition.

Fear that Luke might not be able to handle her being with his brothers. Loss at an old way of life—of one man and one woman living happily ever after.

And excitement, too.

She needed to face reality. Times had changed, and the Claiming Law could be just what she needed to protect herself from the government labs.

Uneasiness replaced her excitement.

But what about the one-month waiting period? She hadn't even given that a thought that other men would be allowed to have sex with her.

There was no way she would have sex with strangers. No way.

Her hopes of being claimed and being safe plunged.

God! Would this nightmare ever end?

"It's been two days, Callie," Colter broke into her tumultuous thoughts. "Is Luke well enough to travel?"

She wanted to tell Luke's brother that if Luke was well enough to fuck her senseless for two days then he was well enough to travel.

She nodded.

"Then get your stuff. We're going home."

Colter didn't give them too much time to pack, telling them that the Barlows had sent out a search party for their brother early this morning, and it wouldn't be too long before they came here asking questions.

He gave them a few minutes.

Just enough time for Luke and herself to pack those sex toys he'd bought for their honeymoon, along with a couple of changes of clothing.

A tight knot formed in her throat at having to say goodbye to her little ranch hideout.

She brushed away her tears of sorrow as she headed to the door.

Clearly, it was too dangerous to stay here any longer. Both she and Luke needed the protection of the Outlaw clan.

The walk to the washed-out bridge and the ride back to the Outlaw farm was quiet, yet tense.

Both Luke and Mac held onto their guns, their bodies tense, while Colter drove.

They were taking a huge chance traveling on the road. Although it was private, Outlaw land, anyone could be lurking around ready to strike.

When Callie saw the mellow yellow lights splashing cheerfully from the living room window of the farm, she breathed a sigh of relief.

Now that she was here, surrounded by Outlaw men, she could actually allow herself to think of other things besides keeping herself from being caught and claimed.

Now she had other worries.

The one-month waiting period for one.

She knew she wouldn't be able to go through with the Claiming Law with that provision in place.

And she suddenly began to realize why Luke hadn't told Colter he wouldn't go and see the Barlows.

He was actually considering giving up their ranch.

And suddenly she was beginning to realize why, too.

The Barlows were powerful men. They could buy judges. They could also eliminate the one-month waiting period for them...if Luke gave them what they wanted.

* * * * *

"We're going to have to keep a tight lid that she's here," Luke said after he'd left Callie in his bedroom. "A government scientist is looking for her."

"How was she able to escape? I hear those places are so secure not even a mouse could get in."

"I don't know how. I haven't asked her yet."

It was true. They hadn't even discussed how she'd broken out of the labs. They hadn't even spoken about the Barlow

killing. Or talked any more about this Blakely scientist who'd taken her eggs. Over the past two days, they'd been living in a wonderful fantasy world thinking only of pleasing each other. Now that he thought about it, it had been their honeymoon. Reality totally forgotten.

Unfortunately, reality was staring him straight in the face tonight.

Luke stood and headed for the closest night-darkened window, and looked outside. The full moon had slipped behind the dark ominous clouds making him jittery at the thought that anyone could be lurking around out there. All a group of men had to do was go to the law, tell them the Outlaws were harboring an unclaimed woman and the cops would be searching every square inch of Outlaw land.

"I'm surprised she was able to stay in hiding for so long over at our place without a government team searching the area," Cade said. "Surely they knew she lived in the valley?"

Cade was right. The government must have records that Callie came from Rackety Valley. And what Mac had said earlier about the security at the labs being airtight. They wouldn't let Callie simply walk out of there or make it easy for her to leave. Maybe Blakely had felt sorry for her and decided to let her go? Or maybe something else was going on here?

But what?

Quite frankly, he didn't want to know. She was here, and as far as he was concerned, she was staying here.

Keeping Callie safe was top priority.

"If she's not claimed, there's no way we can protect her, and by the hints you were dropping in the cabin the other day, we figure you both have discussed this?" Colter asked.

"We have," Luke agreed.

"And she's agreed to being claimed by all four of us?"

Again, Luke nodded.

"What's your take on this, Luke?" Cade asked.

Luke glanced back at his brothers who sat side by side on the sofa watching him closely. He knew they wouldn't agree to a Claiming unless he was absolutely sure.

"Luke could take her to Canada," Mac offered quickly, obviously noting Luke's hesitation.

"Canada's adopted the Claiming Law, too," Cade said quietly.

"You could take her away like Jude did with Cate. Go on the run. We could get another boat," Colter offered.

"I'm through running. Luke and I already discussed it."

Luke and his brothers whirled around to find Callie standing at the hallway. She'd changed into a sexy, frilly, white nightgown. A virtual see-through gown he'd purchased years ago for their honeymoon, but had totally forgotten in the bottom of the drawer in his room here at the farm.

Obviously, Callie hadn't wasted any time making herself at home here.

From beside him he heard Mac and Cade's aroused inhalations. Colter swore softly.

Luke swallowed against the dryness claiming his mouth, as he made out the lush outlines of her breasts pressed against the thin lingerie. He didn't miss the pretty pink color of her hard nipples or darker pink of her areolas, nor did he miss the dark outline of her pussy hair.

Beneath the restraint of his jeans, his cock hardened like a piece of molten steel.

She looked directly at him.

"I've already expressed to Luke my wishes of all of you claiming me. So what I'm asking is for an answer from all four of you. Will you claim me? If you say yes, I'd like to be claimed as soon as possible."

* * * * *

Callie had expected Luke to explode when she said she wanted to be claimed. During their last conversation, he hadn't come right out and said he was totally comfortable with the idea, so perhaps she really should have kept quiet. But time was of the essence. Besides, if Luke didn't want to share her with his brothers, she would respect his wishes and bow out.

To her surprise, he didn't protest. As a matter of fact, he'd reacted totally opposite of her expectations.

Instead of anger shining in his eyes, she saw love. And pride.

Not to mention an extremely large bulge pressing against his pants.

The lusty way the other three Outlaw brothers were staring at her made her shiver with both excitement and fear. Fear that maybe she was doing the wrong thing in giving in to the Claiming Law. Excitement that Luke seemed more confident in their relationship than she'd thought he would be.

"Luke?" Colter said in a somewhat strangled voice.

Colter didn't take his hot gaze off her, but Callie could sense he as well as his brothers would only agree if Luke agreed.

"I'm sure only if you're sure, Callie. This is your last chance. Do you want the four of us to claim you?" Luke whispered.

For one split second, she wasn't sure. The urge to change her mind almost won. But that was fear speaking, not reality.

The only way she would be protected as a woman and as an escaped lab rat were for these four sexy, testosterone-ripe men to take her sexually.

Suddenly, she found herself wondering if Luke had told them what she'd done. Had he told them how naïve she'd been in walking into the government labs in her dreams of saving mankind? She'd strolled straight into the lab like some innocent sacrificial lamb.

It was as if Luke sensed her turmoil. As if he knew there could be no lies between her future husbands and herself.

"Go into the bedroom," he said quietly. "I'll tell them everything. They can decide based on the facts."

She nodded numbly.

Ignoring the puzzled expressions on the brothers' faces, she slipped down the hallway and back to their bedroom.

In the living room, she could hear Luke's gentle voice as he began to explain to his brothers what she'd done and what Blakely had done to her.

* * * * *

"She was young and innocent," Luke finished.

"She was stupid," Colter snapped. His eyes blazed with red-hot anger. "Just like she was stupid to trust me out at your place by lowering her weapon. She's still too trusting, Luke. You could lose her all over again if she puts her trust into the wrong person."

"Like you did, Colter?" Luke said gently.

His brother flinched, but by the angry expression on Colter's face, his brother knew what he was talking about.

"She's not you, okay?" Luke continued. "You showed her a valuable lesson by turning on her the way you did. She won't easily forget. Just like you won't easily trust another person, am I right?"

"Shut up, Luke," Colter warned.

"That's why you frightened her that day, isn't it? Because you knew she trusted you. You don't want her to end up hurt like you were because you trusted someone."

The muscles in Colter's jaws twitched angrily, and Luke noticed Cade and Mac edge up on either side of their brother, ready to grab him in case he started swinging like he'd done after Ashley, a conscripted woman he'd fallen in love with one weekend during the Wars overseas, had suddenly left him high and dry.

For a minute, Luke thought Colter might start swinging his fists now, but suddenly the tension visibly dissolved and his shoulders slumped.

"So, sue me for trying to harden her. She's just too damn trusting, Luke."

"It's one of the reasons I love her and why you care so much for her. Do you really want her to change and become bitter and angry?"

Like you? The last two words were left unspoken, but Luke knew Colter got his message by the way his brother frowned.

"Fine. I'll go to the government office tomorrow morning and get the Claiming papers. At least then we can get the ball rolling."

"No, I've got another idea. I'll explain it to you tomorrow. First, I've got to talk to Callie about it."

His brothers nodded.

He wasn't through explaining to his brothers.

When he told them what Blakely had done to Callie in the lab, his brothers looked fit to kill the scientist, but in the end, all of them reassured Luke he could count on them to help him protect Callie and if that meant claiming her then so be it.

To his surprise, having their agreement eased his mind, and he felt as if the world had lifted off his shoulders. Making his evening farewells, he headed to their bedroom.

And to Callie.

* * * * *

"Are you scared?" Luke whispered, as he gently nibbled on her earlobe. He'd come to bed and found her trembling uncontrollably. Trembling because she'd actually voiced out loud in front of the Outlaw brothers that she was willing to allow them to lay claim to her.

"Terrified," she admitted, loving the heated warmth of his cock as he slid slowly into her drenched vagina from behind.

"Are you sure about what we discussed about the deal with the Barlows?"

Her heart said no.

But she knew there was no other way.

She nodded.

"Do you think the Barlows will take to blackmail?"

"They don't have much choice. They only have three brothers left now. If word got back to the government that the fourth husband is gone…there is a chance they could lose Laurie to another group of men. We'll tell the Barlows we know about a certain accidental shooting and that we know where their brother's body is buried. If they don't agree to our terms then I'll tell them we'll go to the government."

"What if the Barlows call your bluff? I mean all they have to do is find the grave, and then we've got nothing."

"Colter and I will move the body tomorrow to a place on Ty's land where no one will find it."

"But what if they don't care about losing Laurie? What if they threaten to kill Tyler? What if—"

"Laurie is a beautiful woman, Callie. They'll fight like the dogs they are to keep her. Besides, there are too many 'what ifs', Callie. Don't worry about it. Let me go to the Barlows tomorrow—"

Panic seared through her. "You're not going there alone. I won't allow it."

"Colter's coming with me. The other boys will stay here and keep an eye out."

"Are you sure it's safe for you to go? I mean with the arrest warrant…"

"Don't worry, I'll be careful. Now let's get back to forgetting all our troubles, shall we?"

"I love the way you make me forget our troubles," she giggled, and arched her backside against his hard hips, allowing

the rest of his thick cock to slide all the way into her warm and waiting pussy.

* * * * *

As the day dragged on and Luke and Colter hadn't come back from the Barlow meeting, Callie grew more and more nervous.

Had something happened to them? Had the Barlows called the police on Luke and gone ahead and pressed charges?

"They're back!" Mac shouted.

A moment later, she heard Mac and Cade's footsteps stomp along the back porch where she'd secured them to shuck beans and peel the potatoes for tonight's dinner.

One quick glance out the window, and her heart picked up a wild pace.

Luke and Colter were getting out of Luke's pickup truck and behind them a black stretch limousine pulled up.

Callie cried out as she watched the three remaining Barlow brothers step out of the limo.

Followed by her sister Laurie.

* * * * *

After Laurie and Callie embraced each other and cried in the kitchen, the Outlaws and Barlows made themselves scarce, telling them they had business to take care of.

Just by looking at Luke's grim face, Callie knew the Barlows had accepted their blackmail deal.

Despite trying hard to stop it, her anger at those Barlows brewed inside her heart. It was obvious they had come for their ranch.

Sons of bitches!

But she didn't have time to waste on them, she wanted to concentrate on Laurie. Her sister looked tired. And thinner.

She'd even lost all of the baby fat she'd been trying to exercise away for years.

Her long, golden-blonde hair was styled in such a way it swept off her neck and curled up top of her head in tiny ringlets with a couple of ringlets dangling at the sides, giving her pretty face a warm, soft look. And she was dressed in a sexy, red-velvet dress that showed off her bare back and dipped down low in front barely covering her full breasts.

She wore no jewelry and hardly any makeup.

She looked absolutely stunning.

"Luke told me the Outlaws are going to claim you," Laurie said softly, her eyes sparkled with excitement. She grabbed Callie's hand and tugged her to sit down at the kitchen table.

"That's the plan."

"It's a good plan. They'll protect you, sis. They're good men. I've always thought highly of each and every one of them."

"Wish I could say the same thing about the Barlows. Luke told me they originally wanted Cate. You should have known they would have figured out some other way to avoid the Barlows from getting her. Why'd you go and take her place?" Callie finally asked the question she'd been itching to ask since she'd heard about her Claiming.

Laurie frowned.

"I have my personal reasons, Callie. Rest assured though, I'm doing the right thing. Please don't worry about me, okay? Promise?"

"How can you be doing the right thing? I don't understand? You were supposed to join the women's resistance. You were supposed to be safe."

"Please, just trust me on this."

"Laurie—"

"We've only got a few minutes. Let's not discuss this anymore."

Callie nodded, but frustration screamed through her.

"How are they treating you?"

Her sister flinched visibly at the question.

"And you don't want me to worry about you? I want you away from them, Laurie."

"I'm where I need to be at this time," she said gently. There was a strange glint in her eyes. It made Callie even more concerned.

"What do you mean you need to be there?"

"Please, don't ask any questions. The answers are private...for now."

Private? What in the world was going on? Before she could put the pressure on her to spill her guts, Laurie continued, "They are demanding. Men who haven't had sex in a while can be tiring—especially with so many of them, and now that there is one less it will be a relief." To her surprise, Laurie suddenly smiled and squeezed her hand. "You'll find out how demanding sexually deprived men can be with the Outlaw brothers...but I'm sure they must make excellent lovers if they're anything like Tyler."

At the mention of Tyler, Callie's heart picked up speed. How she ached to tell her sister about him.

But she didn't know what the final deal was Luke had hammered out. She had to keep quiet for now, and she literally had to bite her inner cheek to keep herself from saying anything.

"Is that a wedding ring, you're wearing?" Laurie's shocked voice made Callie realize she was still wearing the gold band that Luke had slipped back onto her finger.

"Luke and I got married."

"Married? That's not possible. All the preachers and anyone capable of marrying couples have been imprisoned. How did you do it?"

Quickly Callie explained about what had happened after Luke had escaped from the Barlows ranch.

"And he forced you to marry him at gunpoint?"

Callie nodded, and had to laugh as her sister's eyes widened into saucers in disbelief.

"How absolutely romantic. If Ty had lived, he would have been my Prince to my rescue like that, too."

Tyler is alive! And the Barlows know where he is.

She'd figured agreeing to be claimed by four men would be the hardest thing for her to do in her life, but keeping this secret from Laurie was even harder. How long could she keep the information to herself before she actually cracked and told Laurie? But as Luke had said, if she did tell Laurie then the Barlows would have Ty killed.

"Time to go, Laurie."

Callie's head snapped up at the sound of Zeb Barlow's deep voice. He stood in the kitchen doorway watching both of them intently. Obviously, he was making sure Callie didn't tell Laurie about Ty.

Familiar anger began to burn inside her, but she clamped down on it, opting to keep Laurie here with her as long as possible.

"Oh! Couldn't you all stay for supper? Laurie and I have so much catching up to do."

Zeb frowned and shook his head. "I'm sorry, but no. We have other plans for Laurie tonight."

Callie's excitement plummeted. Laurie hadn't even been here for ten minutes and they were already taking her away.

"But please," Zeb continued, as he was joined by the other Barlows behind him, "We'd all love to see your Claiming videos. Feel free to drop by and visit with them anytime."

Callie's stomach tightened.

The Barlows were absolutely disgusting and vile creatures.

As if sensing Callie was about to blow up, Laurie quickly stood and embraced her tightly.

"I have to go," she whispered. "Please come and visit me when you can."

Tears shone in her haunted eyes as she pulled away and gave Callie a watery smile.

Callie nodded, suddenly wanting to grab her baby sister and never let her go.

This isn't right! her mind screamed. *She shouldn't go with them! She doesn't belong to them! She belongs to Tyler. He's alive!*

She took one step forward with every intention of telling the Barlows that as far as she was concerned they could go straight to hell with the brother she'd killed when Luke's hand wrapped around her elbow stopping her cold.

"Let her go," Luke whispered. "She's a strong woman. She'll be fine."

She wished she could believe him. Wished she could trust that Laurie would be safe with the Barlows.

But she couldn't be sure of anything.

Deep down in her very soul she knew there was one thing she was sure of. Only one man could rescue her.

Tyler Outlaw.

Keeping silent, she watched from the kitchen window as the Barlow brothers and Laurie sped away.

"Everything is done. We buried the body over on Ty's land in a place they'll never find it. We can keep the fact that there is one less Barlow hanging over their heads just like they can keep Ty hanging over our heads. The good thing is the Barlows accepted most of the deal we agreed on last night. They've agreed to drop the charges against me and to make the one-month waiting period vanish for you if I gave them our ranch. That's why we were gone for so long. We went with them to buy a judge."

"So they have our little ranch."

He nodded, and she bit her lower lip to prevent from crying.

They'd lost their ranch. Their beautiful future was gone. The finality of it left her with a hollow, empty feeling.

"That's not all. We're not to mention to Laurie that Ty is alive."

"I don't know if I can do this to Laurie. I feel as if I have to tell her the next time I see her."

"Hear me out, Callie."

"What?" Callie stamped her feet in frustration.

"It's only for nine months. We keep quiet for nine months, and they'll tell us where Tyler is."

"Why nine months? He could be dead by then."

"I tried for less. But they wouldn't go for it. They figure in nine months they'll have her pregnant, and she'd be less likely to leave them when he came back."

Callie felt like screaming.

Luke's arms curled around her waist and he squeezed her tightly. His warm body pressing lovingly against her did little to douse the hatred she felt for those men who would betray Laurie in such a way.

"If we tell her within that time frame, the Barlows have threatened to have Tyler killed."

"Can we really believe that they even know where he is?"

"Oh, they know where he is."

Anger spiked his words and he let go of her, digging something out of his shirt pocket.

He held up a photograph of Tyler, and it just about broke her heart. His face was bruised, one eye swollen shut and he was holding up a copy of last week's edition of Rackety Valley's newsletter.

"You think they have him hidden close by?" Callie asked, as she ran a finger over the picture, tracing Tyler's black eye. Despite the fact he looked awful he was smiling, if only to defy whoever was taking his picture.

"Close enough so they can get a picture of him with last week's town paper, but far enough away where it'll take us one

hell of a long time before we find him. If you'll notice the background is a white wall. It could be anywhere."

"I don't know, Luke. So many things can go wrong in nine months."

"We have to trust them, Callie. We have no other choice."

Even when he said it, Callie could hear the doubt lacing his voice, and Callie knew he was trying really hard to make himself believe Tyler would be all right.

Perhaps he believed the same thing she believed? That the odds of Tyler making it back home alive were pretty bleak.

"Something else the judge ordered. This will probably come as a shock, but he's ordered the Claiming right away. The minute he gets the tape, he'll approve it. If it's okay with you, I'll tell the boys and we'll do the Claiming tonight."

At Luke's words, Callie's breath backed right up into her lungs and erotic weakness splashed through her, along with tremors of nervousness.

Tonight? So soon?

Better to get this over with as soon as possible. She wanted to be safe, and she wanted to be with Luke.

And she wanted to be close to her sister.

"Will you be there always?"

"Right beside you. We're in this together, sweetheart. Every step of the way. Go on into the bedroom and get ready. I'll bring Colter in first."

Callie blew out an anxious breath, and headed for the bedroom.

Chapter Eleven

Tension knotted Luke's shoulders as he listened to Callie's shower running.

He'd told Colter, Mac and Cade about the plans.

They'd been visibly shaken that the Claiming was taking place so quickly, but after reassurance from him that this Claiming was something that needed to be done in order to protect Callie, they'd retreated to their rooms to get ready.

Shoving his fingers through his hair, he closed his eyes and wondered again if he was doing the right thing in allowing this Claiming.

Maybe he should have simply thrown Callie over his shoulder and dragged her off to live in some cave with him like their ancestors had. But Callie said she'd run enough. She wanted stability. A life. Peace and security.

Luke had explained to the judge about Blakely wanting Callie. The judge had reassured Luke once she was claimed she would be legally safe from Blakely's wants. At present, in the government's eyes, a man's sexual satisfaction was top priority.

Sex kept the men happy.

Kept them out of trouble in a world that had gone topsy-turvy without a woman to gentle a man's fierce needs or keep his bed warm at night.

Luke sat there listening to the running shower, and imagined how warm Callie's flesh must feel after being naked under the hot spray. He could imagine her hands soaping the curves of her breasts, over her belly and lower.

He hadn't missed the familiar tremors or arousal coursing through her as he'd held her earlier in the kitchen and told her the Claiming would take place tonight.

A little stab of jealousy had ripped into him at the thought his brothers would be so intimately involved with Callie but he'd reined his emotions in, making himself grateful that at least Callie's Claiming would be consensual and not forced as it might otherwise have been had she been caught by some strangers.

"Luke?" Colter's soft voice ripped into his thoughts.

He opened his eyes to find Colter standing in front of him wearing nothing but a pair of black track pants, the material stretched tight over an impressive bulge between his legs.

Maybe he should have warned Callie that Colter was a hell of a lot bigger than he was?

Oh, hell, she'd find out soon enough.

"Ready?" Luke asked.

Colter nodded tensely.

"Okay, let's go."

* * * * *

Callie looked down at her empty ring finger with a strange loneliness clutching her heart as she placed the disposable razor onto a nearby soap dish, and allowed the pulsing shower spray to wash away the soap and curly hair from her pubic area. She'd left the ring on the dresser not wanting the camera to pick it up and have the judge asking questions.

She hadn't realized that taking it off would have such an impact on her. The lack of it making her feel as if her future with Luke was gone forever. In a way, it was, but she wanted to believe this new way of life would be just as fulfilling. Time would tell.

She'd shaved her pussy as quickly as possible, but considering it was such a sensitive area, she'd taken much longer than expected, dipping the razor on both sides of her

soaped-up pussy lips and over her mons, making her privates nude so she could bare herself to Luke, his brothers and to the camera.

When all traces of hair and soap were gone, she stepped forward until the hot fingers of water poked roughly against the sensitive flesh of her breasts, massaging her nipples until they enlarged with arousal and hardened into thick pebbles. She turned around allowing the heated spray to knead the anxious muscles in her back and shoulders. The tenseness knotting her flesh slowly dissolved, making her skin tingle with fire.

Callie found herself smiling.

Tonight would be the beginning of her new life. She'd be free.

Well, as free as a woman could be in a world gone mad.

Free, nonetheless.

Despite the way Colter had acted toward her when he'd told her not to trust any man, deep in her heart she knew she could trust the Outlaw brothers to protect her from Blakely.

Callie grabbed the bar of fresh-smelling soap, and ran it along the scar on the right-hand side of her abdomen, compliments of that last surprise experiment.

The bastard had drugged her, cut her eggs from her belly, sewn her up and dangled the fact that he would use her eggs and his sperm to create future fetuses for his experiments to cure the women.

The man was mad.

But then he had to be to create the X-virus and hand it over to the highest bidder. And now he was being commissioned by her own government to find a cure or a vaccine against the sickness he'd created.

Despite those disturbing thoughts, Callie found herself smiling.

The night she'd escaped she'd exacted her revenge.

He'd left her isolation lab and for the first time since she'd been there she hadn't heard the familiar click that indicated the door locking. She'd waited only a few minutes before trying the door.

To her ultimate excitement, the door had opened.

The corridor had been quiet and dimly lit, allowing her to tiptoe out into the hallway. She'd been surprised to discover she was being housed right across the hallway from the lab.

It had been empty when she entered it and searched it frantically. Eventually, she'd found the vials containing her eggs and had smashed them on the floor, effectively destroying any chance of him ever using her eggs for experiments.

To her surprise, getting out of the building had been easy.

Almost too easy.

She'd slipped into a nearby storage room where she'd been able to don a lab coat, a pair of slippers, a mask and hair net to cover her hair.

Then she'd found a package of cigarettes and a lighter on a lab bench, grabbed them and followed the Smoking Areas signs, which led her directly to an unlocked back door, where she'd lit a cigarette and casually strolled outside into a yard where a few smokers were puffing away.

Dressed in her garb, they didn't even give her a second look.

A twelve-foot-high chain link fence surrounded the yard, but she'd found a corner easily enough to keep away from prying eyes, climbed the fence and hopped over.

The lab had been in the business district of Bangor, Maine.

She knew an old friend who she could trust who lived in the area and finding a phone, she'd called her collect. Her friend had been shocked to hear from her, had known she'd gone missing and had come right away to get her...with her four new husbands.

Helping an escaped lab rat was a criminal offence, and her friend's husbands had been wary, but her friend had been persuasive and they'd driven her to Rackety Valley where they'd promised her to never reveal they'd helped her.

She'd gone to Laurie who at the time had been readying herself to flee the newly invoked Claiming Law and join the resistance. She'd spent one night with her sister who had put her in touch with the town preacher who had come for her and taken her to the cabin where she'd stayed until now.

Perhaps by destroying her eggs that night in the lab she'd delayed Blakely finding a cure for the X-virus. But she'd never agreed to the experiment, and he'd had no right to do what he'd done to her.

Now that Luke and the Outlaw brothers had agreed to claim her, her protection from Blakely would be secure or Luke would have told her otherwise.

Not to mention she could now spend the rest of her life with Luke, a man she'd loved more than she ever thought she could love someone.

Two shadowy figures on the other side of the clouded shower glass made Callie's heart pick up speed. From the silhouettes, she recognized Luke's broad shoulders and Colter's taller frame.

Oh, sweet heavens!

The Claiming was about to begin.

Luke entered the steamy shower first, the water spray crashing against his big muscular chest and peppering his smiling face.

"Thought I'd join you first. Get you in the mood."

Callie dropped her gaze.

Her heart fluttered wonderfully at the sight of his engorged cock, but sudden anxiety overshadowed her arousal.

"I'm nervous," she admitted.

"It's okay, sweetie. We'll go slow. Just you, me and Colter to start."

Oh, God!

He grinned at her shocked expression.

"One more thing. We get lots of points if you act submissive and do everything we say."

"You like that don't you? Me being submissive."

"I'd rather have you fighting me as I rip your clothes from your body," he whispered huskily.

"I'd rather like that myself, but I'm also curious to see what you and your brothers have cooked up for me tonight."

He chuckled and cupped her waist with his hot hands, maneuvering her around so that the shower was splashing against his back. Grabbing the soap from her trembling hand, he smoothed the slippery bar over one of her breasts. His free hand began a slow, erotic massage of her other breast.

"Spread your legs wide, Callie," he instructed. "Colter will be stepping inside with the government camera any moment. He'll mount it on the wall in here. Just act natural and pretend it isn't there."

She did as he instructed, her heart pounding frantically in her ears, her abdomen clenching with anticipation.

Then his head lowered and he was kissing her.

His hot mouth seared against her lips with wild abandon while his hands soaped her breasts.

Suddenly she felt a new pair of hands at her hips.

She couldn't stop herself from stiffening at the intrusion.

"It's just me," Colter whispered, as his warm hands sensuously cupped her ass cheeks.

"The first Claiming requirement is a double penetration," Luke said softy, as he broke the kiss. "We'll do it here in the shower."

Oh, boy.

"And then the next requirement is —"

"Don't tell me. It'll just make me more nervous."

He grinned mischievously.

"We'll keep you in suspense then. Your orgasm is always stronger when I surprise you with things."

She was about to be double penetrated and he was in a teasing mood? She found herself relaxing at that realization.

Her relief lasted only moments when Colter's hand slipped between her widespread legs, and he slid a finger lightly against her pulsing clitoris.

A shiver of arousal slammed into her pussy.

Confusion gripped her.

Should she be feeling sexual pleasure at another man's hand if she loved Luke so much?

"Luke?"

She wanted to pose that question to him, but it seemed as if he was reading her mind.

"I want you to enjoy yourself. Don't hold back. Be natural. We want the government video to see how much we all belong together."

At the mention of the video, she automatically stiffened. Where was the camera? Was she ready for this? She thought she was. Thought she was prepared to allow numerous strange men to view the video, and see her having sex with Luke and the Outlaw brothers.

Maybe she wasn't as ready as she thought?

But the erotic way her swollen clitoris pulsed against Colter's finger, the wetness seeping from her channel and the sensual way her hips automatically gyrated against Colter's ministrations made her realize that yes, she was ready for this.

Luke's tender caresses turned her breasts into swollen globes. Her nipples ached as he brushed his chest back and forth against them in a sensual rhythm that had her whimpering her approval at the pounding pleasure.

Soon she writhed between the two men, their eager hands sliding soapy suds all over her tingling flesh. "Bend over so Colter can take out the butt plug," Luke groaned into her ear.

Callie swallowed as the eagerness inside her mounted.

She bent over, grabbing the backs of her knees and drew in a sharp breath when Luke's thick erection wavered mere inches from her face, his purple mushroom-shaped cockhead swollen with desire. The blue veins pulsed down each side of his shaft like slithering snakes.

Her mouth watered at the idea of taking him into her mouth, but she couldn't. She had to do what she was told. It would show the government she was a willing and subservient wife. Being submissive would give them more points for the Claiming.

For a split second, she realized that the terrorists had won.

They'd unleashed the X-virus among the world's population in a desperate effort to make all women submissive to men. It was ironic. In the end, their own governments had given into the terrorists and enacted the Claiming Law making women property of men to do with them what they wanted.

Her thoughts were broken as the thick, plastic butt plug slowly slid out of her. She felt Luke's hands curl around her upper arms as he helped her to straighten again.

Colter's large hands slipped around her waist, a hot brand reminding her of what was to come.

"Lean back into Colter," Luke whispered.

She began to tremble with excitement, with need as she leaned against his brother's hard, hot, wet body.

His aroused breath fanned warmly against the nape of her neck.

And then she felt it.

Felt Colter's fiery erection, his thick, generously lubed cock prodding the entrance to her back door.

"Oh, God!" she hissed as the erotic fire from his slow penetration took hold of her senses.

She'd been taken in the ass many times by Luke over the last two days at the ranch, but Colter…was thicker than Luke.

So much thicker.

Her ass muscles scrambled to stretch to this new invasion as he continued to impale her.

Sensing her apprehension, Luke's mouth clamped over hers, sending powerful sensations slicing through her. It was as if Luke was sending her a message loud and clear.

Telling her that despite the fact that another man's cock was buried in her ass, Luke was claiming her with his warm mouth, branding her with his eager lips, making sure she remembered to whom she really belonged to.

As Colter slid even deeper, Callie kissed Luke back with an eagerness she found highly erotic.

She needed to show him he was still her main man.

Luke's hands dipped between her legs to slide over her drenched clitoris. His touch was harder than his brother's.

Fiercer.

More confident.

He had her perched on the edge of bliss within seconds. His engorged erection parted her labia and he thrust into her tight channel in one solid stroke that had her moaning her approval into his hot mouth.

"Sounds like you just enjoyed that." he breathed harshly, as he broke the passionate kiss.

She wished she could find the words to explain the awesome feeling of having two pulsing cocks buried inside her, but all she could do was moan and hold firmly to Luke's shoulders.

Her eyelids felt heavy with lust.

Her body trembled with desire.

Colter chuckled from behind her. His large hands tightened on her waist.

"You're doing fine, Callie," his voice sounded strangled, as he began a slow torturous slide from her ass. Before he was completely free, he slammed back into her again, making her cry out in surprise as her asshole convulsed with pleasure-pain around the rigid impalement.

Luke was on the move now, too, staking out his territory with his own fiery strokes.

Heat arced through her as he plunged in and out of her like a frantic piston.

Her heart crashed in her ears, and she barely heard the sound of flesh slapping against flesh as the brothers discovered the perfect rhythm for impaling her.

She could feel her body preparing itself for the impending orgasm.

Could feel her vaginal muscles clamping around Luke's hard, long cock. Her anal muscles stretching impossibly wider with Colter's every deep plunge.

Erotic tendrils spread throughout her.

Her thighs tensed.

She could smell the scent of their sex searing through the warm mist.

And then it hit.

Her inner muscles clenched and pulsed around the massive intruders.

Her head fell back, and she convulsed violently against the two men, crying out her arousal into the steamy shower stall.

Her fingers dug into Luke's shoulders, her grip tightening as she writhed in an achingly sensual dance.

First, she heard Luke's guttural cry, which was quickly followed by an erotic shout from Colter as they both joined her in a mind-blowing orgasm.

She didn't know how long her mind and body were ripped apart with the frenzy of pleasure but finally the joy ebbed away.

Her anal muscles were still quivering erotically when Colter withdrew his thick cock.

A moment later, she heard the water taps shut off and he stepped outside the stall.

"I'll move the camera to the bedroom." She heard Colter say.

That's when she noticed the mini digital camera stuck on the shower stall wall.

It was no bigger than a silver dollar.

"You did real good," Colter grinned at her, as he pried off the camera then quickly left.

"You okay?" Luke asked, keeping his cock buried inside her and curling his arms snugly around her waist, bringing her closer to him.

She hugged him and nodded. "It was wonderful. Awesome. Something I would never have imagined."

To her surprise, she was eagerly looking forward to the next requirement of the Claiming.

"Sweetie, we're going to have to move into the bedroom. Cade and Mac are out there waiting for us."

Callie pressed her forehead against Luke's and blew out a breath. "Give me a minute to get my bearings. I swear if you weren't inside me, I'd be on the floor in a heap of satisfied lust."

"So would I," he chuckled.

"Are you okay with this?" she asked, suddenly wanting to be reassured the Claiming was okay with him.

"Don't worry about me, Callie. I'm willing to do whatever it takes to protect you."

Warmth swept through her at his soft-spoken words.

He made her feel so secure. So safe. It was something she hadn't felt in a long time.

The door to the bathroom opened and Colter stuck his head inside.

"Don't mean to intrude but we're ready for the next requirement."

Butterflies suddenly swooped inside her lower abdomen. For a moment panic struck, but it quickly disintegrated as she remembered Luke would be with her and he was okay with everything.

"We're coming," Callie said, surprised that her voice sounded so steady when Luke's brother was watching them standing naked in the shower still joined as one.

She figured she'd better start getting used to it fast because there were two more brothers who would be seeing her naked very soon.

Colter nodded and closed the door.

Luke slid his once again hardening cock out of her.

Suddenly she found herself wishing he would stay buried inside her forever, but there was a Claiming to be done and no time for getting snuggly with the man she loved.

They toweled each other off, Luke drying her in her most intimate places, arousing her all over again.

By the time he was finished with her, her pussy was sopping wet and she wanted to have sex with him again.

Bad.

He draped a warm robe over her shoulders, and she clasped the ends together, covering her nakedness.

It gave her a small measure of confidence.

She could do this. Really, she could.

On the other side of this door were three Outlaw brothers who in mere minutes would be getting very intimate with her.

The warmth of Luke's hand pressing through the soft robe against the small of her back kept her anchored in reality.

"You ready?"

Callie nodded.

His hot fingers intertwined with hers.

"You sure?"

"Yes, I want to do this."

She took a deep breath mustering her courage and as Luke stepped naked through the doorway he pulled her into the bedroom with him.

Colter stood naked at the head of the bed, his huge cock sticking straight out from his body with full arousal as he mounted the government camera to a bedpost. To her shock, she noted his nipples were pierced with tiny, silver nipple rings and there was a fist-sized tattoo in the middle of his lower abdomen just above his shaft and balls, a lone rose blossomed from the one of the skull's eye sockets. Shivering with excitement she wondered what the story was behind that tattoo and those nipple rings.

Cade and Mac sat on the bed, completely nude, their hands boldly stroking their long, thick, fierce-looking cocks readying themselves to claim her.

When they looked up at her, their eyes dark with lust, she trembled at the desire coursing through her. Oh, boy! These men really wanted her!

Sudden doubts assailed her and she felt paralyzed with fear.

What if she wasn't good enough sexually for them because of her lack of experience with men? She'd only been with Luke. How would they take her inexperience?

How would it look to the viewers who watched their Claiming tape? Would the judge that the Barlows hired decide not to grant the Outlaws the claim because she was acting so timid?

Suddenly she realized it was time to get her act together.

She knew Luke had told her to show herself as being a submissive wife, but surely if she appeared to want sex they

would gain more favor with the judge and whoever else viewed the Claiming?

It was a chance she was willing to take.

An unusual boldness calmed her butterflies and she called out, "Come on, boys, don't be shy. Make love to me."

Their eyes widened in surprise.

She couldn't help but giggle nervously.

"They haven't had a woman in months, Callie, and they want you real bad. Go easy on them," Luke chuckled into her ear.

They hadn't had a woman in months?

All those pent-up sexual urges ready to be unleashed on her.

The thought was dizzyingly erotic.

Luke's warm hands slid sensuously over her shoulders, and she took it as her cue to let go of the front ends of her robe.

Both Outlaw brothers licked their lips as Luke slid the garment off her shoulders, revealing her nakedness to them. Colter groaned his appreciation.

"The next phase is a triple penetration," Luke whispered into her ear. "I'm going to watch while the boys do all the work. You just enjoy."

Oh, my God!

* * * * *

Seeing Callie naked and surrounded by his attentive brothers was the most erotic sight Luke had ever seen in his life, and it took every ounce of his strength to stop himself from joining the ménage in progress.

One of the requisites of the Claiming was the triple penetration.

While he and Colter had met with the Barlow-bribed judge, they'd been informed a double penetration and a triple

penetration with the fourth husband looking on, would be the minimum sex acts required to clinch the claim.

They'd been truly lucky.

Luke had heard stories of other women who'd had to have sex with several groups of men during the one-month waiting period. The group giving the women the most orgasms in the most varied ways always got the claim.

And now as he watched Colter instruct Callie to sit her cute rounded ass upon Mac's engorged erection as he lay on the bed, flames of need licked Luke's cock at the pleasure-agony shining on her face.

She gasped as Mac's massive cock disappeared into her ass.

Then she obediently opened her mouth as Cade's long cock slid between her eager lips and into her mouth.

With Mac's cock now buried up her ass, she lay backwards on top of his hard body, his hands came up and he began a slow sensual massage of her breasts, squeezing her ripe, jiggly globes and pinching her pink nipples until they were peaked with desire.

She, in turn, began rubbing her clitoris, moaning as her pleasure quickly began to crest.

She saw Luke watching the foursome and smiled sexily.

Spreading her legs wide open, she gave Luke a full view of Mac's cock buried deep in her ass. The pink petals of her swollen labia looked so appealing he wished he could suck them right into his mouth. And the damp, tiny slit that dripped with the cream of her arousal would soon welcome Colter into her writhing body.

Luke shuddered pleasantly as he watched Colter, his shaft already as hard as a rock, come over between Callie's open legs.

His engorged cock parted her drenched labia and hurriedly disappeared into Callie's luscious cunt.

Soon the suctioning sounds of flesh slapping against flesh, his brothers' groans of arousal and Callie's sensual whimpers split the air as the three men made love to her.

Breathing harshly at the awesome sight, Luke's eyelids became heavy with lust, and he could barely contain the chills of pleasure raking through his own penis as he imagined himself thrusting into Callie.

Each powerful plunge of Cade's cock between Callie's luscious, eager lips made Luke groan as he remembered the satiny feel of her hot mouth devouring his erection.

Every solid thrust of Colter's thick erection into her suctioning pussy had Luke's hands massaging harder at the length of his engorged flesh.

And each aroused groan from Mac, who by the way his eyes were closed tightly with bliss, was experiencing quite the erotic pleasure merely lying there with his penis buried inside Callie's oh so tight ass while he enjoyed the movements of Colter thrusting in and out of her, had Luke crying out his own gratification as his orgasm drew closer.

He watched his three brothers make love to his wife and saw Callie's lips move sensuously around Cade's cock. He noticed her body tense as she neared her own orgasm.

Every nerve and fiber inside him short-circuited from the erotic show.

His body grew taut with desire.

His balls felt terribly tight, heavy and full as his fingers kneaded and squeezed them.

Perspiration dampened his skin.

Callie whimpered as Colter's hips heaved, his cock plunging in and out of her like a piston.

Luke's hands increased their pressure around his own rod trying desperately to climax himself.

But he couldn't do it.

Not without Callie.

He needed her so badly it hurt.

He cried out in anguish and suddenly Colter was standing in front of him, his cock ready to burst as he urged him toward Callie who lay writhing on the bed, her fingers desperately massaging her wet clit again as she attempted to bring herself off.

Obviously, she couldn't climax without him either.

With his legs shaking so badly from pent-up emotion, Luke could barely scramble onto the bed to get to his love.

When she saw him coming to her the anguish of unfulfillment left her face, and she smiled around Cade's cock, once again eagerly sucking and bringing his brother closer to release.

Luke came over Callie, savoring the sight of her cream of arousal branding the insides of her thighs.

His thumb pushed hers away and he slid easily against her engorged red clitoris, slick with the juices of her cream.

Her hands came up and curled over his shoulders, her nails raking painfully against his back as she pulled him down upon herself and Mac.

He kept his eyes glued to her flushed face as he thrust his cock into her tight pussy.

Watched the way her mouth opened in a tortured gasp as she climaxed instantly.

She bucked against him like a wild woman gone mad, screaming out his name as her pussy muscles wrapped so tightly around the heated length of his penis that Luke thought he'd died and gone to heaven.

He powered his cock harder into her soaked pussy.

In and out.

Faster.

Deeper.

Until he had her crying out, over and over again.

Her climaxes were long and hard.

Feral.

One after the other they slammed into her.

She writhed beneath him, weeping out her pleasures as his cock continued to piston into her tight, triple-penetrated body in long and hard thrusts.

Soon he heard Colter cry out his release, quickly followed by Mac and then Cade's shout of release.

When his brothers' climaxes slowed and he felt Callie's orgasms begin to weaken, he finally allowed himself to explode inside her, giving himself into a killing pleasure that urged him to call out the name of his lover as he spilled his hot sperm into her warm and welcoming body.

Chapter Twelve

Perspiration covered Callie's flesh as Cade removed his spent cock from her mouth.

He'd tasted wonderful.

Hot and sticky.

Salty and sweet.

A wonderful combination she knew she wanted to taste again.

The scent of sex hung heavy in the air as a moment later Luke rolled off her and helped her to get off Mac, whose large, hard cock had impaled her ass beautifully.

She knew what they'd experienced together had been something awesome.

And she'd experienced the wildest orgasm ever when Luke had finally thrust inside her.

She'd tried to climax with Colter's huge rod plunging into her eager pussy, had hung on the edge of bliss, but when Luke had entered her, he'd been the one to push her over that carnal edge.

He'd made her tumble into something so darkly erotic she knew she wanted to experience a triple penetration again.

She had to admit this Claiming Law wasn't as bad as she'd first thought.

With willing partners, it would be a beautiful union for husbands and wife.

Her heart burst with a new love for these three brothers who had decided to save her by agreeing to the Claiming. Her feelings weren't as passionate as her feelings for Luke but

something different. Something gentler. Something she would enjoy.

Although Luke would always be *the one* who took up most of her heart, his brothers would forever hold a special piece, especially after what she'd just experienced with them.

* * * * *

The morning dawned bright with sunshine and the house was totally silent. When Callie opened her eyes, she was surprised to discover only Luke in bed beside her.

"You look so beautiful when you've been properly fucked by four men," Luke grinned.

Callie giggled, her face heating up with an erotic embarrassment. "I didn't know my Outlaw lovers would be such experts in the art of lovemaking."

"And you, my sweet, are our goddess."

"Keep those compliments coming big guy and I'll be putty in your hands in no time flat," Callie whispered and reached up, her fingers lightly stroking the raw, red edges around the healing bullet hole in his shoulder. Sometime during their sexfest, he'd removed the bandages or maybe they'd fallen off in the shower. In all the excitement, she couldn't remember when.

"Is your shoulder sore?"

He grinned. "I'm fine. Absolutely perfect."

"You sure?"

He nodded. "Colter took a look at it before he left. He says I'll live."

"Speaking of Colter, I'm dying to know about the story behind that tattoo and those nipple rings," Callie giggled.

"I've asked him on several occasions."

"And?"

"He won't say too much. He gets this funny look on his face and changes the subject."

"I bet you there is a woman involved."

"Well there was a conscript woman named Ashley… Something happened between them."

"A torrid romance, I bet."

"Something along those lines."

Callie pouted. Obviously, Colter wasn't the only one who didn't want to talk about it. She felt like trying to pry the information out of Luke, but held back. She didn't want to appear nosy. Besides, it wasn't her business. Not unless Colter decided to confide in her sometime in the future.

"So where are they anyway? It's awful quiet around here."

"Cade went to deliver the video and Claiming papers to the judge. He'll stay there and wait for the papers to be signed. Colter got called away to doctor some farmer who cut off his hand while haying, and Mac had some work to do out in one of the fields. They'll keep busy while I tend to my newly claimed bride."

Muscles bunched beautifully in his biceps as he reached out and curled an arm under her neck, encouraging Callie to nuzzle closer to him. Inhaling the strong scent of male, she shivered at the sensual outline of his thick erection sliding up against her hip.

Gosh! How could she be so lucky to have a man like Luke all to herself?

As always, it was as if he knew what she was thinking. "You gave the boys some much-needed relief by wanting the Claiming, and I'm not just talking sexually." He tangled his long fingers into her short hair, and pulled her closer so their lips were mere inches apart. His eyes blazed with such love it twisted her heart. "You've brought a sense of stability into their lives. Before you came back to us, my brothers were lost. Colter was brooding over a woman. Cade and Mac were unable to accept a way of life without dating and romancing women. So, you've pretty much saved them from a fate worse than death."

Warmth spilled through Callie at his honesty, but he was leaving someone out. "And what about you? Did I save you from something?"

"You've saved me from endless bouts of masturbating."

She saw his chest heave slightly and knew he was trying to contain a teasing chuckle.

Feigning anger, she jabbed her finger into the tender flesh around his wound, hard enough to make him wince, but not enough to hurt him seriously.

"Is that all?"

"What do you mean, is that all? I'll have you know carrying around a permanent hard-on isn't easy on a man, especially when women are scarce."

Callie pouted. "So? That's all I am to you? A warm pussy?"

The teasing left his face and he turned stone cold serious. "You're my life, Callie. I knew it the minute I saw you that first year in high school. Then it really hit home when we were separated."

"I'm so sorry, I did what I did," she whispered fighting back the anguish of what her actions had done to them.

"You did what you did because you felt it was the right thing to do, sweetie. I had no right to dictate to you. I should have understood your passion to help the women."

"You were scared for me, Luke. And I shouldn't have snuck off behind your back like I did. I promise I won't ever do that again."

Her thumb caressed his nipple and his breath quickened, his hot eyes held hers captive. Instinctively, she knew he wanted to tell her something very important.

"Do you know how many times I didn't care if I lived or died while I was out there in the desert fighting the terrorists? I had so many close calls out there. One day shortly before the government ordered us back home, I was out in the desert scouting for landmines ahead of the troops. We usually did the

landmine sweeps in pairs, but that day my usual partner was sick so I went out alone. The monitor always beeps to let me know there is a landmine up ahead. I'd locate it on the computer screen, go out, find it with the handheld detector and flag it so someone from the team behind me could defuse it. Then I'd drive around it and continue onto the next one.

"On this particular day, I'd just flagged the mine and decided to take a leak. I'd shut the handheld detector off because my computer had only signaled one mine in the area. I'd walked a few feet away from the flagged mine when something happened that made me realize I wasn't sure I wanted to die after all... I stepped on something, and I heard the click."

"You stepped on one? On a land mine?"

He nodded. "To this day I don't know why it hadn't registered on the computer, but yeah, I sure stepped on it."

A cold wave showered over her as she pictured the explosion that might have ripped him to shreds, left his crumpled body all alone in the desert, his lifeblood draining into the grains of sand on foreign soil.

"What...what happened?"

"I could have stepped off of it so easily, and let myself be blown apart so I could forget about you. I'd be lying to you if I said I didn't think about doing it. But then your smiling face appeared in front of me as it always did when I was in danger... Now that I think about it, maybe that's why I was always putting myself into unsafe situations, so I could see your face."

Luke inhaled, and gathered her closer against him as if he wanted to make sure she was really there with him.

A new kind of fear, one she'd never experienced before, slipped into her.

"What happened with the mine? Someone must have come along and helped you in the nick of time, because I can attest to the fact that all your important parts are in great working order."

"No complaints?" he grinned.

"None at all, Mister Very Well Hung."

"Mister Very Well Hung, huh? I think I like the sound of that," he nibbled on her earlobe, making sweet shivers shimmy up her spine.

"So who came along? I want to thank him for saving your life."

"Somebody you'd least expect..." He chuckled and continued, "I'd left the radio in the jeep so I couldn't radio for help. I figured I could wait until the landmine defusers showed up. But later that day I saw the sandstorm in the distance. It was coming in and coming in fast. I had my goggles and mask in my jeep. I knew if I didn't do something soon that looming sandstorm would choke me to death. So I prayed."

Agony powered through her.

Not a day went by while she was incarcerated in the lab that she didn't wonder what Luke was doing at any particular moment. She'd heard from the various nurses that took samples from her that many men had gone overseas to fight in the Terrorist Wars.

She'd prayed so hard that Luke hadn't been one of them. Instincts had told her he wouldn't be sitting idly by. Deep in her heart, she'd known he'd be fighting for his country. Until now, she hadn't realized he'd also been fighting himself. Struggling with the decision of whether he should die because she wasn't in his life anymore. A love like that was powerful. A love like that would last forever.

And she would do everything in her power to live up to that love.

"I prayed like I'd never prayed before," he continued. "Told the Big Guy upstairs that if he got me out of this situation alive I'd be forever in his debt and then I said something else... I told him that if you were dead I wanted to be dead, too. I told him it was up to him now. Did he want me to die out here? Or, did he want me to live and do something else with my life? So I stepped off the landmine and nothing happened."

"The mine was faulty?"

"It was faulty to a certain extent. I'd walked about ten yards then it blew me right off my feet. I knew the Big Guy was trying to get my attention. Realized he must have something in store for me, and that's why he let me live. Exactly what, I wasn't sure, until that night when I got shot.

"I'd heard the Barlows' whispering about killing me, and so I knew I had to escape. I remembered how the Big Guy had saved my ass out in the desert. I figured he didn't want me to have it end at the hands of the Barlows either. They thought I was too injured to run, and so when they turned their backs, I found my strength and hoofed it back to my truck. I thought about our church. I could barely drive there. The preacher found me slumped over in one of the pews, and I guess I was delirious or something. I'd been having visions about you. When I aimed my gun at him and mentioned your name, he spilled his guts. Told me he knew where you were. Told me he'd take me to you if I didn't shoot him. At first, I didn't understand what was going on, and then I realized he was serious. He knew where you were. I know it sounds kind of dumb and mushy, but that's when I realized why He let me step off the landmine and why He let me survive the Barlows. It was because He wanted us married, Callie. So I married you...even though I don't remember much of it, I was so drunk."

"You were a cute drunk, hiccupping all over the place." Callie whispered, and gently kissed his warm lips.

"How about I get cute with you right now...unless your pussy is too sore to accommodate me."

"Deliciously sore," she purred, and slipped her hand beneath the sheets to softly scrape her fingernails along his thick erection.

He inhaled sharply.

"And I plan on making you deliciously sore, too, before I give you relief," she promised, and nipped sharply at his bristly chin, giving him a prelude of things to come.

Then she lifted up the covers and slid her head underneath.

* * * * *

It was the distinct sound of a familiar, heavy breathing that she'd been tormented with in the last several weeks of her stay in the government labs that drifted through the layers of Callie's sleep.

At first, she thought it was just another dream of Blakely, but when a cool finger trailed up along the side of her neck and settled beneath her chin, she knew it wasn't.

Her eyes snapped open and terror filled her as a familiar face hovered above her.

Blakely! He was here!

Before she could scream a warning to Luke, Blakely's hand clamped over her mouth, pushing her head into the pillow.

More faces hovered into view. She felt hands slip around her wrists and ankles, pinning her arms and legs down into the mattress.

From beside her she heard Luke's surprised shout, "What the hell—" It was quickly followed by a sickening thud and a yelp of pain from Luke.

Then silence.

My God!

Luke!

What did they do to him?

She tried to turn her head against the death grip clamping over her mouth to see, but the hand wouldn't let her budge an inch.

Blakely hovered into view.

He grinned down at her from beneath that black handlebar moustache she detested. Obvious amusement sparkled in his coal-black eyes as he chomped on a stick of tobacco gum.

"You didn't think I'd let my prize bitch get away from me, did you?" he chuckled, and turned his head slightly to spit a

stream of tobacco juice from between a wide gap in his two front, yellow-stained teeth.

She screamed into his hand, wanting to tell him he was a dirty pig, but all that came out was a garbled shriek.

Blakely frowned his disapproval, and his pockmarked face lowered until it was inches from her, the horrid smell of tobacco splashed sickeningly into her nostrils making her gag.

"You're mine, Callie. And that baby those Outlaws put into you is mine, too. You didn't think I'd let you escape the lab so easily, did you?"

What?

"Since I consider myself such a gentleman, I could never force myself upon an X-virus resistant woman to make her pregnant, so I had to let you go. I knew you'd end up here. I knew one of these boys would do the job of mounting you... I didn't expect all of them to do it before I could get to you myself."

Oh, God! She was going to throw up. How did he know the Outlaws had claimed her?

He lifted his hand off her mouth, but her legs and arms remained pinned by the goons.

Immediately she turned her head to see what they'd done to Luke, and her breath caught in her throat.

He lay sprawled on the bed, unconscious. A large, red, horizontal bruise blossomed across his rib cage.

Standing over him was a man cradling a very large bat.

"Don't worry," Blakely said. "He's not dead. Just out of commission long enough to allow us to do what we came to do."

"What...what's that?"

"Take you back to my new laboratory, of course. You'll be safe and secure there, while I run more tests on you, and on that fetus you're sure to be carrying."

Panic sliced into her brain.

Think fast, woman! Think!

"There's…there's no fetus. We used protection."

"You've forgotten that I have contacts with the government, my little bitch in heat. I got a copy of the Claiming video the instant one of your husbands filed the claim."

Callie's stomach lurched.

"Mind you, I was quite jealous to see you writhing in pleasure beneath all those well-hung lovers."

He ran his clammy fingertips up the length of her naked arm. The feel of his flesh on her skin blew red-hot anger into her.

"Get away from me, you creep!"

Once again, she struggled against the two men holding her down. Her efforts proved futile. Their lecherous gazes roved over the tangled sheets that surely must be giving them glimpses of her nakedness.

"Such endearments will change, my sweetie," Blakely chuckled. "Especially when you've been locked up for months without men fucking you. Then you'll come to me willingly. By then you're belly will be swollen with child. Your sex hormones raging through your system. Your orgasms will be unlike any you've just experienced with your new husbands. Did I mention that I prefer to fuck pregnant bitches? That's another one of the reasons I let you go. So you'd get pregnant and then I could come for you."

Sick bastard!

Callie closed her eyes as a wave of dizziness swamped her. God help her, this had to be a nightmare. Blakely wouldn't dare hurt an unborn child, would he?

But she knew the answer to that.

He was a madman. Madmen would do anything.

A sharp pinprick to her inner arm made her eyes snap open. Her blood froze when she saw the needle in his hand, watched in absolute horror as the pinkish fluid drained from the needle into her vein.

The urge to scream stopped dead in her throat, and she felt the familiar sleepiness sweep through her.

"You bastard," she whispered, as the fast-acting sedative shrieked through her.

Blakely smiled down at her. "Just like old times, isn't it?"

Before she could protest, she was being swaddled into the sheets.

"You can't do this. I've been claimed! I belong to the Outlaws," she tried to say, but only a whimper of protest escaped her quickly numbing lips.

Blakely answered her with a cold chuckle that made shivers of fear crawl up her spine.

"Come darling, let's get out of here. I don't want you to see what Lurch here will do to your lover with his prized bat. It might leave a bad opinion of me when I'm fucking you."

He easily lifted her into his arms, his eyes glazed over with satisfaction.

Oh, God! No! Please help Luke! Her mind screamed her silent horror, as she spied the other man pounding the baseball bat into his palm, the sharp sounds of wood slapping against flesh gave her the distinct impression he was only moments away from using it on a totally defenseless Luke.

Once again, she tried to yell a warning, but despite her trying to, no sound emerged from her lifeless mouth.

Then Luke's helpless figure disappeared from her view as Blakely carried her out the bedroom, down the hall and out of the house.

* * * * *

Luke's ribs ached like a son of a bitch every time he inhaled a breath, but he forced himself to remain stiff as a corpse, as he listened to a person moving at his side of the bed.

The instant he'd awoken and realized Callie was in danger he'd been hit smack across his ribs. The brutal force had

knocked the breath clean out of his lungs, incapacitating him. He hadn't fully gone unconscious but he'd been close.

While Blakely had confessed he'd let Callie out of the labs on purpose so she would become pregnant, he'd fought the overwhelming impulse to smash his fists into the mad scientist's face. But he'd controlled himself, waiting for an opportunity to increase his chances of successfully getting Callie out of this nightmare.

He didn't know what Blakely had done to her, but he'd done something or Callie wouldn't have allowed him to take her so easily from the house.

He'd probably drugged her.

Maybe it was best that way. At least she wouldn't feel the terror of being kidnapped.

At the sound of her slurred protests as Blakely had carried her from the room, he'd wanted to bolt from the bed, but he'd held tight to the thin fragment of control.

His restraint had paid off.

Now *he* had the element of surprise.

He could hear the goon whistling softly, and Luke opened his eyes slightly to see what was going on.

The man was leaning over the nearby dresser picking up Callie's wedding ring.

Son of a bitch!

Now that the goon was preoccupied, it gave Luke the perfect opportunity to make his move.

Gritting his teeth against the sharp pain searing across his ribs, he swung his legs up and over the bed. Both of his feet made solid contact with his attacker's hard thigh. Luke pushed with all his might sending the guy flying across the room. He hit the far bedroom wall with a thud and slumped in a daze to the floor, the baseball bat dangling from his fingers.

For a moment, Luke thought the guy would be out of commission long enough for him to retrieve his gun from the

drawer, but the man shook his head then sprung to his feet as if nothing had happened to him.

The bat was held firmly in his powerful hands.

Oh, shit!

"I'm going to knock your bloody head right off you," the man chuckled as he took a couple of steps forward, readying to swing the bat.

"Go ahead, make my day." Luke growled, finding a strange courage in those familiar words from a popular Clint Eastwood classic as he readied himself against his attacker.

"I'm going to make ground beef out of your face," the man threatened, and took another step closer. "And I'm going to squash that cock of yours so you can't fuck Blakely's woman ever again."

"Blakely's woman, over my dead body, asshole," Luke growled.

The man swung the bat, and despite the pain clawing at his ribs, Luke managed to duck the swing giving him the perfect opportunity to sucker punch the guy right in the gut.

"Oomph," the goon groaned, and bent over in pain.

Luke moved in for the kill. Latching his arm around the man's neck, he gave it a quick jerk.

The snap of the spine breaking made Luke grimace.

He hated that sound. Had heard his share of it in the army when they'd eliminated terrorists, one-by-one.

He dropped the lifeless body to the ground. The man's hand unclasped and Callie's wedding ring shone brightly up at Luke.

Sucking in a sharp breath as he bent over to pick it up, he quickly donned his jeans, retrieved his gun and headed toward the back door of the farmhouse.

When he got his hands on Blakely and the rest of his henchmen, he was going to make sure they never forgot the name Luke Outlaw.

* * * * *

"I paid a high price to buy you for my research project," Blakely cooed, as he placed Callie into the backseat of his awaiting vehicle and slid in beside her. Her neck felt so numb she couldn't even keep her head straight. It lulled sideways giving her a perfect view of the bastard who'd just kidnapped her.

Go to hell! her mind screamed.

The urge to run was so great she swore she was doing it, yet her limbs could barely move an inch.

"The instant I saw you when I was first hired at the laboratory I knew I wanted to have you for my very own harem of pregnant bitches. My wife, she's a scientist like me; she will really enjoy fucking you, too. We love threesomes."

Someone actually married this creep? And from what he'd just said she was obviously just as sick and twisted as he was.

She tried to convey her contempt to him by staring at him long and hard, but he just kept smiling at her, his frosty eyes boring into her very soul making her feel so cold she couldn't stop herself from shivering, or at least she thought she was shivering.

"We have to run some tests to make sure you are indeed pregnant. I don't see why you wouldn't be. You are a very healthy woman. Your eggs had been very receptive to my sperm in the laboratories."

She closed her eyes against the wash of nausea at his words.

"But then of course you took care of my experiments when you smashed the vials. When we get back to the lab I'll extract some more eggs from you, and of course, we'll have to take some vaginal swabs to make sure those Outlaws didn't infect you with something dangerous, what with all those women they've been with during their stay in the army."

At the mention of the Outlaws, Callie couldn't stop the tears from rolling from her eyes.

Oh, Luke, I'm so sorry. I'm so very sorry. I should have stayed away. I should have left you and your brothers instead of getting you all into trouble. For all she knew Colter, Cade and Mac could already be dead.

And Luke…

Oh, God! She couldn't think about what was being done to him in there.

"Those soldier boys were very well taken care of by the government while they were away from home. The government knew they'd have to keep those troops satisfied if they wanted the job done right. They even purchased and conscripted women. I sold my very own stepsister to them with the stipulation they turn her into a whore." His voice turned angry as he looked back out the window. "That'll teach her for rejecting me."

He'd dared to try to have relations with his stepsister?

He was sick.

"I've no doubt she's serviced hundreds of men by now. A fitting end for such a beautiful, uptight woman. I'm sure every man in the army enjoyed her."

Blakely frowned, and pressed a nearby button on the armrest. The window whirred downward.

"What's taking Lurch so long to get the job done?" he called out to one of the two men who stood beside the car.

"Maybe he's enjoying himself too much," came a reply.

"Go inside and get him. Make it fast!"

One of the men nodded and loped away.

The window whirred up again.

Callie stiffened as Blakely turned his sights on her again.

"I'm going to enjoy the internal exam to see if those cocks damaged your insides."

Internal exam!

"Or maybe I should do an exam right now? I always enjoyed fingering you while you were under anesthesia on my table. I would have fucked you, too, while you were under but I'm not that callous. I enjoy watching my bitches' faces scrunch up with pleasure while I fuck them senseless."

His confession made her feel dizzy, and her eyes widened with fear as he made a move to lift up the sheets covering her nudity.

Suddenly the car rocked violently.

"What the—?" Blakely screamed.

Through the front window, Callie saw the henchman who'd been standing near the front of the car, slumped over the hood.

He didn't move.

In a split second, Blakely had a gun in his hand. The finger on the trigger tightened as he aimed it at his side of the window.

Callie tried to scream a warning to whoever was outside but all that escaped her lips was a sickening whimper.

"No fucking way you're going to get my bitch!" Blakely yelled.

The side window disintegrated in a roaring blast as he started shooting.

Her heart pounded against her chest so hard it hurt.

Who was out there? Who was he shooting at?

Please, let it be Luke, she prayed. *Let Luke be alive.*

No! If it was Luke, Blakely would kill him!

The gunshots continued as Blakely went wild, frantically shooting out all the windows in the car.

Finally, he clicked on an empty chamber.

Silence filled the air.

He looked at her.

Fear raged in his eyes. Fear and a powerful anger that made her believe he would kill her before he ever let whoever was out

there take her away from him. "I'll never let you go, you little bitch," he echoed her thoughts.

She sensed he was about to harm her when without warning an arm slid through the open window, grabbing Blakely around the neck.

Blakely's eyes bulged round with terror, his face reddening with every beat of Callie's heart as the arm tightened.

She cringed at the sickening snap of a neck breaking.

Blakely's mouth dropped open. Spittle oozed out the side of his lip. His eyes went glassy and lifeless. Lightheadedness swept over her at the horrible sight.

At the same moment, her side of the door opened and Luke's strong arms slid under her ass and he swept her into his arms.

As he lifted her from the car, she snuggled against his bruised, naked chest, relief pouring through her every fiber.

It had all happened so fast she wasn't sure if this was real or if the drug Blakely had given her was screwing with her mind.

She blinked up at Luke, not quite believing he was alive and well.

"Are you okay?" he asked.

She could barely nod and tried to speak but nothing came out.

"He drugged you?" Colter's voice sifted from nearby.

Again, she could barely nod. The effort to fight off the drugs was taxing her quickly.

"I'll get a blood sample from you and see what I can do to counteract the effects."

She heard running feet, and assumed he was heading back into the farm.

She wanted to cry out a warning, to tell him there another man inside the house, but then she saw Mac and Cade dragging out a couple of bodies.

Thank God, her Outlaw lovers had come to her rescue.

How had they known there was trouble?

It was as if Luke could read her mind.

"Cade was waiting at the Claiming office when someone tipped him off that Blakely had viewed our claiming video. He called Colter and told him to hightail back home. Cade parked his truck out on the main road and hoofed it over to get Mac, and they met me as I was leaving the farmhouse to come and get you. They took care of the other guy who came inside. Then Colter came running in from the other direction indicating he would take care of Blakely and I could rescue you."

Callie grinned.

"Thank...you," she said. At least she thought she said it.

Then she closed her eyes and allowed the sedative to finally whisk her away.

Chapter Thirteen
Two months later…

"So are we pregnant?" Callie asked Colter.

She held tight to Luke's hand searching Colter's face as he read the results of the early pregnancy test he'd asked her to take.

Since the Claiming, the Outlaw brothers had brought her to sexual fulfillment on a daily basis, but only Luke had vaginally penetrated her so she knew if she was pregnant then the baby was his. She turned to Luke and noticed how awfully pale his face looked as they awaited the answer. Since she'd told him and his brothers she thought she might be pregnant they'd begun worrying themselves silly over everything, making sure she ate all her meals, making sure she slept her eight hours a night, took afternoon naps and helped her around the farmhouse with pretty much anything and everything.

She'd reassured them constantly that she was fine. Told them she might be pregnant, but that didn't mean she was a fragile china doll.

Despite her reassurances she felt fine, aside from the occasional queasiness, they'd even stopped having sex with her because they were afraid to hurt the baby. Something she would rectify as soon as she found out if what she suspected was true.

There was no way she would go months without having sex. No way!

Not after all the sexual joy she'd been experiencing over the past two months on a daily basis. She was hooked on sex with her Outlaw lovers.

Baby or no baby, she wanted to be sexually satisfied by them.

They'd had to wait several days for the early pregnancy test to be delivered. Because of the bad economic situation in the United States, Colter was unable to get the medical supplies he so desperately needed to treat his patients. He'd finally managed to purchase an early pregnancy test through the ever-growing black market.

Now as they sat in the tiny room adjoining the living room that Colter used as his doctor's office, Luke looked as if he might faint dead away. She could only imagine how he'd be when the baby came.

If the baby came.

If she was pregnant.

"So? Is she?" Luke asked.

Hope filled his voice and love for him filled her heart.

Colter smiled warmly. "According to this test, Callie is pregnant. Congratulations to both of you."

"Sweet shit," Luke whispered from beside her. "We're going to have a baby."

Suddenly his eyes rolled into the back of his head and he fainted.

* * * * *

"Is he all right?" Mac's concerned voice washed over Luke.

"I think he's waking up," Cade replied.

"Here, I think this will help," Colter's amused voice whispered through Luke's grogginess.

Suddenly a harsh spray of cold water splashed over his head, sweeping away his wooziness.

He blinked, open his eyes and found Colter standing over him with an empty bucket in his hands. His other two brothers snickered nearby.

"W…what happened?"

"You passed out," Colter said, extending his hand and helping Luke up.

Water dripped into his eyes and he blinked the liquid away.

"Shit! I've never done that before in my life."

"You better start getting used to it, or at the very least, try to control your breathing. Callie said she's decided she wants lots of kids."

"She's pregnant." He still couldn't believe it.

"Yes, you're going to be a father...in about seven months."

"I'm going to be a father?" Suddenly he felt woozy again.

"I recommend bed rest, Luke," Colter said, as he steered Luke out of the office and down the hallway. "Lots of bed rest."

He stopped in front of the bedroom Luke and Callie shared.

"And I've given Callie a prescription. It'll be up to you to make sure she gets it filled out on a daily basis."

"Prescription?"

Colter pushed the door open and quickly shoved Luke inside. "Callie will show you what I mean."

The door shut behind him and the sound of the door locking made him frown.

"Now why would they lock me in —?"

"Oh, lover boy," Callie's sultry voice whispered from behind him.

He turned to find her lying in the king-sized bed, a sensual smile curling her luscious red lips.

His cock roused to life, and his eyes widened as he spied the flowery sheets slowly moving up her very naked luscious legs.

"Colter said he's given you a prescription, and I'm supposed to make sure you get it filled, so what is it? Prenatal vitamins? Where are they?" He scanned the room half expecting to see a bottle of vitamins on the nightstand.

There weren't any.

"Come here and fill my prescription, lover boy," Callie whispered, as the sheet slipped further up revealing her nude pussy.

Oh, boy!

His heart picked up speed as she spread her legs wide.

Her labia were plump and juicy looking, and her clitoris, a tight, swollen, red knot aching to be touched.

"We can't, Callie." Although right now he wanted more than anything to mount her and bring her the sexual release she was obviously craving, he didn't want to hurt the baby.

"It's doctor's orders, Luke."

"That's right, Luke," Colter called out from the other side of the bedroom door. "And I'm not letting you out of there until you fill her prescription, which is keeping Callie very happy with plenty of sex and tender loving care."

"Get lost!" Luke shouted at the door.

He heard his brothers snicker and then they stomped down the hallway.

"I'm pregnant, Luke. My sex hormones are going into overdrive. At a wonderful time like this, the last thing I want is to be deprived of your lovemaking skills, now get your ass naked and start showing me some TLC. Can't not follow the doctor's orders now, can we?"

He grinned.

The last thing he wanted to do was not follow the doctor's orders.

He got himself naked.

Fast.

And headed for the bed.

And for Callie.